POWER OF
PERSUASION

TITLES BY STACEY ABRAMS
WRITTEN AS SELENA MONTGOMERY

Deception

Reckless

Secrets and Lies

Hidden Sins

Never Tell

Power of Persuasion

The Art of Desire

Rules of Engagement

POWER OF PERSUASION

STACEY ABRAMS

WRITING AS

SELENA MONTGOMERY

BERKLEY

NEW YORK

BERKLEY
An imprint of Penguin Random House LLC
penguinrandomhouse.com

Copyright © 2002 by Stacey Abrams
Foreword copyright © 2025 by Stacey Y. Abrams

Library of Congress Cataloging-in-Publication Data

Names: Montgomery, Selena, author.
Title: Power of persuasion / Stacey Abrams writing as Selena Montgomery.
Description: Berkley hardcover edition. | New York : Berkley, 2025.
Identifiers: LCCN 2024015896 (print) | LCCN 2024015897 (ebook) |
ISBN 9780593439456 (hardcover) | ISBN 9780593439470 (epub)
Subjects: LCGFT: Romance fiction. | Novels.
Classification: LCC PS3601.B746 P69 2025 (print) | LCC PS3601.B746 (ebook) |
DDC 813/.6—dc23/eng/20240408
LC record available at https://lccn.loc.gov/2024015896
LC ebook record available at https://lccn.loc.gov/2024015897

Arabesque Books paperback edition / November 2002
Berkley hardcover edition / January 2025

Printed in the United States of America
1st Printing

Book design by Laura K. Corless

To those who dream, who dare, and who do.

FOREWORD

Twenty years ago, I visited my dear law school classmate Jaya Ramji at her childhood home in Northern California. Her gracious family allowed me to wander around their house for a weekend, poke my way into conversations, and ask lots of questions. One discussion in particular caught my interest. Jaya's older brother, Samir, was studying computer science and talk turned to his research. I'd grown up in a time before computers were easily attainable, when the architecture of programming had only begun to move into the mainstream of our parlance. Most of my knowledge of artificial intelligence came from Isaac Asimov and *Star Trek: The Next Generation*. Thus, I found his work fascinating and the inquiries compelling, and he was kind enough to answer my barrage of questions. I enjoyed that time so much that a few years later, when I sat down to write the third installment of the ISA series, Sam Ramji's tutelage on artificial intelligence became the core of A.J. Grayson's story.

A.J. and Damon meet in a moment when neither is ready for the other, and when the world is not prepared to let them fall in love. Telling their story then meant delving into geopolitics, history, art and then translating what little I knew about AI and Markov decision processes (based on lurking around MIT's website for weeks). As always, I welcomed the chance to dive deep into areas I didn't know much about, one of my favorite parts of writing. In retrospect, though, I am doubly glad that I chose to use the juxtaposition of artificial intelligence and political intrigue to get to the heart of one of my most treasured romantic suspense tales.

What AI means and what it can do reveals itself anew seemingly every day. But the core issue is about how we allow technology to shape our worlds. In a different way, A.J. has planned out her life by her own internal algorithms, only to find Damon has upended her sense of self and forced her to confront her subconscious worry that she might not be enough. Damon finds a worthy partner in A.J. at a moment when he has discovered his entire life has been built upon lies and sacrifice. Two decades ago, their derring-do was about technology's potential and flights of fancy. Today, their romance is one small glimpse into a fast-changing world, one still anchored by the most basic of technical mysteries: falling in love.

As someone who has been privileged to blend my competing passions for storytelling, politics, public service, and good old-fashioned romance, *Power of Persuasion* is probably the novel that brings them together best. Just as A.J. and Damon must work hard to make their differences fit and reveal themselves to find each other, I am grateful for the chance to reintroduce their royal love story to another generation of readers.

With affection,
Stacey

POWER OF
PERSUASION

A thousand lights glittered, incandescent stars twinkling in celebration. Golden champagne, the potable required by the night, flowed endlessly into fluted crystal. Mirth floated above harps and flutes, blended with conversation. Dazzling couples circled the parquet in elegant steps. In approbation, the heavens offered a full moon and cloudless sky, a gentle breeze to stir the summer night. Held in the home of Liz and Robert Walton, the wedding reception of Raleigh Foster and Adam Grayson had demanded no less.

A.J. remembered seeing him enter.

In a sea of dashing gentlemen, he caught her eye, stuttered her heart. It was a face of memory, the lines and curves too beautiful for lethe. Sculptors for pantheons had drawn the slash of cheekbone; poetry immortalized the sensual mouth. She knew instinctively the heat of the tawny eyes, before she felt them light upon her.

Intentionally, she turned away.

Later, when her pulse had evened, she joined her family and the newcomer. He watched her steadily, taking in the sinuous gown, with its waves of emerald flowing and clinging to dips and curves.

Admiring hazel locked with intrigued brown, and both recognized their connection. At the moment of introduction, when he took her hand to dance, she appreciated the unsophisticated phrases of lust she'd read but never grasped. Wrapped together, they glided across the floor. Melody drifted into melody, and they did not pause. Soft words whispered between them. With her head tucked into the taut muscle of his shoulder, she felt the susurration of sound before words wholly formed. The lovely accent stoked the romance of the evening, and she wondered at its source.

Damon led A.J. into a waltz, their steps light and nimble. He examined her face closely, memorizing each feature. "You're exquisite."

"Thank you," A.J. demurred. "Flattery is an excellent start."

He steered her into a complicated turn, which she easily matched. "An excellent start to what?"

Coquettish, A.J. fluttered her lashes, the effect ruined by the mischievous grin. "A new friendship?"

"Is that what we'll become?"

"That depends," A.J. answered as long fingers traced lightly over the sensitive skin of her back.

"Upon?"

"The fates, I suppose."

Damon suspected she believed in nothing so ephemeral. To tease, he responded, "It is appropriate then that you are a sprite, is it not?"

"A sprite?"

"Absolutely. A fairy creature, clad as a wood nymph." Satisfied with the description, he twirled them across the floor and caught the attention of other guests. A.J. found herself laughing delightedly at the dizzying sensation of the dance and his embrace.

Damon did not laugh, but studied her carefully as they flowed into another number.

"What do you do, A.J. Grayson?" The question trailed off as he folded her closer. Above the scent of magnolias rose a headier perfume. A determined connoisseur of women and their trappings, Damon felt surprised that he could not name the fragrance, but he imagined she smelled of sunlight.

"I'm a scientist at GCI."

"Do you enjoy your work?"

Her job as an executive in R&D, like every job before, had been carefully planned and quickly attained. She saw no reason to do a job one did not love, and no sense in not being the best. "Absolutely. And you? What do you do?"

"I run an art gallery."

A.J. finally recalled why his name seemed familiar. "Oh, you were the one to sponsor Alex's show!"

"Yes." Damon spoke against the tender shell of her ear. It was small and well-shaped, exactly like the woman in his arms. Lust, primitive sheer lust, rocketed through him. From their positions, he could easily discern that she was at least half a foot shorter than his own six feet, likely more. He'd always preferred tall, but no longer.

To distract himself from more brazen thoughts, he asked huskily, "And your field at GCI?"

"Research and development. I specialize in cognitive science."

"Which means?"

A.J. considered giving him the rote answer, but the intelligent eyes demanded more. "Cognitive scientists focus on understanding the nature of the human mind. Some through anthropology, others through linguistics, psychology, and other disciplines. My field is artificial intelligence."

"Some might say that it is the only kind."

A.J. toyed with the strip of silk at his throat. "Cynics."

"Realists."

Amused, and half-convinced, she conceded, "Perhaps, but such a dreary thought for an artist. What brings you to our fair city?"

"I am here on business, and I came to visit Alexandra. However, the rather formidable Mrs. Downey chastised me for missing the wedding and commanded that I join the reception."

A.J. commiserated with a solemn look. "The Waltons pretend she is the housekeeper, but the truth is that she allows them to remain here on sufferance."

"She frightens you too?"

"Oh, I'm terrified of her. Once, when I was fifteen, Liz hosted a dinner party here. On a dare from my cousins, I snuck into the wine cellar. Mrs. Downey discovered me."

"Had you imbibed much?"

"Half the bottle. But unfortunately, I chose to uncork a 1955 Château l'Angelus to prove myself."

Damon winced at the image. "The '55 Château l'Angelus? *Mon dieu! Il tres incredible.*"

Enchanted by the smooth, rapid transition from impeccable English to comfortable French, she asked, "You are from France?"

"No. South Africa, but I spent my formative years in Senegal. At the knees of a wine collector. Had I been the culprit in your Bordeaux crime, I would have found sitting difficult for several days."

"I did have that problem," she admitted wryly.

Damon lifted their clasped hands, and brushed a kiss over the delicate flesh. And felt the tremble. "Was it worth the punishment?"

"Of course," A.J. responded in a smoky voice, edged by an emotion he longed to explore. "Sometimes danger is its own reward."

Passion flared suddenly, glowed solid and hot, catching him unprepared for its force. Damon paused mid-step, but effortlessly caught A.J. as she stumbled. Silently, he led them from the dance floor, toward the house.

Perhaps he could steal time away from fortune, he thought recklessly. The crown had waited twenty-five years, surely it could spare him a flash of stolen bliss. "Inside, there is the wine cellar?" He rasped over the question, as desire tightened its vise.

"Yes."

"Show me."

A.J. led him through a maze of rooms to the kitchen, then down two flights of stairs to the basement. The chilliness sharply contrasted with the heat of the evening. A.J. shivered in the thin emerald gown, with its slender straps. Damon shrugged out of his jacket and settled the material around her shoulders, lingering over the task.

A.J. whispered her thanks, and he took her hand again.

Together, they wandered through the rows of bottles collected by the Waltons. Damon regaled her with legends of vintners who'd crafted the wines. Eventually, they returned to the steps, and A.J. perched on an edge.

"Tell me about your family," she instructed.

"It is much like your own. I was adopted by my aunt and uncle."

"How old were you?"

"They adopted us at birth. My parents died later."

"Us? You have siblings?"

"A twin brother," he answered shortly, and A.J. didn't probe.

"I grew up with my cousins. Adam, Rachel, and Jonah. Maybe not in the conventional way, but they are as close as siblings."

"Were your parents also a part of GCI?"

"No. My mother was a teacher, and my father was a construction worker. Aunt Carolyn is my mother's sister."

"So, you grew up in one social strata, then moved into another." Thinking of what was to come for him, he asked, "Do you ever feel like an interloper? A changeling?"

"Like I don't belong? No."

But Damon heard her hesitation. Unable to leave the subject, he said, "But you are not one of them. You do not share a common background."

"It doesn't matter," A.J. denied. "At least, I have to believe it doesn't." She checked the slim band of gold on her wrist, and said politely, "We've been gone for nearly an hour. Guests will be leaving soon, and I'm sure my family is looking for me." She emphasized *family* as she scrambled to her feet. "I need to go back."

"A.J.?"

"It's time to go, Damon." She stood on the floor beside him, and refused to meet his gaze. "A bridesmaid's work is never done," she quipped sarcastically.

In the dimly lit space, Damon pulled A.J. to him, annoyed by the distance she created, confused by its source. He could feel her withdrawal, and was determined to stop it. Body to body, flesh to flesh, he held them together. "What happened?"

"I don't know what you mean."

"Don't lie to me, A.J. Where did you go?"

"I'm right here."

"A.J.," he breathed, the name a craven desire he could not ignore. He did not believe in instant attraction, in the fallacy of love at first sight. Love, romance, were the stuff of myth. Lust, desire, the chemical reactions necessary to fuel the conceit. Yet, holding A.J., he wondered at forever and mourned. "Come back to me."

"Damon," she murmured, relenting, her hands lifting to his shoulders to steady herself, though she stood still.

"You feel it, don't you?" he asked harshly as he planted a chain of kisses along her jawline. "You must feel this, this magic between us."

"Yes," she whispered, unable to deny it, and she angled her head to offer greater access to skin longing for his touch. When he pulled away, she lifted her head to meet his eyes. "Are you alright?" Concern darkened her voice.

"I did not expect—" he murmured.

A.J. comprehended at once what he did not say. "Nor did I. But perhaps it is—"

"Fate. If so, she has odd sensibilities."

She smiled at the palpable irritation. "At a wedding? It seems appropriate."

"Perhaps if we were different people." He sighed, tugged her deeper into his embrace. "With different destinies, at a different time."

"Are we so different?" she asked softly, as strong fingers twined with her own.

"My life is—is beyond what you can imagine. And more than I can explain."

"I understand," A.J. said haughtily, breaking away from his hold. "I don't need to be told more than twice."

He turned her, spun her, and her breath caught. "You don't understand. It's not you."

She pulled away again, leveled her eyes to his own. "Cryptic is only romantic in novels."

Damon smiled dryly. "Unfortunately. But it will have to suffice."

She heard the certainty of goodbye, but would not accept it. "Give me a reason."

He shook his head, frightened by how badly he wanted to remain and how assured he was that he had to go. Now. Before he abandoned his pledge to a legacy centuries in the making. He'd already endangered the life of a friend to fulfill his promise. Could he dare abandon duty for desire? And if he hurt her in the process, could he forgive himself?

His entire life, he'd been the responsible one. Only once had he dared take something for himself, when he'd assumed leadership of the Toca Galleries and molded it into a premiere institution. But even that would end soon, and he might possibly perish in the attempt. It was unthinkable to risk A.J.'s life for what he imagined in a stolen moment.

"Damon? What's wrong?"

"It is nothing."

He couldn't have her, not even for a night, because in the morning, it would be impossible to let her go. But he would have a memory. He deserved to taste what was forever denied to him. Then, decision made, Damon tipped her head back, her hips into his.

She gasped, but did not draw away.

Eyes met, held. "You are beautiful. Too lovely to hold and let go."

"Then don't," she countered firmly.

"I must. I have no choice." He had no choice in the matter. Any bargains with destiny had been made years before. "But first—"

Mouth met mouth, and immediately both recoiled at the shock of encounter. Suddenly ravenous, they braved the flames again, a frantic mating. He searched the supple cavern hidden behind impossibly wanton lips. Tongues stroked in a sweet tangle of heaven. He raced his hands over compact curves, moaned aloud as she too explored him.

A.J. forgot to think, forgot to breathe. All she knew of that instant was the perfect union of planes and angles, of hard to soft. She touched greedily, kissed hungrily, wanted desperately, afraid of the end.

But it came. He broke away, lingering for a final second over the contact. Then setting her aside, unsure of whether minutes or hours had passed, he turned away.

"Sometimes, the difference is too great and the danger is not reason enough." Damon understood his lot. *"Au revoir, ma fée."*

———

A.J. had watched as he ran up the stairs, taking them in pairs. Her hands gripped the jacket lapels and she inhaled deeply, in part to settle wild nerves, in part to drink in the scent of forest and man that clung to the fabric.

The same hands had wrathfully tossed the jacket into the trash chute, when she read of the ascension of Damon Toca to the throne of Jafir. Suddenly, his enigmatic remarks about "difference" and "social strata" became clear. The ache that had been longing hardened into antipathy. If she never heard the name Damon Toca again, it would be a day too soon.

CHAPTER ONE

A.J. stared at the short, stern man, incredulous. The patience so antithetical to her nature and so necessary in her job was sorely strained this morning, and she was in no mood for even the most absurd humor. Certainly not the ludicrous story she'd just spent the better part of an hour digesting. The tepid coffee in the unmarked black mug sloshed a bit as she raised the rim to the soft mouth thinned into a line of disgust. She didn't have time for this . . . this farce. Anger warred with good manners as she stared at the older man, curbing her tongue with effort.

The morning had begun at four thirty a.m., the shrill summons of the bedside phone rousing her from a fitful sleep. She had tumbled into bed a mere three hours before, after spending most of the night in the laboratory. Bleary-eyed, she'd grabbed a plastic-wrapped suit from the closet and what she had luckily guessed were matching shoes from a jumble beneath the bed. The jet left the private hangar half an hour later, arriving in DC in time for a glossy obsidian car to spirit her to a nondescript building in Dupont Circle.

Early morning meetings were nothing new to A.J., but she had a firm policy against the unexpected. She despised the un-known; loathed surprises. Particularly those surprises that sprung up the day before the most important meeting of her twenty-five-year-old life.

On Monday morning, she would have to convince thirty people that cognitive science was the wave of the future and a natural complement to their product line. The brainchild she'd slaved over in secret for more than a year would be revealed. Even more, she'd have to cajole the board of directors for one of the world's most powerful corporations into turning over com-plete control of research and development to the youngest exec-utive in Grayson Conglomerate International.

A.J. didn't doubt her capacity to handle the job. More than anyone, she was vibrantly aware of the responsibility she sought. R&D was the lifeblood of the GCI empire, particularly its ad-vanced computer technology. Under her command, Poppet would be the next wave in artificial intelligence.

But instead of preparing her presentation to the board or fine-tuning her prototype, she was seated in a bureaucrat's office at an ungodly hour of the morning, listening to a preposterous tale about secret agents and international intrigue.

"Let me get this straight. You wake me at an unconscionable hour. Fly me five hundred miles in a rainstorm. Whisk me to a clandestine meeting all to tell me that my cousin is James Bond?"

With a withering glance, A.J. pushed back her chair and rose. "Goodbye, Mr. Russell."

"Sit down, Athena," the man quietly instructed.

"No one calls me that," A.J. growled, but she sat immediately. Not that she was at all afraid of the man behind the desk. At least fifty years old, Russell had black hair sprinkled liberally with gray, a color that matched the thoroughly unnerving eyes.

"The name is A.J.," she grumbled. She crossed her arms in a petulant pose familiar to her family, and pouted full, glossed lips. "What other fairy tales do you want to tell me? That Adam and Raleigh met on a secret mission and fell madly in love?"

"Well, that's true, but beside the point." James "Atlas" Russell favored the young woman with a grin. "Of course, they broke up when she refused to save his partner, but yep, that's how it started." The Texas drawl revealed his amusement with the story. "Damnedest romance I ever saw."

"Raleigh's a spy too?" Now A.J. knew the man was a lunatic. Raleigh Foster, the newest member of the Grayson family, was entirely too sensible and, well, staid, to be Emma Peel to Adam's Mr. Steed.

Atlas leaned back in the massive leather chair and steepled stubby fingers on the jumbled desktop, with its odd ring of letter holders, files, and pencils carefully situated around the outer edge. On his left, what resembled a mangled bear claw sprawled next to a half-eaten donut. Amused by her perusal, Atlas grinned conspiratorially. "Yes, your cousin's new wife is also an agent with the International Security Agency. One of the best."

In response, A.J. pasted on her most engaging, placating smile and again rose from the chair. She slowly inched toward the door, fully prepared to turn and run if necessary. "Mr. Russell, I don't know why Adam put you up to this, but I really don't have time for pranks. Please let him know that the next time he tries to pull a practical joke on me, he should pick a better time for it. Now, if you'll excuse me."

As her hand closed around the cold, metal knob, it twisted beneath her grip. She jumped sideways to avoid a collision. Her hip rapped smartly against a mammoth globe, which teetered on its pedestal. Clutching her hip with one hand, she steadied the globe with the other. And glared when she saw who had knocked her aside.

"I told you to let me tell her," Adam announced as he entered the room, his arm draped around his wife's waist. Raleigh crossed to A.J. and brushed her cheek with a kiss. Adam soon did the same, and he steered A.J. to her recently vacated chair.

"Adam? Raleigh? What's going on here? Who is this man? What is the ISA? Why does he know so much about GCI?" A.J. demanded in rapid succession. "And don't tell me that nonsense about you two being secret agents."

Raleigh dropped into the chair beside A.J., and Adam perched on the arm. Raleigh spoke first. "A.J., I know this is a lot to take in, but we needed to tell you."

"Yeah, kiddo. This is rather important, and you're the only one we can trust," Adam said as he patted her hand. "Just hear us out."

Right before I kill you, she imagined happily. Then she'd hide the bodies, check in to a hotel for a few hours of sleep, and head back to Atlanta. "I'm listening," A.J. lied.

Adam smiled despite the distrust. "As Atlas has told you, Raleigh and I work for an extra-governmental organization known as the ISA. I've been employed by them since law school. Raleigh joined a few years later. The ISA collects intelligence and runs counterterrorism missions, among other things."

"Other things?" Oh, this is just getting better and better. Perhaps she was still in bed in Atlanta, engrossed in a bizarre nightmare. She had been getting very little sleep lately, and it was bound to take its toll. With a surreptitious gesture, she pinched a length of skin exposed by her skirt. And yelped.

"You okay?" Adam asked with concern.

"I'm fine," she replied, not at all convinced. But this was no dream.

Adam looked at Atlas then. "GCI has a strong working relationship with the ISA. It's primarily information sharing, but we occasionally develop technology for them."

"So you're like Q?" The legendary British gadget maker had fueled her childhood fantasies. A.J. could easily recall marathon sessions of the 007 movies. She had little interest in the espionage, but she lived for the introduction of the newest toys. *Mission: Impossible. The Avengers. Alias.* She'd never dreamed of living the life of the secret agents. It was the thrill of invention that caught her imagination. "GCI makes equipment for spies?"

"Not exactly," Atlas interjected. "But we're veering way off course here." He lifted a sheaf of papers and extended the pages to A.J. "Take a look."

A.J. accepted the packet warily. On the first page was a dossier. Name: Athena Josephine Grayson, née Calvin. Age: 25. IQ: 167.

The page continued, laying out the bare facts of her life in stark phrases. "Parents killed in a train accident, subject unscathed. Responses to parental death include irrational reactions to mild exposure to fire, including candles, fireplaces, and other controlled flammable devices. Attempted therapy to overcome phobia unsuccessful. Displays initial signs of compartmentalization. Tends to relegate upsetting or discordant aspects of life to a separate mental place—may find it difficult to assess the impact of work life on personal life. May overcompensate or disregard incompatible emotional responses."

Mortified by the report and its implications, A.J. leapt from her seat, tumbling the chair to the floor. She threw the offending papers across the desk and darted to the door, intent only on escape. The weakness shamed her, and she'd tried everything to combat it. To have her failure documented for a stranger's eyes, and to know he'd have access to other, more personal records, overwhelmed A.J. Embarrassment galvanized her, and she blindly hunted for an escape.

"A.J.," Adam began as he intercepted her at the entryway. "Wait a minute. What are you so angry about? It's just a dossier. They have one on all three of us."

A.J. poked him in the chest, embarrassment melting into indignation. "You told him?"

"Of course. I gave him your file." Adam ran a placating hand along her arm. "It's an informational tool. They needed to be sure we could trust you."

"Trust? You bastard. Take your hands off me." The words were low, husky, deadly.

Confused, Adam squeezed her captive wrist. "Sweetheart, hear me out. There's nothing to be upset about. The information is public record."

"Public record?" A.J. whipped her head around to look at Atlas. "You stole medical files that were none of your business. As soon as I get back to Atlanta, I'll slap you with a lawsuit so quickly, your head will spin." She impaled Adam with a deadly glare, and Adam recoiled as though struck. "You'll have my resignation on your desk in the morning. I'll explain it to the family, but I don't ever want to speak to you again."

"Why the hell are you resigning? Because of a few medical records? For goodness' sake, don't be ridiculous." Adam shook his head, irritation plain. "If you don't want to help us, fine, but don't overreact."

A.J. jerked her arm, trying to free herself. "Take your hands off me, Adam."

"A.J., stop being stubb—"

Adam doubled over in pain as she landed an elbow in his solar plexus. She whirled around and shot a fulminating glare at the gasping man. "I'm not overreacting. I quit." She tore open the door of the office and rushed out.

Inside Atlas's office, Raleigh stood behind her husband, gently stroking his back as he tried to catch his breath. Assured that he was merely winded, she said matter-of-factly, "I told you she wouldn't be impressed by this cloak-and-dagger stuff, Adam. You have always been so melodramatic."

Adam scowled at his wife of eight months, eager to retort but unable to form the words. The blow had been solid, delivered exactly as he'd taught A.J. when she was fourteen and being bullied at school. He simply never expected her to use the maneuver on him, he thought as he rubbed the point of impact. But neither his ministrations nor those of his bride soothed the initial pangs of guilt forming in his gut. Raleigh was right about the meeting.

He'd remembered his introduction to the ISA fondly, blithely ignoring how intrusive the entire interview seemed at the time.

Atlas had detailed his family history, his hobbies, moments in his life to which few were privy. It made him angry, but not violent. Adam lifted the dossier, interested in seeing what had caused A.J.'s temper tantrum.

The psychiatric profile narrowed his eyes. "Damn it, Atlas," he cursed, shaking his head. "You should have warned me." He passed the page to Raleigh.

She skimmed the words quickly, then looked at Atlas across his desk. Atlas sat stiffly, arms folded. "That wasn't necessary, Atlas," she admonished.

"You above all people should know it was," he coldly replied. "Childhood traumas interfere with judgment. I needed to see her reaction."

"And?"

"And I think we need to rethink this mission. She skittered out of here like a frightened doe. This is too delicate to leave to an amateur."

"We don't have a choice," Raleigh reminded him. But to Adam, she said, "And he is right. This could be dangerous, and if A.J. is unstable . . ."

"She's not unstable! She's angry and justifiably so. What if you'd read about your father on a sheet of paper handed to you by a stranger?"

Raleigh became rigid, her eyes clouding over with memory. She'd finally come to terms with her father's death, but only after years of avoiding the matter. Had she been confronted with the truth of that night by an outsider, her reaction would have been just as violent.

"What do we do now?" she asked as she gave Adam the sheet.

"Let me handle it," Adam demanded of Atlas. "She's still our best chance. I'll talk to her."

Adam reread the cold summary of the phobia caused by the most devastating night of A.J.'s life. He still remembered the crisp winter evening that brought her fully into their lives. The nine-year-old had shown up at the Grayson house after a commuter train derailed and collided with the family car. The impact threw A.J. from the vehicle, but the resulting explosion killed both of her parents. The police had brought the skinny, traumatized child to her only living relatives.

For weeks, she'd been nearly catatonic, a reaction the therapists described as survivor's guilt. It had taken time and patience to coax her out of her room, to help her find her place in the Grayson household. And now, she thought he'd shared her darkest fears with a complete stranger.

Adam rubbed the spot where she'd belted him, and sighed.

In the plush antechamber to Atlas's office, A.J. struggled to calm herself. Sensible black pumps lay discarded on the Chinese rug that covered pale hardwood floors waxed to a high shine. Anguish twisted her stomach as she huddled in a butter-soft leather chair, slim legs drawn beneath her. Long, slender fingers trembled as she pressed them together to control violent tremors.

"How could he?" she whispered in a pained voice to the thriving rhododendron in the corner. How could Adam betray her so easily to strangers?

She longed to flee the building, with its dark panels and

callous secrets. Unfortunately, her original plan to rush out and catch the next flight to Atlanta had been thwarted by a keypad that secured the door. The presence of the security system did not pose an insurmountable obstacle; with concentration, she could decrypt the system in under ten minutes, fifteen on the outside. But at the moment, running number permutations in her head seemed beyond her reach.

Instead of the poised, brilliant A.J. Grayson she'd painstakingly created, she curled into the chair, a mass of insecurity and fear.

For years, she'd carefully repressed the night of the fire and its myriad meanings. Like her namesake, A.J. imagined she'd emerged from the ruins of her childhood a tiny adult Adam nicknamed A.J., forever abandoning her parents' preferred name "Athena." Yet, in mere seconds, a single sheet of parchment destroyed the carefully constructed fantasy she'd so meticulously built.

A sob caught in her chest, strangled her. Yes, she did tend to focus on her work, but not out of fear. She was busy, and she had goals. That didn't mean she—what had the psychiatrist called it?—*compartmentalized* her life. She merely understood that one had to have focus, and she concentrated her efforts on building GCI. Wringing her hands, A.J. dismissed the idea of overcompensation, oblivious to the telltale gesture. She was a perfectly healthy young woman with a dislike for fire, surely a natural reaction.

The memory built quickly, the leap of amber and red flames, the tinkle of glass as it erupted from the windows. When her breathing quickened with panic, A.J. summoned other memories with effort. Their solid familiarity stilled the trembling.

Inhaling deeply, A.J. recalled the seamless integration into the tightly knit family of five. Aunt Carolyn and Uncle M.G. offered her the option of Mom and Dad, and they understood when she declined. Rachel and Jonah, at ten and nine, respectively, had welcomed their only cousin easily.

But it was Adam, at sixteen, who had taken on his new sibling with determination. It was he who'd sat by her bedside at night before she could sleep in the dark. He taught her to ride a bike, to throw a punch, to build a computer from scratch. Adam was her cousin by blood, but in every way that mattered, he was her brother.

Now, to help an organization she knew nothing about, he had turned her secret confessions into a profile for outsiders. And he expected her to help him.

A shadow fell over her, and she looked up from her hands with tears shimmering in liquid pools. Adam stood in front of her. She hastily dashed the moisture away. "Why'd you do it, Adam?"

"I didn't, honey. I swear." Adam inched closer to the chair, uncertain of his reception. "Raleigh and I knew that Atlas intended to see you this morning. He said he wanted a chance to talk to you, feel you out. I didn't know about the dossier, kiddo. I wouldn't— I'd never let anyone hurt you like that."

"You didn't give them my files?" she asked, needing reassurance.

"Of course not." He seemed annoyed by the question. "Besides, Atlas wouldn't need my help for something so simple. He's a powerful man, A.J., and he's investigating you for a good reason."

A.J. dashed away the moisture with the back of her hand. "And the whole stealth thing? His idea?"

Adam grimaced, chagrined. "Well, uh, Raleigh and I were flying in from Belize and thought it would be better to meet you here." He shrugged with discomfiture. "It seemed funny at the time."

"You're an idiot, Adam," A.J. said mildly. "A big, dumb idiot."

"You can't tell me you're not impressed." Adam reached out a hand and chucked her beneath the chin, a familiar gesture. "I'm sorry to spring this on you. I'm even more sorry about the dossier. I honestly didn't know it would say that."

"So someone has been researching me? What the devil for?"

"We're quite serious about the ISA, A.J. And about needing your help." Adam stepped away from the chair. "Take a couple of minutes. If you can forgive me, we'll tell you all about it."

Adam walked into the office. Waiting a beat, A.J. uncurled her legs and stood. She'd listen, and if what they said didn't make sense, she'd use the other fighting techniques he'd taught her.

Resolved, she slid her feet into the plain shoes, adjusted the hem of her conservative black Italian wool suit, and crossed to the office door.

With a warning knock, she opened the door and entered. A.J. ignored Atlas's speculative look and moved to stand in front of Adam. "I'm not sorry I hit you," she said brusquely.

"I know, short one," he replied, brushing a hand over the ebony hair sleeked into a bun at the nape of her neck. At five four, A.J. was a full head shorter than her exceptionally tall cousin. The diminutive "short one" had been a private nickname between the two of them since her entrance into the Grayson family.

"Are you alright, A.J.?" Raleigh asked quietly.

A.J. turned and offered a wan smile. "I'm fine. Seeing my psyche summarized like that is a bit disconcerting. I guess I got a little upset."

"You guess?" countered Adam, rubbing at his injury. "You almost cracked a rib."

"For your sake, you should be glad that 'almost' doesn't count," A.J. sneered. To Atlas, she said, "Now, where were we?"

Atlas chuckled appreciatively. He lifted the reassembled file, the dossier removed from the stack. A.J. accepted the papers gingerly, and opened the stiff leather cover. The top page now contained a miniature map in the upper right-hand corner, and a detailed litany of facts on the remainder of the page. Two items caught her attention this time.

The map depicted the island of Jafir, the site of the trials for Praxis, GCI's latest innovation.

The other name was its newly crowned King. Damon Toca.

Heat flushed A.J.'s face and tightened her stomach. "Damon Toca? You need me to help him?"

"Not simply Damon, but the entire country." Atlas scooted his chair back on its coasters and walked to the oversized map that covered the expanse of wall behind his desk. He lifted an old-fashioned pointer, a product of his refusal to use the laser contraptions his assistant, Lewis, tried to foist on him regularly. With the metal tip, he tapped Jafir on the map.

"As you know, Damon Toca has ascended to the throne as King of Jafir. And in the past two years, the nation has served as the fulcrum for the successful negotiations of the African-Arab Alliance and the first trials of Praxis." Atlas paused, and looked at Raleigh.

"Next month, the Alliance will begin final talks with Israel, and they hope to iron out a peace agreement throughout the region by the end of May. Because of the success of Praxis, Jafir remains the natural center of discussion."

Adam interjected. "Unfortunately, there are a number of factions in the area and throughout the world who are terrified of such an agreement."

"Do you know why?" Atlas prompted.

A.J. lifted an arched brow. "Is this a game of spy *Jeopardy?*"

"Athena."

"Stop calling me that," A.J. snapped, but at the look in the steely gray eyes, she answered, "I would assume it's because a successful treaty would diminish the need for illegal weapons and other terrorist hardware. And it would secure Praxis."

"Correct." Atlas nodded. "The defeat of Scimitar has left a power vacuum in the region, and several groups are scrambling to fill the void. If the Alliance signs a treaty with Israel first, several players in the terrorism game will have to find new outlets."

"I still don't see where I come into this," A.J. said quietly. "I don't deal in weapons, explosives, or anything that is remotely connected to Praxis."

Adam spoke up then. "For the past year and a half, the ISA has been monitoring your research on cognitive science. Your work on artificial intelligence is magnificent."

"And I thought it was secret," A.J. mumbled in annoyance.

"It's my company, A.J.," Adam reminded her blandly. "Your newest innovation, Poppet, may be exactly what we're looking for."

"It's an R and D device, Adam," A.J. corrected. "I designed it to predict consumer wants based on existing products and customer responses to market shifts. It has no weapons application."

"The algorithms you designed for Poppet are spectacular, A.J. You've created a simulated model of the prototypical consumer, complete with variates based on age, socioeconomic status, and familiarity with technology. And it models multiple consumer bases simultaneously. Your use of POMDPs to overcome the state of the system issues were inspired."

"POMDPs?" Atlas repeated.

"Partially observable Markov decision processes."

"Which means?"

"MDPs, or Markov decision processes, allow the researcher to reason out an AI's actions when the system is faced with multiple uncertainties, that is, if the agent makes a decision at times determined by external events. But there is the added difficulty of the state of the system, where, for example, an AI can't observe its own state, just the complex data fed to it. POMDPs are a framework for modeling the system."

"Forget I asked." Atlas rolled his eyes, then squinted. "Is Poppet a robot?"

"No. Just a very advanced, complex computer system with interactive components. It doesn't simply compute data and spit it out to me. It will model behaviors, query options, and predict user probabilities in infinite variations."

"Remarkable."

A.J. preened. "It is fairly ingenious, but that's not all. It can learn and adapt, which is the major barrier to artificial intelligence. POPET is an acronym for power of persuasion experimental technology. We call it Poppet. Poppet can understand changes in market forces and reason out not only what the next product should be, but why. It can predict how we should market the products we develop, who the consumer should be, and why she'll buy three."

"And that's why we need it, A.J." Atlas tapped the map lightly. "Factions both inside and outside the region have joined forces with remnants of Scimitar to create new partnerships. Deadly ones. We think you can adjust Poppet to anticipate what the partnerships will look like and how they will target Jafir and the Alliance."

A.J. snorted in disbelief. "You want me to do what? Poppet isn't a military tool. It would take copious amounts of data on the existing threats to Jafir, the data on all the major and minor terrorist groups, their cells and their members. Not to mention, I'll need to construct a model based on at least three or four of the most notorious terrorists to establish a baseline for the learning curve. That information alone will take months to accumulate."

Holding out a flash drive, Atlas simply said, "This should get you started."

"Huh?"

"The reason we've told you about the ISA, A.J., is because we knew you'd need this information. We have every possible statistic you can imagine, and we have intelligence on every criminal mastermind, geopolitical psychopath, and urban terrorist in the known world."

"And you have GCI's president. So why do you need me?"

Adam shrugged sheepishly. "Because I couldn't figure out how to make Poppet work. Raleigh tried, as did some of the brightest AI minds in the business. What you've developed is beyond them."

"You want me to become a spy?"

"Not a spy. Just a consultant. For six weeks. After the summit, if the treaty is signed, it will be much harder to destroy the Alliance."

"And where does Damon fit in?"

"He'll be your liaison. Both he and President Robertsi are

familiar with the ISA, and we have briefed the President on your work. As far as the rest of the Cabinet knows, you'll be conducting an audit of the government. The full cover story is in the folder, and it will guarantee you access to sensitive information. You'll undergo training for the next two weeks; then you'll leave for Jafir."

"I can't disappear for two months! I have a presentation to the board on Monday. And I've got work to complete."

Adam interjected, all operative now. "I will take care of GCI. The board will be told that I've sent you on a special project to Jafir. Given our ties, it will make complete sense. In addition, it will only improve your status in their eyes, making it easier to sell them on Poppet."

Casting about for another excuse, A.J. argued, "Two weeks can't be enough time for training. I've never fired a gun, and I don't know any karate."

Raleigh smiled. "You handled Adam well. I'll instruct you in a modified course of hand-to-hand combat. You'll also be briefed on select operations in Jafir, and I'll introduce you to the rules of engagement, our protocol guide. Adam is less comfortable with his command of the procedure."

"Some of us aren't so hidebound." Adam scowled, the argument an old one. "I will conduct your weapons training. My wife doesn't like guns."

"They're clumsy," Raleigh retorted. "I didn't hear you complaining last—" Remembering their audience, Raleigh stopped herself. "Instruction begins at noon, A.J."

Adam handed an overwhelmed A.J. a flat keycard. "Lewis will show you to your quarters. We'll pick you up there. Do not go exploring."

Tapping the silver plastic against her palm, A.J. realized she could think of no further excuses. "Where would I start?"

Satisfied with her grudging acquiescence, Atlas circled the oversized teak desk and leaned against its surface. "Get some rest. Your code name for this mission will be Cipher, and the mission will be referred to as Iota."

"Why?"

Adam explained, "It's the Greek letter J. Atlas isn't terribly imaginative."

Atlas glowered at Adam, the gruff expression belied by the paternal twinkle in the gray eyes. He returned his attention to A.J. "This afternoon, we'll reconvene and fill you in on the players and the history. It's a long story, and one you cannot reveal to anyone else. You'll be undercover for the duration of this mission, and breaking cover will have dire consequences. Do you think you can handle the secrecy?"

A.J. grinned dimly, accepting her defeat. "Who'd believe me if I tried?"

CHAPTER TWO

Power seduces with the softest of touches. It entices with silky words of command; enthralls with the promise of authority. In the proper setting, power weakens the knees, beguiles the senses. And with trappings of crown and glory, power reigns supreme.

For Damon Toca, novitiate to the throne, the lure of power proved imminently resistible. Hour after hour, he sat in stuffy, long-winded meetings, listening to reasonable people justify unreasonable expectations. Briefings from State, then Treasury, from Military Affairs, and Human Services flooded his days. Assistants daily pressed thick files brimming with facts and figures upon him. Gross national product information, pollution data, treaty provisions, export numbers, and crime statistics peppered his dreams. Nighttime ushered in a never-ending parade of state visitors to the grand marble halls of the palace, with black-coated servers tending to every need.

Damon Toca endured the bows and scrapes. He tolerated the eager presses of flesh and fustian conversation generated by his unusual ascent to the throne. When wine flowed and highborn guests jockeyed for his favor, he smiled and nodded and charmed.

And longed desperately for his art gallery and his home in Durban.

Today, he'd risen at dawn, unable to sleep. With the silent trail of armed guards a respectable distance behind, Damon wandered the grounds of the royal palace. White stone glistened in pale light and morning dew. Towers rose straight and tall, sentinels of the Mediterranean. In the lush courtyard, palms, jacarandas, and dragon trees grew in dense groves. A few feet away, a profusion of flowers bloomed in the garden, no, the Asphodel, he reminded himself sternly. His great-great-grandfather had named the garden in honor of his wife's favorite flower. He wandered between the rows of tulips and king's spears, stopped to caress the climbing roses.

Lowering himself to a stone bench in the midst of the Asphodel, Damon draped his suit coat across his lap and studied the exterior of the palace. The artist in him admired the cleverness of stained glass in the double-arched windows on the sea frontage. The monarch appreciated the skill of architecture that disguised sentry posts and buttresses. Hidden cameras tracked movements from beneath cloaks of granite and marble façade. Wires ringed terraces and turrets, constantly communicating with the security station in the south and north wings. There, in sharp contrast to the ancient castle, a digital maze of monitors and bays tracked enemies of state and their potential allies.

The estate housed the National Assembly and the presidential mansion, all dwarfed by the royal palace. Inside the palace, the monarch's offices and residence dominated the north wing and central building, but ceded the south wing to the President's headquarters. After nearly a year in residence, he had yet to accustom himself to the vastness of the property or the constriction of movement required by his post.

Whims no longer existed. Freedom shimmered as a distant memory. Wrought iron gates and invisible bands of heritage stood between his past and his present.

Resentment rose quickly, its taste acrid and bitter. He clenched a fist in impotent rage at the fate that had bound him to a land he barely knew. Damon had been brought to Jafir by a duty to parents he'd never known. Thirty-two years before, Jaya Toca and Nelson Tebbe, the royal family, had hidden Damon and his twin brother, Nelson, with relatives for their protection. A prescient move, as only five years later, they were brutally murdered by Kadifir el Zeben.

Zeben headed the insurgent group Scimitar, an organization bound by profit, not politics or religion. For decades, Scimitar had cultivated friendships with poor countries, providing medical aid and stolen weaponry to foment civil wars across the Middle East and Africa, and north into Eastern Europe.

It was a successful venture until, over the years, the formerly shrewd Zeben became a fanatic, intent on controlling the political fortunes of Jafir. He'd betrayed former allies in a quest for supremacy. The year before, Zeben had stolen blueprints for a potent environmental system in order to convert it to a devastating chemical weapon. ISA agents foiled his plot and incarcerated him, until Zeben escaped.

Zeben partnered with Damon's younger twin brother in a plot to steal the throne of Jafir. According to Jafirian custom, the monarchy passed to direct descendants who possessed proof of their heritage. A long-hidden obelisk and a sacred stone attested to the rightful heir. Damon had uncovered the conspiracy and, with the help of the ISA, thwarted Nelson and Zeben's plans of usurpation. Now his brother and Zeben were imprisoned on opposite ends of the island, and Damon had assumed the lost throne.

A throne he'd been unaware of a year ago, and was convinced he did not want. Yet, if he refused to take the throne, Nelson would surely launch a claim of right that could destabilize the nation. It was a chance he could not take. Thus, a circumstance of birth had conspired to steal his life away and demand he sacrifice the autonomy he prized above all. And he had no choice.

"Sir?" The uniformed guard halted before him and waited for the signal to speak.

Damon looked up. "Yes?"

"President Robertsi has arrived. They have escorted him to your office."

Damon shook off the dark emotion, and nodded politely to the guard. "Please tell the President I will join him shortly."

He pushed himself up from the cool stone, brushed at the gray slacks with their light dusting of pollen. Shrugging into the jacket, Damon took a deep breath. A quick mental roll through his schedule reminded him of the six thirty a.m. meeting with the President, to be followed by a security briefing from the Minister of Military Affairs at seven forty-five. After a breakfast meeting with the Arts Council and a tour of Desira with the city commissioners, he had an afternoon conference with the Cabinet.

May as well begin the torture, Damon thought as he strode along the cobblestone walkway to the palace doors. He entered the south wing, guards signaling his movements along the wide corridor lined with paintings of relatives he'd never known. Damon ignored the twinge of loss. He turned onto the short hallway that led to the Monarch's Suite, a collection of opulent offices where he met with staff and dignitaries.

In the main chamber of the suite, Damon pushed gently at the polished mahogany doors, which swung silently on well-oiled hinges.

"Good morning, President Robertsi." Damon crossed to the older man standing stiffly by the fireplace and extended a hand. A formally beautiful man of sixty-five, with smooth coffee skin, Lawrence Robertsi had the bearing and carriage of a military man. His ascent to power began during a stint in the Jafirian Navy, where his heroics saved a shipload of crewmates. Soon, he advanced through the ranks to become Chief of Military Affairs, then Minister of State. The high esteem showered upon him by the citizens had been reaffirmed by his reelection to the presidency. Robertsi was respected by his peers and feared by his rivals.

Damon was dubious of the category in which Robertsi placed him. "My apologies for the wait."

Robertsi shook his head in demurral. "I arrived early. No apology necessary, Your Highness."

"Damon, please. I find myself longing to hear the sound of my own name these days," Damon complained as he dropped into a wing chair upholstered in brocaded Chinese silk in muted reds and greens. "Please sit," he instructed, gesturing to a matching chair behind Robertsi.

"Of course," Robertsi murmured as he settled into the chair. "I hope you have not found your adjustment too arduous, Your Highness," he responded intentionally. "It would be unfortunate to have exhausted our new King so early in his tenure."

Damon noted the continued formality, but decided to let it pass. Instead, he replied, "I am not yet exhausted. Only slightly overwhelmed. The rigors of governing do not leave much time for reflection or other pursuits."

Robertsi followed Damon's gaze to the Tanner hanging above the carved granite mantel. "You miss your gallery."

"Desperately," Damon said with a self-mocking smile. He gestured to the Matisse on the far wall and the Cuevas sculpture displayed near the central panes of the window. "Surrounded by such glorious art, I cannot help but imagine myself as its curator. Not its owner."

"Caretaker," Robertsi corrected sharply. "The national treasures housed here and in the National Gallery are the property of the people. However, your parents acquired an enviable private collection. Your meeting with the Arts Council will address how you intend to dispose of those pieces."

"Never fear, Lawrence. I do not intend to abscond with the State's art and pawn them on the underground market." Neither spoke aloud the fact that his brother, Nelson, could not have made the same declaration. Nelson had built his fortune and reputation on art smuggling and fraud.

"I have no doubts about your *artistic* integrity, Your Highness," Robertsi replied.

"But you do have qualms about my ethics in other matters," Damon muttered as he levered himself from the chair and stalked over to the fireplace.

"The qualification of 'artistic' was inappropriate. Forgive my lapse."

"You are allowed to have your concerns, Lawrence. I cannot fault you for that."

"Of course not. However, certain proprieties must be observed."

"Proprieties? Is that what the cold chill between us is? Propriety?"

"Your Highness—"

"Damon. My name is Damon," he ground out, and jumped to his feet. "For thirty-two years, I have been Damon Toca. Now, suddenly, I am reduced to a title wielded like a shield between us. Treat me like a friend, for heaven's sake! After almost a year, I have at least earned that courtesy, have I not?"

Robertsi, who had risen as soon as Damon leapt from his chair, shook his head. "With all due respect, Your Highness, I cannot."

"Why not?" Damon rounded on Robertsi, eyes flashing with annoyance. Tempestuous hazel, a gauzy brown shot through with emerald, narrowed with impatience. When Robertsi remained silent, Damon waved a hand imperiously. "Speak freely, man! Why not?"

Robertsi spoke harshly, months of antagonism edging his words. "Because you are not my friend, Your Highness. I have spent my entire adulthood defending Jafir. For decades, I have guarded its shores and protected its people. In that time, I learned to choose my friends carefully. You have agreed to serve your people, and for that I can respect you. But your family has wreaked havoc on my people, and that I cannot forget."

"I am not my brother!"

"No, but I am not yet confident of who you are." Robertsi stopped abruptly. The patrician posture, with its ramrod-straight back and dutifully squared shoulders, slumped a bit. "Damon," he began quietly, "I do realize that you have given up a great deal in loyalty to a nation you barely know. However, I do not have the luxury of trusting you yet. I offer you this candor only once." He walked to the younger man and laid a hand on his shoulder. "I am the leader of this nation, but you are its head. We must share a power I alone have borne for years. It is a difficult transition."

"I understand that."

"What I do not understand is why one with no ties to my homeland except a family he does not recall and a threat he has evaded would accept this role. Is it for the power? The money? The title? Or is it, as you claim, out of respect for your parents' sacrifice?" Robertsi squeezed the captive shoulder meaningfully. "Until I am convinced, you may have my fidelity but not my friendship."

Damon looked at the hand on his shoulder, the skin taut despite its age. He then met Robertsi eye to eye, despite the older man's superior height. Robertsi did not waver, and in the obsidian depths, Damon thought he saw something murkier than suspicion. He dismissed the concern as pique and nodded. "I understand, President Robertsi. No informalities between us. Colleagues and nothing more."

Behind them, at the doorway, a discreet cough sounded.

McCord, Damon's aide, waited politely. "President Robertsi, there is a call for you."

President Robertsi nodded. "Thank you. Shall I meet you in the conference room?"

"When you are finished," Damon agreed.

"Then if you'll excuse me." Robertsi bowed slightly, then walked from the room. As he passed McCord, he nodded.

McCord was a man of indistinct years, but Damon guessed him to be in his early seventies. The lived-in face, with its wrinkles and lines, were evidence of service; the wiry white hair, proof of its difficulty. If McCord had a first name, no one used it, and Damon's furtive investigations had yet to produce one. Short, stocky, with a boxer's rolling gait, McCord moved easily between regal and provincial.

He'd headed the Tribunal of Ascension for thirty-one years, a job he assumed after the death of the royal family. When Damon ascended to the throne, custom dictated that McCord serve as his Chief of Staff, as he had to Damon's mother, the Queen.

McCord had taken an instant liking to Damon, who reminded him of his Jaya. The chocolate hair and lighter eyes were gifts from his mother, and she too possessed a volatile temper quickly controlled and a commitment to honor demanded of royalty. In him, McCord also saw traits passed on by his father, the gentle humor and quick intelligence. Serving Damon struck a deep chord of fond sadness, and deeper loyalty.

"You fought with the President," McCord declared as he closed the double doors, sealing out the guards.

"'Fought' is a strong term. I believe saying I was 'rebuffed' is the appropriate term. He doesn't trust me."

"You must allow for such hostility, Your Highness. You have ejected him and his family from the home they occupied for years," he said, referring to the President's relocation to the mansion. "They thought the monarchy was a myth, and then you arrive and alter the dynamic of power. You have forced him to divide an authority that once belonged solely to him. Robertsi is a proud man, and although he has accepted the situation, you cannot expect much else yet."

"Simple friendship is not such an unreasonable prospect after months of collaboration! We have shared meals and sleepless nights. I am not asking to become his boon companion, but he refuses the most innocuous of friendships."

"As is his right," McCord stated baldly. "You cannot force him to like you, Damon. Not even by royal command."

Damon gave a short laugh. "A royal decree that he has to like me. Death to he who dares disobey."

"Give him time."

"How much time? How long until I am able to build a life here? I am not an automaton, McCord. I need friends, comrades, something. Instead, I am surrounded by colleagues and sycophants. Other than you, I am alone, and even you refuse to relinquish that stubborn formality of distance between royalty and subject."

"I am sorry, Damon, but this is how it must be. And not only between you and I, but for your sake, between you and everyone. The people have made you King, but they have not yet accepted you. Until you have earned their trust, your obligation is to them. This leaves no room for friends, for fraternity."

"So I am to be isolated in this palace?"

"For a while, Your Highness. That stubborn formality you

deride is required of your role. You are more than a figurehead, but you are indeed a symbol." McCord coughed abruptly, then admonished, "And, ah, Damon, your life must be above reproach, and your liaisons discreet."

"What liaisons? I haven't enjoyed even a dalliance with a serving wench," Damon quipped. "My closest encounter was—"

"Your trip to London last month. The barrister. Learn to be more wary of reporters."

Damon shifted uncomfortably. "Nothing happened. Particularly given the constant shadow of guards."

"But the tabloid reported—"

"A lie. Judith O'Brien is a trusted friend of the family."

"You cannot always be certain, Damon," cautioned McCord. "It will be difficult for the next few months, but after the coronation, the strictures will ease. Then we can begin to seek out a suitable mate for you. I have taken the liberty of reviewing candidates. They will be included on the Coronation Ball invitation list."

"A suitable mate?" Damon scowled. "I don't need you trawling for wives on my behalf. I will control my personal life, McCord."

"Your Highness, you have no personal life."

With an arrogant arch of brow, Damon corrected, "I control what happens in my bedroom."

"No. You do not. Particularly not in such unstable times. Trouble comes cloaked as a paramour as often as an enemy. And she may not know she is being used to harm you. Your Highness, until the coronation in May and the summit, you cannot risk it."

"This is ridiculous!" Damon barked.

"This is your duty."

"Duty be damned!"

"As will we all if you abdicate the throne or place it in jeopardy."

By degrees, Damon drew himself in, the stormy eyes calming, the flat line of his mouth regaining its natural curve. McCord watched with admiration as Damon bit off his retort.

"Very good, Damon Toca," McCord said beneath his breath. The young man had so much to learn, and barely any time to absorb it all. A sophisticate of upper-middle-class society, Damon had mingled with royalty, grown up among the wealthy. Yet his new role required an understanding of nuance, of subtlety, that would prove the making or demise of the King.

Surrounded by parasites and foes, Damon would need to be wary of not only those enemies he knew, but of saboteurs in his inner circle. McCord started to utter the warning, but then he caught the slowly clenching fists. Damon may have schooled his expression into submission, but body language spoke of less settled emotions.

"Your Highness," McCord said quietly, "we should rejoin the President. You have a meeting with Teresa Wynn about the military attaché visiting from Israel to oversee preparations for the summit."

Damon released his balled fingers slowly, a trick learned in childhood. With effort, he relaxed tense muscles in his neck and jaw. The smooth veneer he'd cultivated as a counter to Nelson's more aggressive style slicked over temper and disguised irritation. He inclined his head regally in assent. "Let us go."

Together, the men climbed the shallow staircase to the conference room in silence. On the second level, stained glass poured in streaks of colored light from insets lining the upper tiers of windows. The palace had a third and fourth floor in the central building, with the dual leveled wings flanking each side. As with the other stairways, hand-carved marble and rich traditional Berber lined the steps.

A lovely prison, Damon thought bleakly. Day after day, he pretended to be its master, vibrantly aware he was merely its slave.

He played no true role in the machinations of state. Indeed, he struggled vainly to recall the reason for this early morning conversation with Robertsi, as they reached the landing. The schedule had only indicated state affairs.

Likely another visiting dignitary and his homely daughter, or a warlord seeking absolution for an ill-fated alliance with Zeben. The former would result in a luncheon or a dinner where idle prattle disguised as small talk would bore him silly.

The latter would yield a parley attended by Wynn as Minister of Military Affairs, Santana as Head of State, Robertsi, and Jean-Louis Bayrout, the Minister of Treasury. Damon was often present for the negotiations, but he was intimately aware of his limited role in decision-making.

Damon didn't begrudge his exclusion. He was vividly aware of his status as an interloper in matters of government. Like a child at his parents' dinner party, Damon was granted the thin courtesy of attendance, but held no sway in deliberations. He had no right to expect more.

At their first meeting, President Robertsi had cautioned Damon that while the monarchy was the heart of the people, Robertsi was its head. People may pay obeisance to him, but to no avail. Damon, King of Jafir, had only a limited Constitutional role as monarch. The President and assembly governed, with his feckless advice and regardless of his consent.

Thus, Damon rarely spoke at these meetings, relying instead on Robertsi to rule.

The rigors of politics did not intimidate him. He understood people and their needs. According to the Constitution, the King had no real role, and he accepted that.

To the world, to the government officials, he was a gallery owner, not a politician.

Beyond the glass, the Mediterranean crashed against the craggy shore below the Desira Plateau. Life for the government wouldn't change at all if he skipped this meeting and escaped to the stables for a ride along the rocky beach. The thought cheered him, and Damon turned to inform McCord of his decision. Why should he sit in a meeting with a man who had little use for him, and then endure a briefing from Wynn about decisions he could not make?

"McCord." The older man stopped and turned to face Damon. Damon spoke softly, aware of the constant listeners. "Inform Robertsi and Wynn that I will not be attending the morning briefings."

"Excuse me, Your Highness?"

With an imperial shrug, Damon repeated, "I will not attend the morning briefings."

"And why not, may I ask?"

"Because I am not needed. You and I both know my participation is simply a pretense. As soon as the briefings are completed, I am whisked off to another Very Important Meeting, while the adults remain behind and conduct the business of Jafir."

"Don't exaggerate, Damon. You have a responsibility."

"Yes, yes, I know. A responsibility. A duty. A commitment. And I have done my level best to honor it. However, the public image of an engaged King can be maintained without us believing the lie." I'm a prop and I know it, Damon thought silently. If no one else will admit it, I will.

"These briefings are important," McCord argued. "Vital information."

"Which I will have no part in acting upon. Jafir is a democracy with duly elected heads of state. I am not one of them."

"Begging your pardon, Your Highness, but that is not entirely correct." McCord checked around him, noted the guards waiting patiently at the base of the stairs. He gestured toward the receptionist's office. They entered, dismissed the curtsying young woman, and closed the door.

"What is not entirely correct?" Damon demanded.

"That you are not a head of state."

"I know I am the monarch, McCord. I may be useless, but I'm not stupid. The Constitution is very specific about my job description. I attend laborious dinners and smile for photo ops, while my mind is filled with useless clutter in an attempt to keep me occupied. Ah, the veritable wonderland of being King."

"Oh, do cease being tiresome, Damon," McCord interrupted with exasperation. "Self-pity does not become you."

Surprised by the breach in protocol, Damon was speechless. A sudden grin broke over his countenance, and Damon chuckled aloud. "Tiresome, McCord? I don't believe that is the proper way to address your King."

McCord flushed with embarrassment. "You do frustrate me, Your Highness. My apologies."

"No. It was well worth the rebuke to see the chink in your perfect armor. Now, what was it you were explaining to me?"

"Robertsi wanted to speak with you about several items today. Before the meeting with Wynn or the Cabinet meeting this afternoon."

"The schedule said affairs of state. I assumed it would be another briefing."

"Not exactly." McCord hesitated, then sighed. "Attend the meeting, Damon. It is important."

"What is going to happen?"

"I am not at liberty to say."

"McCord!"

"Attend the meeting," McCord repeated flatly. "Robertsi is waiting."

Muttering, Damon shook his head in frustration. "Come on."

Inside the conference room, President Robertsi waited with the Minister of State, Isabel Santana. A tall, striking woman of forty-five, Santana had been appointed by Robertsi to the ministry's top position five years before, after years as his aide when Robertsi had been the Minister of State.

She came gracefully to her feet when Damon and McCord entered the room. "Your Highness. Mr. McCord." Her words were polite, cold. Damon felt the chill confirmed by her icy stare.

"Minister Santana." He inclined his head and took a seat that allowed him to observe both politicians. McCord silently moved to a chair along the wall. "I was not aware you would be joining us. I hope I did not keep you waiting."

"Not at all," Isabel replied in the same frosty tone, clearly communicating her displeasure.

"Your Highness, I asked Minister Santana to join us this

morning because what we need to discuss directly affects both of you."

Damon stiffened, sensing an ambush. "I do not understand."

Robertsi glanced at McCord, who Damon knew sat just beyond his shoulder. Damon resisted the urge to turn and look at the older man. Whatever the two had in store for him, he would listen now, react later.

"The Constitution of Jafir is quite clear on a number of matters. It deliberately separates the power of governance from the monarchy. The President maintains executive power in almost all matters."

"Almost all?" Damon echoed.

"Yes. The drafters wanted to maintain the monarchy as a viable tool for ensuring state security and as a connection with the world beyond Jafir's borders. To that end, the Constitution provides for the president to appoint the ruling monarch as Minister of State, if the President feels such an appointment is warranted."

"I know that. And I know that you have already selected your Cabinet and your allies."

Robertsi paused, and met Damon's wary eyes with his own inscrutable expression. "Despite our earlier discussion, I do believe it is in the best interest of the country to appoint you as Minister of State. I have discussed my decision with the Cabinet, and most concur. McCord has provided a rather glowing assessment of your progress. You have done an admirable job of familiarizing yourself with every aspect of government. However, to ensure continued stability, the people of Jafir and its neighbors need to believe that we have confidence in you."

"The monarchy is a titular role, Robertsi. There is no need for this," Damon countered. "You merely needed someone to occupy the throne to prevent Zeben or Nelson from making a claim."

McCord spoke then. "That was true, initially. Yet, with the coronation and the summit coming so soon, questions have emerged about your loyalty and commitment to Jafir. As heir to the Tocas and the Tebbes, you own nearly one-third of the national lands, including mineral deposits and other natural resources. Your holdings also extend north to Spain, France, and Greece and south to several African nations. You have interests in Arabian oil wells as exchanges between the royal houses from centuries ago."

"So, in order to demonstrate that I am not simply a figurehead with no real ties to the stability of Jafir, you're giving me a political stake in its future," Damon deduced.

"Yes," Robertsi answered unequivocally.

"And if I act in a manner contrary to state interests, you can have me deposed and arrested as a traitor."

"Yes." Robertsi's second response came as quickly and matter-of-factly as the first. "We are at a critical moment, and we can ill afford to lose allies now."

Damon turned to face Isabel. "You can't possibly be pleased by this."

"My first duty is to Jafir. Personal ambition has no place," she answered grimly, as though in doubt to his opinion on the same.

"If I am correct, I am being offered a position by a man who doesn't trust me, taken from another who will necessarily despise me. How could this be any worse?" Damon said aloud, though mainly to himself.

Unfortunately for Damon, McCord possessed a wicked sense

of humor that had served him well for fifty years in the palace. "Ah, Your Highness?"

Damon twisted in his chair, and he dreaded the gleam of amusement lighting the man's blue eyes. "Minister Santana will be your new deputy."

———

In the gathering shadows of late afternoon, the Cabinet convened to welcome their new Minister of State in the Presidential Suite. The head of the National Assembly, Leslie Joycean, read the acclimation from the body accepting the change of position. Polite applause followed the swearing-in ceremony, and Damon struggled not to laugh at the farce of the occasion.

The newly demoted deputy Minister, Santana, watched him with banked hatred, and President Robertsi examined him with a mixture of distrust and resignation. The remaining Cabinet members surreptitiously inspected him, as though trying to determine if he had wielded a Svengali-like control over the two. And Damon waited for the next shift in the affairs of the Jafirian government.

He didn't have long to wait.

"Ladies and gentlemen," President Robertsi intoned quietly. Instantly, the murmuring ceased. "We have additional matters to discuss. As announced last week, the King and I have decided to hire a consultant to conduct an audit of our capacity and structure. GCI has agreed to provide this service at no cost, and their consultant will be arriving in the morning. In the folders being passed to you now, you will see the consultant's CV as received today. Also included in your packets is the information she will require from each of your departments."

Damon flipped through his report, then stopped dead at the name of the consultant. "A.J. Grayson?" Damon asked uneasily. An image of that night flashed in his head, and coiled in his gut.

President Robertsi answered tersely. "Yes."

"I thought her area was research and development."

"It is," President Robertsi explained. "She is the Vice President of Research and Development for new markets at GCI. Before that, however, she worked in their organizational development division. And, given the sensitive nature of our concerns, we are fortunate to have someone so experienced." Oblivious to the panic in Damon's voice, Robertsi announced, "She'll be here in the morning."

CHAPTER THREE

She didn't often judge people, A.J. reasoned, as she waited for her appointment in President Robertsi's anteroom. She typically accepted them at face value, foibles and all. As a result, it was she who defended the termagant or made excuses for the curmudgeon. Wasn't that why she was often stuck as the family representative at tedious social functions?

She could encourage smiles from the intractable and calm the fractious because she instantly engendered trust. To her cousins' delight, her poker face had cost her thousands of dollars in Monopoly money before she swore off the game. A.J. had little talent for subterfuge and less patience for snobbery.

But in her newly cast role as a spook, she'd have to conceal her feelings and disguise her ulterior motive for helping the government solve its terrorist threat. The ISA suspected that no matter who on the outside wanted to disrupt the summit, they would have to secure assistance on the inside. Although Robertsi and Wynn assumed the same, they did not consider themselves or their inner circle to be culprits. The ISA did.

Already, her brain teemed with questions about Jafir and its power. President Robertsi, a decorated admiral turned politician, angry at the loss of solitary dominion over the nation he'd guided for years. Damon Toca, a gallery owner conscripted to be King and brother to a convicted thief and terrorist collaborator. The lesser players in the game like Minister Wynn, who'd summoned the ISA, and Minister Santana, who would negotiate the treaties with Israel, were also possible moles, as was Damon's Chief of Staff, McCord. Either one could be responsible, or it could be none of them.

The scientist in her demanded open inquiry and full information. But, as Adam and Raleigh had drilled into her during her abridged training session, she couldn't let anyone know what the ISA suspected. Nor could she make any determinations on her own. Her role was simply to run the analysis and report her results. And to observe.

A.J. cringed a bit when she thought about the rules of scientific observation. The researcher had an obligation to discard preconceived notions not based on fact, and to ignore guesses in lieu of evidence.

But she didn't trust Damon Toca as far as she could throw him.

True, A.J. admitted grudgingly, her opinion owed less to the file Atlas had given her than to their aborted flirtation at the wedding. On paper, Damon struck her as an intelligent, focused man. Educated at Oxford and Yale, his facility in art history and a natural talent for portraiture had netted him a prestigious internship at the Louvre. Ambition was also obvious, given the success of his transformation of the Toca Galleries. From their evening together and the background file the ISA had assembled, she'd learned about the redesigned gallery, which now showcased native artists rescued from obscurity and young emerging talent.

A.J. consoled herself with the knowledge that on paper, at least, Damon Toca seemed to be the type of person to whom she would undoubtedly be attracted.

If he weren't such an arrogant snob. It wasn't the fact that he'd snubbed her, A.J. decided as she sank into the chintz sofa. She'd been rejected before. She wasn't so conceited as to think every man should or would want her.

But the fact that Damon Toca obviously considered her beneath him rankled. It still boiled her blood to remember his arrogance that evening. How he'd flirted with her so boldly, muttered some obscure nonsense about timing, then brazenly kissed her before he vanished into the night.

She frowned and crossed her arms, her mouth in a petulant pout. How dare he come on to her and then traipse away as if she were some distasteful peasant? The nerve!

A discreet cough from the efficient secretary in the reception area indicated that her muttered imprecation had been audible. A.J. offered her an apologetic smile, and continued to ponder her loathing.

It was the snootiness that incensed her, she justified to herself, not the fact that her lips sizzled for hours after the contact. Not the memory of his beautiful voice calling her "my fairy," in French no less. And not that he lingered in her mind for months afterward, generating a mixture of regret and self-loathing.

No, it was the fact that he thought she was beneath him, a

plebeian to his King. Clearly, he thought he was above common courtesy and—she purposely ignored the leap of illogic—perhaps he also thought he was above the law.

As she felt annoyance at the memory build, A.J. hurriedly removed a notepad and began to doodle. A habit from childhood, some of her best inventions had been crafted while she idly drew on scraps of paper or the back of homework. Slowly, the scrawls and curls organized themselves into words, then equations. At the same time, A.J. felt her temper cool.

It wouldn't do to snap at His Royal Jerk at her first official meeting with the President, she reminded herself. President Robertsi had been nothing but gracious since she'd first spoken with him three days ago. Besides, she had a mission to accomplish.

The thought brought a hastily strangled giggle to her throat. She might have imagined a multitude of futures for herself, but none had ever involved acting as a spy for a secret organization.

She'd always envisioned running GCI one day, a tribute to the Graysons. She'd prove that they were right to take her in, to make her theirs. It was more than a goal. It was her calling. For them, she'd slaved away through high school and college, never receiving a grade lower than an A. In graduate school, she'd studied twice as hard as her cohorts. Rather than computers like Adam, the law like Rachel, or medicine like Jonah, she'd picked a field that would make GCI better and stronger. Her dissertation had resolved a schematic design flaw in a GCI product that had been recalled. Every project, every class, had been designed to make her indispensable.

The Graysons would never have cause to reject her. Not if she had her way.

A brisk knock at the door signaled the arrival of President

Robertsi. She stood, aware of the protocol. The President entered. Two guards followed unobtrusively behind, taking up their positions in the hallway.

"Dr. Grayson." He enveloped her hand in a warm greeting. "It is a pleasure to welcome you to Jafir. I trust your flight was uneventful."

"Of course, sir," she answered, her eyes cutting toward the door that stood slightly ajar. "Your country is breathtaking."

President Robertsi followed her gaze. "His Royal Highness will be joining us shortly," he explained with a polite smile. "I understand you two have met previously."

A.J. flushed, but answered steadily, "Yes, at Adam's wedding to Raleigh. It was a lovely ceremony. They were sorry you could not attend."

"Unfortunately, the affairs of state will rarely yield to affairs of the heart." He gestured toward a closed door at the opposite end of the room. "Shall we go into my office and get acquainted?"

"Thank you." She followed him, and entered the office. The large room greatly resembled Atlas's sanctum, except for the utter lack of clutter. Pens and pencils stood at attention in an ivory holder. Gleaming desktops and tables were clear of papers and files; not a single stray item marred the perfection. She thought of her own office, with the stacks of files leaning drunkenly into space; the sticky notes with their illegible scribble dotting every free surface.

"Please, sit." He gestured to the coffee service set up on a stand she recognized as Duncan Phyfe. "Coffee? Tea?"

A.J. declined. "Nothing, thank you. Mrs. Adams was kind enough to offer earlier."

"Very good," President Robertsi answered, and he opened a

drawer, removing a blue file. A sound at the door made him lift his head. "Ah, Your Highness."

Robertsi rose to his feet, and A.J. followed suit. With effort and anticipation, she turned toward the door.

Damon quickly schooled his expression, erasing the longing he knew had tightened his features. His muscles tensed as cool brown eyes slid over him, then dismissed him. He deserved it, Damon thought wryly. After their last meeting, he expected no more.

What he had expected, however, was that the wanting had ended. That the sight of her reed-thin body in muted jade would not move him. That the lithe, silk-clad legs would not make his pulse race. That the mutinous line of mouth would not make his own water.

Well, he thought fatalistically, expectations were untrustworthy creatures. Because he wanted A.J. Grayson as much at that moment as he had that night. He wanted to clasp firm, sleekly muscled shoulders, now covered by the severely tailored suit. How effortlessly, he thought, she could evoke both boardroom and bedroom. He wanted to feel the sweet curves hidden beneath its lines press against him. He wanted a dark room lit only by candlelight, and an eternity to savor each touch.

He wanted the impossible.

"Dr. Grayson," he said quietly as he strode into the room. When she curtsied in elaborate motions, he barely restrained the urge to kiss the mocking smile from the lush, glossy mouth.

As though she could read his thoughts, she replied, "Your Highness. Or is it, Your Majesty?" The words were polite, but he alone could see the scorn.

"As you prefer." He took the seat beside hers, and the scent of her perfume hung in the air between them. The fragrance of sunlight twisted his gut. Desire, thick and hot, curled into him. "I hope I did not keep you waiting," he managed tautly.

"Not at all. I had some work to keep me occupied. I realize you must be quite busy."

From the barely polite tone, Damon understood that she evidently wished he'd remain that way for the duration of her stay. "Never too busy to greet a guest. However, duty does call constantly."

"Uneasy lays the head that wears the crown," she quipped.

Damon lifted a coffee cup from the tray. "Shakespeare knew of what he spoke. Which is why we are glad to have you here. Your audit will speed along my tutelage." He didn't add that with any luck, she'd finish in a couple of weeks and be on her way.

At the mention of the audit, A.J. seemed perplexed. "My audit?"

"Yes. The reason you are here." Damon turned his attention to President Robertsi. "She does know why she's here, doesn't she?"

"Dr. Grayson is well aware of her purpose, Your Highness. However, I have not been completely candid with you."

His spine tingled with foreboding. "You haven't been honest with me?"

"Dr. Grayson is here to conduct a research project, but not the one that I have led the Cabinet to believe." Robertsi folded his hands atop the desk, the knuckles relaxed. "Minister Wynn and I have asked the ISA for its assistance."

Damon tensed at the mention of the ISA. With reluctance, he remembered running through the forest in Crete and scaling cliff faces with Alex, Phillip, Raleigh, and Adam. While he had only high praise for the organization, their presence signaled trouble, and part of him knew it might involve his brother. "She is an agent?"

"Yes," answered Robertsi.

A.J. modified, "Temporarily."

"Robertsi, what is going on?" Damon demanded. "Why is the ISA sending a temporary agent to Jafir, and what good can she possibly do with her 'audit' system? If Jafir is facing a credible threat, shouldn't we have real operatives working with us?"

President Robertsi stiffened at the imperious tone, but he responded, "With the summit approaching, security has been on high alert. In the past few months, we have received threats from several different international factions. However, despite a thorough investigation, it is impossible to anticipate who is bluffing and who intends actual harm."

"They've threatened only the summit?" Damon asked calmly.

"Not only the summit. You were mentioned by name."

His life had been in danger, yet no one told him? A cold fear gripped him, dissipated quickly by indignation. "Why wasn't I informed about any of this?"

"Information was shared on a need-to-know basis."

And as a figurehead, he had no real need to know. The words hung unspoken between them, but Damon heard the contempt. He opened his mouth to retort, then recalled A.J.'s presence. A quick glance revealed her avid interest in their discussion. Reining in temper, Damon said instead, "And now?"

"You are the King. Your position requires that you remain apprised of our situation. Also, we determined that the Minister of State should be involved. The delegates will have to be handled delicately if we wish to avoid an incident or a fracture in the Alliance."

"Is this why you decided to appoint me? To compress the two functions?"

"It was a primary factor. Other than Minister Wynn and myself, no other Cabinet member is aware of Dr. Grayson's actual purpose in being here. I had planned to bring in Isabel, but we must maintain the highest security. The three of us only."

Damon accepted the explanation, but the thought of working with A.J., particularly given the danger of the assignment, disturbed him. "She's a scientist," Damon protested. "I don't understand why the ISA didn't send a professional, if the situation is so dire."

"Dr. Grayson has created a program that may help our security team determine who the real threats are. If you will, Dr. Grayson?"

A.J. rifled through her briefcase for the presentation, fascinated by the exchange. It seemed King Damon had not yet earned the trust of his people or the President. In fact, the waves of hostility flowing from President Robertsi had been palpable as soon as Damon entered the office. And the briefing left little question of Robertsi's opinion of His Royal Highness. She noticed also that Damon didn't seem surprised by the revelation of the threats. Curious.

But not as curious as how her pulse skittered at the sound of his voice.

He'd taken her by surprise with his arrival. She'd steeled herself for the tug of attraction, but her last encounter had been months before. Today, when she saw him lounging in the doorway in a gray suit that emphasized the lean, rangy body, she recalled the powerful arms that held her as they danced. Spare and trim, Damon Toca was a clothier's dream.

She wasn't ready for the wickedly beautiful face, with its dark honey eyes and firmly molded mouth. Somehow, she'd forgotten the mellifluous voice, its charming baritone purring over words, its timbre sliding into her bones.

And she wasn't ready for the ache of yearning. A chance encounter had no right to leave such persistent desire. Exasperated by her own ungovernable reactions, she launched into her presentation. After handing out the documents, she explained Poppet and its capabilities. Robertsi asked a series of probing questions, but it was Damon's inquiries that surprised her. He instantly grasped the dynamics of the system, and asked questions a fellow scientist would have posed. She responded as curtly as she could within the bounds of good manners, and struggled not to be impressed.

Finally, after a ninety-minute interrogation, both men seemed satisfied with her plan. "Are there any further questions?"

"I have one more." Damon skimmed the sheaf of papers, then watched Robertsi carefully. "Why would she need access to the entire Cabinet if the threat is external?"

"Because in addition to verifying outside risks, Wynn has suggested an analysis of the internal hazards as well."

"She suspects a mole?"

"The more plausible threats have included internal information, which suggests that an ex-employee or a leak is collaborating with our enemy."

"Which is why I was kept uninformed for so long. I may have been the leak," Damon concluded.

"You are now Minister of State, Your Highness. You are completely . . . in the loop. In fact, as Minister, it will be your responsibility to assist Dr. Grayson with her project." President

Robertsi pushed away from his desk and circled around to stand in front of A.J. "Dr. Grayson, unfortunately, I have another engagement. I leave you in more-than-capable hands."

Alone with her, Damon turned to A.J., who busily collected her materials. Prepared to wait, Damon reclined negligently, enjoying the sight. Tendrils of black hair, loosened from a bun clasped at the nape of her neck, fell forward. A.J. pushed the offending tresses away, and Damon smiled as they slithered forward again. After the fifth time, Damon leaned toward A.J. and tucked the errant hairs behind her ear.

Face-to-face with her, Damon saw the soft brown eyes widen in reaction. The guileless face he'd once likened to a sprite was only inches away. Without volition, he stroked his hand along the curve of her cheek, marveling at the silky skin beneath his palm. The gamine face, deceptively open and inviting, beguiled him with the possibility of mystery. The crimson lips trembled, then parted.

The space of a breath separated them, and he longed to plunge inside, to satisfy a greed that had lain dormant since the wedding. His eyes held hers, and she did not pull away.

"Ma fée," he whispered tenderly, their mouths infinitely close.

The venomous look she aimed at him shocked him, as did the small but effective hand that shoved him away.

"What was that for?" he asked in genuine confusion as he teetered in his chair.

"I am not your fairy." Her words were irate, succinct.

Damon shifted away, puzzled by the acrimony. "I intended no insult," he explained quietly. "I am sorry if I offended you."

"Offended me?" The hard laugh A.J. choked out belied any notion of humor. "You may not recall our initial meeting, Your

Highness, but I do. I am not your fairy, nor do I intend to become your concubine or whatever it is kings have as playmates. I'm here to do a job, and once it is finished, I will happily leave." Rising to her feet, A.J. slung the strap of her bag over her shoulder. "If you'll have someone show me to my room, I'll be on my way."

"A.J., wait."

Ignoring the command, she stalked over to the door. Damon quickly followed. Before she could exit, his hand shot past her for the knob and slammed the paneled oak with a thud. The sound reverberated, but Damon didn't care. For a tantalizing moment, she had been as ready as he to explore whether their attraction had been a fluke. He would know right now what had precipitated this sudden tantrum.

"What the devil?" he exclaimed as he crowded her against the wood. "Who said anything about playmates?"

Her fingers scrabbled against the door, searching vainly for the handle. "Get out of my way."

The quiet fury should have warned him.

"Not until you explain that last remark."

"Which one? 'Get out of my way'? It means move!" She shoved at his chest, but it felt as though she were moving granite. She thought recklessly of punching him or stomping his foot, but at the last second remembered where she was and with whom. With Herculean effort, she forced herself to calm and to ignore the violent and traitorous urges coursing through her. She'd thought that she felt only suspicion, but when he whispered the endearment, she saw red.

The sting of his rejection, so carefully forgotten, flooded back. What shamed her, though, was that when he touched her, where he touched sizzled from the contact. "I'd like to leave," she managed with feigned composure.

"Not until you explain yourself."

"Explain myself? I'm not the one who led someone into a wine cellar, partially seduced her, and then vanished into thin air with some inscrutable tripe about destinies and fate, now am I?"

"Is that why you're so livid? Because I only partially seduced you?" Damon streaked a tempting hand under the now-unraveled bun. "I can certainly remedy that oversight."

"Don't you dare!" Forgetting her resolve, A.J. twisted her face away wildly, eager to avoid the marauding lips aimed at her own. The hand tangled in the thick skeins of hair tightened and forced her head into quiescence. "Don't," she demanded raggedly.

"Fine," Damon agreed, "I won't. But I'm not letting you go until you let me explain."

"I neither want nor need an explanation, Your Highness," she sneered, her chin jutting out proudly. Despite being pinned to the door and the riotous urge to succumb to temptation, she still had her dignity. She'd tell him in plain terms what she thought of him, he'd release her, and she'd be on her merry way. Then she'd take a cold shower. "I understand exactly what happened."

"And what, pray tell, happened?"

"You saw a pretty girl at a wedding and decided to have your last fling with a commoner before assuming your title." She flung the words at him, bitterness coating her tone.

"Go on."

"But you decided that I was even too common for you."

"What the devil are you talking about now?"

"Don't be coy, Your Highness." The title sneered in insult. "We both know you couldn't bring yourself to dally with a peasant."

"Peasant? Your family is richer than Croesus."

"But I'm not, am I? I'm the, what did you call me, *interloper. Changeling.*"

"I did not mean it that way," Damon argued.

"Well, you said it!"

"I was comparing our situations. How you moved into a foreign environment, much like the one I was about to enter."

"Sure."

"Honestly, A.J., do you think me such a cad that I would insult you, then try to make love to you?"

"Yes!"

"*Mon dieu!*"

"Stop swearing at me in French!"

"When you cease to be an imbecile!" Damon paused, and drew a deep breath. "This rancor is because I called you a name?"

No, she seethed silently, because you spoke aloud what I fear every day. "Not rancor. Distaste. I may have to work for you, but I am not here for your dalliance, Your Majesty. I will not be trifled with, and absolutely not as a convenience. Now, if you will kindly step out of my way, I'd like to go to my room." A.J. was proud of her measured tone, the wounded feelings hidden by bravado. She desperately hoped he was satisfied with her explanation, because contact with his lean hardness was unraveling her disgust.

"First of all, Dr. Grayson, having you here is anything but a convenience. You are a distraction and I'm not convinced your system will have any luck in solving Jafir's problems." A.J. gasped in indignation, but Damon continued. "Secondly, to clear my besmirched name, I did not mean to hurt your feelings. I drew parallels without explaining why. And at the time, I couldn't."

"Adam told me about the rites of ascension," she offered warily. "Is that why?"

"I was sworn to secrecy. Lives were already imperiled. I couldn't risk telling you openly about my fears. But I wanted to." He lifted her chin and stared into eyes wide with twin lights of doubt and expectation. "As to my partial seduction, *ma fée*," he added deliberately, "I will endeavor to remedy my oversight right now." The last words were jagged, intentional, and he pressed her firmly against the rough wood, his mouth temptingly close to her own.

"Damon." A.J. gathered her wits about her with effort and resisted the urge to close the distance between them. She had a job to do, one that did not include kissing the King, as much as she wanted to. Needed to. Her mind closed in on the one comment guaranteed to quell desire. "You have doubts about Poppet?" she asked roughly. "I'll have you know—"

Frustrated, Damon lifted his hands in defeat. "Of everything I said, all you care about is your damned— What is it?"

"It's an artificial intelligence system."

"All you care about is your system? *Tu es emmerdant!*"

"I'm annoying?" A.J. tipped her head back to glare at him. "You have me pinned to a door like some Regency maiden. You Tarzan, me Jane Austen."

Abruptly aware of their positions, Damon stepped away, freeing her. Dark color flushed his cheeks. "Forgive me. There is no excuse for my vulgar behavior."

"No, there is not," A.J. said haughtily, straightening her clothes. But at the sight of his discomfiture, she relented. "You didn't hurt me, Damon."

He rejected her reassurance. His face settled into a cool mask of politeness, any hint of passion erased. "There is no justification for terrorizing anyone in such a manner. I will have Felice escort you to your rooms." With efficient movements, he summoned the young woman who'd be acting as A.J.'s assistant during her stay. It was Felice who'd picked her up from the airport and had whisked her bags away as soon as they arrived.

She appeared at once. "Yes, Your Highness?"

"Please see Dr. Grayson to her quarters. And arrange for a meal to be sent to her room. Whatever she'd like." He stood near the phone, his posture stern and unyielding, his words stilted and dismissive. "I will review your materials, Dr. Grayson, and we can speak in the morning."

Suddenly too tired to argue, A.J. nodded just as politely. With leaden steps, she followed Felice from the room. She scarcely noticed the trip through the corridors that connected the Presidential Wing to the remainder of the palace. Plush navy carpet cushioned her feet, fine silk wallpaper lined each hallway. The passageways wound serpentine through the buildings, linked by marble staircases and inconspicuous elevators. At last, they reached the quarters allotted for her stay.

The trio of rooms was the most opulent she'd ever seen. The guest quarters consisted of a parlor, an office, a bedroom, and a sybaritic bath. Decorated in muted tones of sapphire and pale yellow, the sitting room contained a luxurious chaise upholstered in brushed velvet and a matching settee. More importantly, in a tasteful cabinet carved of ebony wood, there was a large flat-screen television. On opposite sides of the cabinet, books lined a series of shelves. The volumes ran the gamut from Spanish literature to American fiction.

A.J. ran a covetous finger over the title of a first edition she adored. "The palace has a wonderful collection," she told Felice, who waited in the archway separating the office and parlor.

"This is part of the King's personal collection."

"Oh." A.J. lifted a novel from the shelf. "His tastes range wide."

"Yes, they do." The young woman waited a beat, then asked, "Is there anything else I can do for you, madam? Your bags have been delivered and unpacked. Also, I have arranged for your dinner to be delivered shortly."

"Wonderful."

"My pleasure, Dr. Grayson. If you have any needs, please dial extension seven-three-three."

"Thank you, Felice. And please call me A.J."

"Certainly." After assuring herself that A.J. was settled in, Felice left the room.

A.J. locked the door, then quickly began to set up the counter-surveillance equipment Raleigh had given her. They were disguised as knickknacks and personal items, so anyone watching would assume she was merely settling into her new home. On the top shelf of the bookcase, she gingerly laid a clothbound novel written by her favorite author. Hidden inside was an emitter that sent out a high-frequency pulse to distort voices. Near the window, she placed a chubby gnome who came equipped with a power source to light its purple eyes. Once activated, the gnome would tap into any video feed and disrupt transmission. Throughout the rooms, she arranged the equipment and activated the devices.

Anyone watching her quarters would know she'd interrupted their observation, but they wouldn't be able to do anything about it without admitting to it. The gnome's purple eyes would indicate any interference, and the novel would show prints when held under an ultraviolet light she hid in the bedroom.

Finished, A.J. sunk onto the chaise, and lifted the remote control. After the day she'd had, television would be a welcome respite. Maybe it would help her unravel the jumble of emotions clouding her exhausted brain.

Two weeks ago, she'd been a dedicated scientist and businesswoman, plotting her career ascension. Less than an hour ago, she'd firmly determined that Damon Toca was vermin and that she had no use for him. But a pet project had altered her plans, and a simple explanation had knocked the wind out of her righteous indignation. Now, she was a counterfeit spy jamming signals in a magnificent castle and harboring a yen for the King.

The ridiculousness of the situation tickled her, and A.J. broke into uncontrollable laughter. The tinkling sound wafted into the hallway where Damon stood, his hand poised to knock. The notes sank into him, tiny claws pricking his conscience and his libido. Just as it had been that night at the wedding, A.J. Grayson drew him, but he could not give in to desire. Too much rested on the next six weeks. Lives and fortunes hung in the balance.

He lowered his hand and turned away.

―――――――――

How much longer will I be in here?" Nelson Toca paced inside the maximum-security cell, hazel eyes flashing. "He's sitting in a palace, basking in the adulation of lemmings. What the hell does he know about politics? About government? About anything except those damned paintings of his?"

"It will only be a while longer, Nelson. Calm down."

"Calm down? I've been rotting away in this hellhole for months now, while he's living in the lap of luxury." Nelson spun on his heel and gestured angrily at the confines of his cell.

His companion noted the bemoaned surroundings without sympathy. Nelson Toca might have been in prison, but it was quite unlike any other prison in Jafir. The cell walls were hung with fine art, and rather than a single chamber, it comprised a suite of three rooms. While Nelson ranted, they sat in the cell's sitting room, complete with antique bookshelves, Hepplewhite furniture, and Aubusson rugs. In the next room, the bedroom boasted a lush four-poster bed with rich silk sheets and finer silk wallpaper. As for the bathroom, which Nelson decried as a sty, a shallow pool masqueraded as a bathtub. Certainly, the bars on the windows, the constant electronic surveillance, and twenty-four-hour guard limited Nelson's freedom, but inside the spacious chambers, Nelson Toca lived the life of the King's younger brother. Not the life of a convicted traitor.

His former partner in crime, Kadifir el Zeben, was incarcerated in less luxurious environs, denied visitors or contact with the outside world. Nelson faced the same restrictions, but his visitor's position allowed a circumvention of the rules, and a camera blackout at every visit.

Fortunately for Nelson, his twin brother had a soft heart and a weakness for sentimentality. The guest examined Nelson, and wondered silently that the two shared so much in looks and so little in soul. Damon lacked the razor edge of temper, the black abyss of conscience that marked his brother. It was Damon who'd commanded the creation of the plush cells to hold his brother as he served out his life sentence in the Jafirian prison. And it was Damon who visited his brother once a month, without fail.

Nelson always refused to see him, preferring to barricade himself in the bedroom for the duration of Damon's visit.

Still, the two shared the loose-limbed grace; the sharp, beautiful features; the piercing hazel eyes. Only a person close to both could easily distinguish the identical twins from each other. Or one who noted that Nelson was right-handed and Damon preferred his left. But the distinctions between the two would cease to matter as soon as there was only one.

"Sit down, Nelson. We have business to discuss."

"I'm tired of sitting. Tired of waiting. The coronation is six weeks away. I will be crowned King!"

"Yes, you will. But not if I have to spend every other day sneaking in to visit you to soothe your pricked ego. Bribing guards to edit surveillance tapes and their own memories is costly business, and if we hadn't also threatened the lives of their families, both of our friends may have turned us in already."

"But now the nice guards are behaving themselves. Take a lesson from them and do as I say," Nelson commanded with menace, "or neither of us will get what we want."

Undaunted, his visitor snarled, "I'm not the one who fouled up in October. I put you in contact with Civelli, got you access to Jafirian transport. If they'd discovered our connection, I'd be shot as a conspirator."

"They don't shoot traitors in Jafir. Too grisly. No, you'd be in a cell next to Zeben. Or, perhaps given your status, they'd build on an antechamber for you next door." The image amused Nelson, and he sank onto the linen chaise. "We're running out of time. Scimitar is ruined. The summit begins soon. Where is Triad?"

"They're prepared, but your accounts are frozen. They will not agree to extend you credit."

"I'll be the King!"

"But, for now, you are the King's brother. Once you've taken the throne, they are more than willing to assist."

"Bloody hell! What do they want?"

"What they've always wanted, Nelson. They have, however, given me permission to resume our embezzlement scheme. I have begun to siphon funds into an account for our use, but I must move slowly. Damon is taking his tutelage quite seriously, and is reviewing every corner of the government. And there is another problem." For the first time, the visitor demonstrated frustration. "We have a visitor coming to help him."

"How?"

"We have an executive from GCI coming in to conduct an audit. When the idea was raised, I couldn't object without calling attention to myself."

"Do we know who the consultant is? His background?"

"Her background, and she's already arrived. It's one of the Graysons themselves."

"A Grayson? Which one?"

"The youngest. They call her A.J.," sniffed the guest with disdain. "I will never understand the American preoccupation with nicknames and diminutives. This will impede our timetable."

Nelson's face became animated for the first time during the visit. "You worry too much. All it means is that we must proceed quickly." Nelson nodded to the seat beside him. "Perhaps we should cease with words and move directly to action." His feral smile matched the chilling expression of his companion. "I have a few ideas."

CHAPTER FOUR

A.J. spent the next morning supervising the equipment setup for Poppet. Palace staff stacked crates containing fragile parts and routed cables through the office. Her workspace for the next six weeks reflected the opulence of an ancient monarchy. Pale violet and paler gold in silks and other fabrics decorated the carpet, the walls, and the unseemly, wide sofa, which was the size of her bed in college. Tall windows, convex and clear, poured in sunlight as they worked.

Her area contained an outer office and a larger space she converted into a laboratory. To accommodate her gear, A.J. had flanked one wall with the computer's terminal and the second with the borrowed desk she recognized as Boulle. The office space was reserved for meetings and for an aide who'd assist her three days a week. A door connected the two rooms, but for protection, access to the laboratory was controlled by a security code. She'd also installed the countersurveillance devices in the laboratory, disguised as desk ornaments and computer paraphernalia.

Despite the assistance with unloading, A.J. insisted that she install the components herself. Poppet, fully assembled, was composed of four towers linked together by an intricate series of fiber optics, modems and transceivers, plus voice simulators and data processors. A streamlined design was possible, but A.J. preferred the multiple tower arrangement, in case one unit malfunctioned.

The workers rearranged the towers and set up the twenty-five-inch monitor and the massive ninety-six-inch projection screen. After they departed, A.J. calibrated the vocalization patterns and initialized the system. Sarah, a graduate student completing her dissertation on artificial intelligence, toiled cheerfully beside her. Questions about A.J.'s training and career with GCI peppered the conversation, and time flew swiftly.

By the end of the first day, the two women slumped on the carpet, having lost any will to crawl onto the sofa.

"If we ask, do you think they'd carry us out?" A.J. moaned.

"Perhaps. But one of us would have to shout," Sarah reminded her.

"Ah, an intern's work is never done." When Sarah opened her mouth to yell, A.J. grabbed her arm. "I'm joking, Sarah. We'll just lounge here until our saviors come. Or until the smell leads them to us and they find our decomposing corpses."

"With all due respect, Dr. Grayson, yuck."

A.J. grinned and, losing her tenuous hold on gravity, let her head loll against the sofa's leg. "It's A.J. Not Dr. Grayson. Dr. Grayson is my aunt."

Sarah looked over at A.J. "Adam Grayson is your cousin, correct?"

"Mm-hmm," A.J. responded, eyes fluttering closed.

"He's gorgeous. And brilliant. I thought about switching my dissertation topic after the deployment of Praxis." Sarah finished breathlessly. "Do you think the marriage will last?"

"I'm afraid so." A.J. smothered a laugh. By now, she'd grown used to the almost rockstar-like adulation that followed her cousin. Last year, with Raleigh's help, Adam had introduced Praxis, a revolutionary environmental technology that cleansed atmospheres of pollutants and allowed developing nations to industrialize without jeopardizing the lives of their citizens.

The fact that he was stunningly handsome and fabulously wealthy added to his legend. A.J. quelled the urge to smirk, but only with superhuman effort. Instead, she patted Sarah's hand conspiratorially. "He'll be here for the summit, to negotiate the licensing of Praxis. I'll introduce you if you'd like."

A.J. took the shrill, ear-splitting squeal as a thank-you.

"Is everything alright here?" asked a voice from the open doorway. A.J. sprang to her feet. "Mr. McCord."

"Dr. Grayson." He glanced around the office. "I see you've been quite busy."

"With Sarah's able assistance, I should be up and running in no time."

"Please let me know if you require additional resources," McCord offered as he wandered around the room.

"Dr. Grayson, I mean, A.J., if you'll excuse me. I have a

dinner appointment." Sarah gathered her backpack. "I'll see you in the morning?"

"Nine a.m. will be fine." A.J. walked her to the door. "Thanks for your help today. I promise, no more manual labor."

A.J. stood in the doorway, and watched McCord's close inspection of Poppet. "Would you like a demonstration, Mr. McCord?"

"Thank you." McCord shifted toward the window to give her access to the contraption. Less obviously, he examined A.J. as she booted up the computer. At twenty-five, she'd already served in a variety of capacities at her family's corporation. Mailroom clerk. Secretary. Lab technician. Her current position as Assistant Vice President of Research and Development had been the result of a string of innovative projects and a terrifying work ethic.

His information on her also revealed a short list of tepid and dull relationships. In college, it was a fellow student who took to heart the adage about work and play, to his grade's detriment. In graduate school, she'd dated a start-up millionaire who sought to trade on her connections to GCI. The last relationship, a brief romantic negotiation with a tax attorney, ended quietly when A.J. began her development of Poppet in earnest.

A.J. Grayson was intelligent, dedicated, and meticulous. And she posed a grave threat to the King.

"Mr. McCord, over here, if you will." A.J. motioned to a space beside a six-inch microphone. McCord found his mark and waited expectantly. "Poppet, please say hello to Mr. McCord."

The genderless digital voice dutifully responded, "Hello, Mr. McCord."

Uncertain of what to do, he answered politely, "Hello, Poppet."

A.J. smiled at his good-natured response. "And who is Mr. McCord, Poppet?"

"McCord. First name unknown. Birthplace unknown. Age unknown. Recent post: head of Jafirian Tribunal of Ascension. Family records sealed."

A.J. arched a brow at the series of statements. "I see with whom I'll conduct my first interview, Mr. McCord."

"It is McCord. Nothing more."

"I beg to differ," A.J. murmured. "I find it fascinating that someone responsible for such sensitive areas of government would have so many secrets."

"Secrets have their value, Dr. Grayson. Wouldn't you agree?"

With a half laugh, A.J. shook her head, and felt a tiny shiver of trepidation. "Secrets are made to be discovered, though. Inevitably, they find their way to the surface."

"At least, that is your intention, is it not?"

A.J. hesitated. As far as she knew, only Robertsi, Damon, and Wynn had been apprised of her mission. But his questions seemed too pointed to be coincidence. Still, she decided to err on the side of caution. "I'm here to ferret out best practices for an important nation. With Jafir's role in the African-Arab Alliance and the upcoming Summit with Israel, a strong government is vital. I will do my best to help."

McCord nodded in approval. "And I will be happy to assist in any way I can."

"Will you tell me your first name?"

A mild quirk of lips was McCord's response. Taking it as a no, and eager to change the direction of the conversation, A.J. began to demonstrate Poppet's capacities. She had McCord answer a spate of questions about his food habits, when he ate and how much. Poppet then predicted, with dead-on accuracy, his favorite meals and the contents of his refrigerator.

Pleased by his astonished reaction, A.J. told him more about her research and the possibilities of the technology. Before long, though, dusk had settled firmly into night. A.J. powered down the computer and collected her belongings. McCord walked with her to the door, and waited a few steps away while she engaged the security system.

"His Royal Highness requests your presence at dinner." McCord tucked her hand in his arm as they left the Monarch's Suite. "Dinner will begin at eight thirty."

"Extend my regrets, if you will," A.J. said diffidently. "I'm, uh, exhausted. I thought I'd have a meal sent up."

McCord shot her a look that clearly doubted her tone or her tale. Politely, he clarified, "It would be ill-advised to decline an audience with the King, Dr. Grayson."

"Will he force me to eat with him?" A.J. asked sharply.

"Of course not, but it is a matter of protocol."

At the reminder, A.J. felt a tug of impatience. "Protocol," she'd decided, was a nasty word used to make people behave in unnatural ways. Despite her ease in social situations, trained by years at the feet of masters, A.J. chafed at the restrictions. If she had her druthers, she'd spend the evening curled on the sofa, book in hand, sitcom on the television.

Sixteen-hour days for more than a year had worn thin, and she longed for the rare days when soirees and fundraisers yielded to personal time.

But, if she were to be honest, the hesitation stemmed mainly from not wanting to spend any more time with King Damon than her project dictated.

There was something about him, the way he slid from intense to remote in the blink of an eye. She could still feel the pull of attraction when he crowded her against the door. And it chilled her, the sudden withdrawal, the cool veil of arrogance that slipped over his eyes when he apologized.

He quickened her pulse and disturbed her senses. Normally such a good judge of character, she wondered if she had been too harsh in her conclusions, too ready to assume the worst. Surely, she wouldn't be so fascinated if Damon were truly the louse she'd painted him to be.

A.J. weighed her options. If she declined the invitation a second time, it would seem churlish, and McCord might ask for an explanation. To tell him the truth would probably lead to palace gossip about the reluctant scientist and the outraged King.

No stranger to tabloid rumors, if the wrong person got wind of it, she'd spend most of her time in Jafir fending off questions instead of asking them.

And if she accepted the invitation, she'd spend the night fighting the attraction that had not dissipated since the wedding. The hypnotic hazel eyes, the fallen-angel looks, and the incisive wit undermined her single-minded attempts at exorcising those particular feelings.

Resigned, A.J. sighed. "Please let His Highness know that I'd be honored to join him." She pasted on a false smile that fooled neither of them.

With a courtly bow, McCord left her at the base of the grand staircase that led to the living quarters. "I will tell him to expect you. Unfortunately, without our own Poppet, we had to guess at your food tastes."

A.J. laughed appreciatively. "I'm certain there will be

something to my liking." She turned and headed up the stairs, then paused. "Mr. McCord?"

"Yes, Dr. Grayson?"

"Thank you."

"My pleasure," he replied softly.

A hurried check of her watch revealed that she had less than half an hour to dress for dinner. And it occurred to her, as she bounded up the stairs, that she forgot to ask who else was coming.

Twenty-five minutes later, she descended the steps at a more stately pace. Her work attire had been replaced with a simple black dress, draped at the bodice and high at the back. She accented the severe color with an amber pendant, a gift from her cousin Rachel. McCord had informed her that dinner would be served in the King's private dining room on the main floor. She remembered it from her whirlwind tour the day before.

Pausing outside the pocket doors, A.J. fiddled with the pendant and pressed a hand to a suddenly fluttery stomach. Stop being silly and go in, she ordered herself sternly. It's just dinner. With a fortifying breath, she knocked and, at Damon's invitation, pushed them open.

A long, heavy table dominated the dining room. Overhead, crystal splintered light in a chandelier, and tapers burned pleasantly on the mantel. Damon walked toward her, cuff links glinting in the beams.

A.J. ran a quick hand over the matte jersey sheath, grateful she'd chosen the dress. The restrained formality of Damon's dinner attire would have been entirely at odds with her fleeting thought of cotton.

"Your Highness."

"Dr. Grayson. Welcome." He inclined his head and gestured to an intimate setting for two. That answered her question about guests, she thought.

Damon pulled out a chair, and stood politely. "Please, have a seat. Can I prepare a drink for you?"

"I'll have whatever you're having," she demurred. The type of liquor wouldn't matter. She had no intention of consuming it, since her survival strategy included keeping her wits about her tonight. Damon Toca had an uncanny ability to unsettle her thoughts and distract her from her mission. Her singular goal tonight was to survive without an argument.

"I understand from McCord that you've settled into your offices." Damon set a glass of sherry in front of her, reaching from behind. His arm brushed her shoulder, and warm breath softly coursed past her cheek. She released a hiss of breath and tried not to squirm or sigh. Finally, mercifully, he moved away. "Are the accommodations to your specifications?"

"Quite satisfactory." Forgetting her earlier decision, A.J. took a bracing sip of the wine. "I also wanted to thank you for hiring Sarah. She was a godsend."

"You're welcome, but I can't take credit. McCord handled the hiring. Sometimes, I wonder which one of us is in charge." He softened the comment with a self-deprecating smile, and A.J. could not help but respond. Nerves settled and she relaxed. Almost.

Damon Toca stirred her, unlike anyone she'd met before. The potent charm of confidence intrigued her, particularly coupled with the surfeit of new responsibilities. Few men could transform themselves from art expert to Head of State in a year. For Damon, though, command would come as effortlessly as poetry.

Rake or ruler? She studied him from beneath her lashes as he sipped sherry contemplatively from his glass. And wondered.

Damon noted the look of puzzlement, and hid a smile. Their argument yesterday and the near fact of an embrace had driven him to plan tonight's impromptu meal. McCord advised him not to, especially given that Damon had to cancel a prior engagement with a visiting sheikh. But the complicated courtship preceding trade negotiations with the sheikh and his oil had to wait while he dissected his reaction to A.J.

Without question, she tempted his senses. The widely spaced eyes, with their thick fringe of velvet lash, flashed with challenge. Lips, tonight painted a subtle shade of red, scorned as often as they smiled. Willow slim, she resembled nothing so much as the orchids his father tended. Exotic, unique, and deceptively fragile. Hothouse blooms that thrived in the wild, if left to their own devices.

"McCord told me about your demonstration. I hope I can also see a preview."

"Anytime. But I'm sure you'll be too busy to play games with me."

He could tell that his earlier remarks still smarted. "Since we'll be working together for the next month, I'm sure we'll find the time." Reaching beneath the table, he pressed a button to notify the kitchen they were ready for their meal. Black-coated staff materialized with the first course. "I took the liberty of ordering for you."

"I'll trust your judgment," A.J. said cautiously, and he heard the qualification. It seemed she had not accepted fully his expla-nation for the apparent snub.

"On matters of food only?"

"Of course not," she corrected quickly. At his speculative look, she added, "I trust your taste in art and literature too."

"Touché," Damon murmured in appreciation at the dig. "What will it take to earn your trust?"

"I don't know. Very few have done so."

"Why? Are you that suspicious of human nature?"

"Absolutely. People are messy, complicated creatures who act on impulse. They are basically self-interested and organize their lives around gratification. Why should I trust a being that capri-cious?" A.J. spooned soup into a mouth curved in humor. "My opinion disturbs you?"

"Not disturbs. Concerns, maybe. Your description leaves questions about your objectivity, Dr. Grayson. If you have no faith in humanity, how will you determine whether a person is honest or not?"

"I won't. Poppet will. I feed it data and it does the analysis. Without the muddled thinking that plagues people." Lifting her wine, she explained, "You misunderstand me. I have infinite faith in humanity's basically kinder nature, but when emotions are introduced, things get interesting. People are driven by in-stinct as often as logic. Passion vitalizes the timid. Fear stumbles the brave." She took a sip of the drier white wine, its flavor a sharp contrast to the sweeter sherry. Savoring the difference, she added, "I don't count myself as superior to other people, Your Highness, I'm simply more aware of my flawed nature."

"Then you don't trust yourself?"

A.J. toyed with her cutlery, her eyes downcast. "In most

matters, I do. But I can be wrong about my impressions. I've been known to jump to conclusions."

Damon heard the undertone of apology and covered the small, narrow hand. The ringless fingers stirred restlessly, then stilled. "I'm glad to hear it. It would be difficult to measure up to a paragon."

A.J. gave an inelegant snort, dispelling the image. "A paragon? Hardly. My family would disagree, especially my cousin Jonah. He more often describes me as the bane of his existence or even less becoming terms."

"Why?"

"Oh, because I am." A.J. shifted her hand, but Damon refused to acknowledge the silent request for release. She continued, "He's a year older, but we spent most of our childhood together. I imitated him, followed him, and generally insinuated myself into every facet of his life. I think I'm the reason he went to medical school."

Amused, Damon asked, "Why is that?"

"Because he was always developing elaborate ways to kill me so that our parents didn't notice."

"Is he why you became a computer scientist?"

"Nope. That was Adam. My idol. I tormented Jonah, but Adam could do no wrong. When he started his own computer company, I cajoled him into giving me a summer internship. I fell in love."

The last emerged on a husky note that A.J. blamed solely on her companion. Damon traced nonsense lines across the soft skin of her hand, and A.J. thought if he didn't stop soon, she'd melt. Sensations shivered up her bare arms, a direct result of the slightly calloused touch that caressed her captive skin.

"Do you do that often?" Damon asked intently, thinking of Alex.

"Do I what?"

"Fall in love?"

Firmly, A.J. withdrew her hand and tucked it into her lap. "No, I don't make a habit of it. Do you?"

"Never. I enjoyed my youth too much for such weighty sentiment."

"Will you ever?" A.J. heard herself ask the question, but she was only making conversation. The soundless entrance of the servers to whisk away soup and replace it with their entrées prevented Damon's response.

Both were profoundly happy for the reprieve. After they exited, Damon steered conversation to less volatile topics. As in the cellar, their conversation ranged from literature to politics to A.J.'s addiction to television. She entertained him with anecdotes of her childhood in a famous family. Damon returned the favor, regaling her with near gaffes during his tenure as King. One almost-international incident involving a bidet and a new bride elicited peals of enchanting laughter.

Almost as compelling was the meal itself. In wonderment, Damon watched rich course after rich course disappear. A.J. Grayson may have been the size of an elf, but she had the appetite of an ogre.

Her genuine, sensual appreciation of each course was evidenced by the abandoned flick of her tongue over the remnants of decadent white chocolate cheesecake left on her fork. Damon followed the erotic dance and wondered, heatedly, how long it would take to taste her again.

Dinner was cleared, and Damon offered to take her on a

more sedate tour of the palace. Having imbibed more wine than she'd intended, A.J. forgot her resolution and agreed enthusiastically.

In each room, he pointed out art treasures coveted by the finest museums. The library, which rose two stories, faced the main garden, which Damon told her was known as the Asphodel. Architects had built the palace to surround the library so that the separate wings of the main palace rose like turrets above a glass dome that flooded the library with sunlight. At night, moonlight shone through the glass, and the multitude of stars reminded A.J. of a planetarium.

Thousands of volumes circled the oval, and alcoves had been strategically placed on both levels for readers. A.J. kicked off her shoes, hiked her skirt, and nimbly climbed the librarian's ladder that led from one level to the next.

"A.J.!" Damon watched with incredulity as she clung to the thin rails and grinned down at him. "Come back down here this instant."

When she blew a raspberry at him, Damon didn't know whether to be insulted or amused. Or aroused. The shortened skirt revealed long, sleekly muscled legs. Hoarsely, he called up, "Don't move." He opened a door disguised as a bookcase and took the interior stairs two at a time. At the top, he emerged onto the landing for the second level. A.J. knelt on the floor beside the doorway, reading titles.

"How clever!" she exclaimed. Immediately, she brushed past him to examine the door.

Damon shook his head in exasperation. "This is how we reach the second level. The library rails are for decoration only," he lectured sternly.

Dismissing his concern, A.J. poked out her tongue and continued around the landing. On the second floor, the shelves sat along a recessed wall, and the open space was protected by a sturdier rail than the one she'd climbed. Laughing at his strict expression, A.J. cajoled, "Oh, don't be a spoilsport. Rachel and I used to climb trees all the time."

Damon was not mollified. "While you're in my home, you'll use the stairs."

"Or what? You'll send me to my room?" she taunted.

He folded his arms and stared down his nose at her. "No, I won't send you to your room. I'll have the rail removed until you leave. Or ban you from the library."

A.J. tossed her head back and studied him scornfully. "I'm a grown woman, Damon. I can take care of myself. Which includes deciding if I want to climb a ladder or not."

"As long as you are here, you're my responsibility. And I take responsibility quite seriously. So, will you agree not to climb the ladder or not?"

It was a petty argument, A.J. recognized, but she feared capitulating. Nevertheless, the imperious tone caused her to fight. Usually an even-tempered woman, seconds in Damon's presence generated complicated, irrational feelings. She wanted to goad him, to irritate him. To provoke him.

She was trying to aggravate him, Damon recognized warily, watching the conflict flare in her eyes. They stood toe-to-toe, and A.J. glared at him, the pixie face an alluring mask of impudence.

Relishing his superior height, he slid his hand beneath her arm to encircle her waist. "Why are you needling me, A.J.?"

"I don't know what you mean."

With his free hand, he lightly stroked the mutinous lip that pouted in contradiction. "You're angry with someone. I don't know if it's you or me, but I'm not going to play."

"I'm not playing," she argued, but did not pull away. "I simply don't take orders well."

"Let's dispense with the distraction, shall we? I'm asking you not to use the ladder."

"Fine," she agreed, the mutinous line of her mouth contradicting the easy agreement. Then the full lips parted, and Damon recognized the unconscious invitation. He lowered his head slowly, inexorably. A.J., unwilling to be seduced, raised her mouth to meet his.

As with the first time, the contact jolted. Damon ignored the heat and focused on the soft. The sultry curve of lips that fit perfectly against his own. The silken arms that curled around his neck to draw him inside. Sensation shuddered through him, and he fought to maintain focus.

A.J. poured herself into the kiss. She tasted and remembered. How long had it been since she'd only felt, only wanted? With Damon, there was a dangerous, sinful care in the way he explored her mouth. How long had it been since she stood still long enough to accept it?

The answer flickered in the corner of her mind not consumed by the slick slide of tongue, the warm ferocity of hands. Only Damon made her feel this, made her forget her plans. Only him.

"Damon," she panted, pulling herself away, together. "We can't."

"Why not?" He sampled the fragrant skin of her jawline. "We both want."

"Damon, this isn't right. We have a job to do."

Breathing labored, Damon released her. McCord's warning rang in his ears, and he knew she was correct.

Until the summit, there was no place in his life for distractions, and A.J. Grayson would be nothing else. Already, the ache of desire had returned, and she'd been there fewer than forty-eight hours. Unless he stopped now, he doubted he'd ever stop.

"You're right. We can't."

A.J. linked her fingers together, and nodded. "We should stay out of each other's way. That would be best."

An ironic smile lifted the corner of Damon's mouth. "It would be best. If it were possible."

"I can work with someone else. Anyone else." If desperation edged her voice, she ignored it. "McCord could help."

"And he will. But I'm the Minister of State. In addition to reviewing the Cabinet personnel files, there are meetings for you to observe, and I'm your passport inside. We'll just have to resolve to keep our hands to ourselves."

"We can do that."

"Of course."

And both prayed that they spoke the truth.

———

During the next three weeks, they remained true to their oaths. A.J. input personnel data, often meeting with Damon for two to three hours each day. For each Minister, she would key in vital statistics, but more importantly, she'd add Damon's observations. As a new member of the team, he possessed a useful detachment. Unlike Robertsi or Wynn or McCord, his keen observations weren't clouded by history or ties. Together, they sifted through minutes from Cabinet meetings, and Damon explained each Minister's role.

Patiently, Damon sketched out the machine that was the government of Jafir, answering hundreds of questions with clear, thorough answers. The sound of him entering the access code each afternoon brightened her day and shortened her breath. Despite their vows, she waged a losing battle against wanting him. The honeyed voice, with its smooth accent and cool tones, wreaked havoc with her senses. His habit of leaning over her forced her to breathe in the heady scent of forest and man that weakened her knees.

Today, however, Damon had stayed far away. Since his arrival, he'd paced the floor, answering her queries in clipped phrases. Fed up, she said, "Damon? I'd rather not have you replace the carpet while I'm here."

Damon paused, but continued to read the report he held. Offhandedly, he said, "I'll pay for it, if it comes to that."

This would require direct intervention, A.J. decided. She stood, stretched, and crossed the floor to join him. "You've been antsy all morning. What's wrong?"

He rolled his shoulders and focused on the report. "Nothing. I have a full schedule next week, including a preliminary conference with the Alliance and a visit from a British Parliament delegation."

A.J. was skeptical, given his normally hectic schedule. "You do more than that in one day. Didn't you meet with the Prime Minister of the Czech Republic Tuesday and the Sultan of Brunei on Friday?" When Damon didn't respond, she pressed, "What gives? Heads of state don't make you nervous, and you are decidedly nervous."

Damon continued to read, so she opted for the weapon she used on Adam when he tried to ignore her. She sang his name, the singsong an annoying sound, even to her. Hopefully, it would needle him enough to make him confess. "Damon? Your Highness? What's going on?" A.J. laid her hand over the page, blocking the words.

"Cut that out, A.J." He dropped the papers and her hand fell. He turned, to resume reading, and she danced around him.

"Come on, Damon. Tell me what the problem is. I can't help if you won't share." She started to bounce, knowing the manic action would force a response. She didn't have long to wait.

Forceful hands dropped the briefing paper and landed on her shoulders, compelling her to stand quietly.

Satisfied, A.J. peered up at him through curious eyes. "Are you going to tell me?"

Sighing in defeat, Damon muttered, "I need a date."

"You need a what?"

Damon removed his hands and shoved them into his pockets. The suit coat had been discarded upon his entrance, and the tie had followed not long after. In A.J.'s laboratory, Damon imagined himself inside a sanctuary, one as restorative to him as sitting in the Asphodel. Only one other place on the island offered him such succor, but he hadn't been able to escape to its haven in nearly a month.

Instead, he relied on the laboratory and its single occupant to quell the nerves that hummed as the summit grew closer. Day after day, they discussed political dealings, digging beneath for useful nuggets to be fed into Poppet's growing database. Sometimes, though, they simply talked.

A.J. acted as sounding board and as critic. Unlike McCord,

she gave him an unvarnished reaction, unconcerned about his title or sensibilities. It was refreshing, he realized, to know that with her, he was guaranteed the truth. In her short tenure, she'd become more than a colleague. A.J. Grayson was fast becoming his friend.

He was also guaranteed frustration. From the sexy pointed chin to the quick, beautiful hands, everything about her made him want. Her wardrobe, deceptively conservative, contained an endless supply of short skirts that emphasized the smooth length of calf and thigh, the nipped-in waist, and appealing curve of her hips. Sitting behind her day after day, staring at the elegant column of her throat, tied him in knots. A tiny kiss on the velvety nape would satisfy him for days, he'd decided sometime last week. But he'd made a promise, and he'd do his best to keep it.

Unfortunately, the more time he spent with A.J., the less he wanted to spend with anyone else. The women who'd been his guests to various social functions since his ascension no longer drew his attention. One by one, he'd cut ties with them, and he'd filled his calendar with nonsocial functions.

McCord, however, had reminded him this morning that he was expected at the annual Children's Ball on Saturday night. Both as the King and as Damon Toca, he realized he could escort any woman he fancied.

He only wanted A.J.

"Will you come with me to the Children's Ball on Saturday?" Damon asked the question quickly, pierced by something akin to fear.

A.J. blinked, her wide eyes confused. "You want me to be your date?"

"Given that you've monopolized my time for the better part

of the month, you've made it nearly impossible to ask anyone else on such short notice."

Thunder moved into the brown orbs, and Damon regretted his phrasing instantly. "I meant to say—"

"That I'm your last resort?" The silky words contained such menace that Damon took a step backward.

"No, A.J." He held his hands out in apology. "I meant that I haven't had much time for socializing."

"I didn't think you did anything else!" she retorted. "According to the gossip columns, you and Judith O'Brien are quite the item. Why don't you take her?"

"Judith and I are old friends. Besides, she's the date of the British ambassador." In a moment of déjà vu, Damon relived his earlier regret. "But that's not why I'm asking you, A.J." Both feet firmly embedded in his mouth, Damon fumbled for a proper apology before A.J. stormed away. He grabbed her arm and rushed into speech. "Even if Judith were free, I wouldn't invite her. I only want you to come with me, but we promised we'd be colleagues only. But I'd be honored if you'd attend the ball as my date."

A.J. sorted through the hasty explanation, measuring his sincerity. Despite the clumsy delivery, she understood. The tension between them was palpable, but neither had dared discuss it. However, if he was willing to test them at another evening of dancing and moonlight, she'd oblige.

And hope there wasn't a wine cellar in sight.

CHAPTER FIVE

The morning of the ball, A.J. awoke to tapping at her door. She stretched, eager to shake off the last strands of the night's dream, which seemed to follow her into the morning. Unfocused eyes read the clock at her bedside, and she tried to disregard the tiny single digits that told her it was just past dawn. Suddenly, consciousness fully revived, she remembered her day's schedule. In preparation for their evening out, Damon had accepted his role as Minister of State and guide with gusto.

It was sunrise, and he rapped at her door to escort her on a tour of the country. At 349 square miles, the island was twice the size of Washington, DC, and slightly larger than Grenada.

A.J. dressed quickly and mutely, and she remained that way as he bundled her into the waiting car. Coffee and croissants perked her up a bit, and she stopped grumbling about the evils of morning.

"Are you always this grumpy in the morning?" Damon asked in a chipper voice that nearly had her lunging across the seat.

"Unlike Mr. Mary Sunshine, yes, I am." She took a deep draft of caffeine and slathered butter onto the croissant. "Where are you taking me?"

"The day of the Children's Ball is quite an event. I thought you'd appreciate it better if you participated in some of the activities." Then he grinned, a carefree smile that lightened the constantly somber hazel and highlighted the flecks of gold.

If today could ease the strain of worry that he carried, A.J. decided she'd throw herself into it with enthusiasm.

All day, A.J. accompanied him on visits to adoption centers and youth programs, watched from the sidelines as he christened the children's AIDS ward at the Desira hospital and held its miniature patients. He kissed babies at the parade, threw candy from a float.

A.J. had never had more fun in her life. Equal parts royalty and citizen, Damon refused to brush aside a single comer, answering questions with patience. More impressive was his aplomb when accosted by critics and detractors. A.J. watched in admiration as he accepted their censure, and assigned an aide to document their concerns. After nearly a month working side by side, she knew instinctively that he'd respond to every complaint before the week's end.

It was near sundown when they drove back to the palace. Damon had gotten no rest the night before, locked in a marathon conference call with the Vice President of Brazil.

"Why don't you take a nap?" A.J. suggested. "It will take at least fifteen minutes to return to the palace. I promise I won't tell Robertsi that you actually rest."

Damon chuckled and smothered a yawn. "Are you still up for the ball?"

A.J. patted his knee companionably, and watched in amusement as one eye shut. "You won't get out of it that easily, Your Highness. I intend to dance tonight. I bought a new dress and everything."

With one eye open, he speculated, "Green. Silky. Almost indecent?"

"It's a black-and-white ball, Damon. No green allowed."

Slipping into sleep, he murmured, "You're gorgeous in anything. Take my breath away."

A.J. laid her hand over his and bit back a sigh. It had been a perfectly lovely day. As the car sped along, she watched the sun dip down over the horizon. Stunning color edged the indigo waters, and A.J. depressed the intercom.

"Can we pull over for a moment? I'd like to watch the sunset."

The driver hesitated, but Damon spoke suddenly. "Let's give the lady what she wants." The guard agreed, and left the car to secure the area.

"I didn't mean to wake you," A.J. apologized. "I thought I was being quiet."

"You were. Fifteen minutes was sufficient. Thank you for the suggestion." Damon turned his hand where hers rested on top. Seamlessly, their fingers linked. "I like you, A.J. Grayson."

A.J. flushed, but smiled. "I like you too, Damon Toca."

When the guard returned, they left the car and walked along the beachhead, coming to stand on a flat, smooth rock worn down by the tide. A warm breeze lifted palm fronds and scented the air with the sea. Gulls called to their mates and swooped down for dinner. A.J. leaned against Damon's shoulder, and he wrapped her close. Stopped, they watched in mute amazement, and the sun disappeared in a ball of amber and rose.

Ping! Ping!

A.J.'s eyes widened as gravel spurted up from the rock.

"Down!" Damon yelled, and he pushed her to the ground. Throwing himself over her, he heard one of his guards yell out for them to stay put, and the guards began to return fire. For an eternity, he pressed A.J. into the sand and waited for the next bullet to rip into flesh.

An engine roared loud, and Damon slowly lifted his head to check. His guard ran toward him, the face awash in anger. "Your Highness? Your Highness? Are you alright?"

Damon got to his feet and helped A.J. to stand. "Darling? Are you hurt?"

A.J. shook her head, willing her voice to be strong. "No, I'm fine. You?" She ran anxious eyes over the taut, angry frame, searching for wounds. "Did he hit you?"

Damon hugged her close and spoke to the guard. "We're unharmed. Did you get the shooter?"

The guard shook his head bitterly. "He was above, on the cliffs. He shot Neis."

Neis had been on his detail since the beginning. A kind man of thirty-seven, Damon knew he had a wife and young daughter at home. "Is he dead?" Damon asked curtly.

With a vigorous shake of his head, the guard hastened to correct Damon. "No, sir. Wounded only. They are taking him to the hospital now. I dispatched one of the units immediately."

Damon nodded his concurrence with the decision and motioned to the guard that they were ready to go. The guard bowed and led them up to the vehicle. Bundled inside, A.J. listened as Damon made a series of calls, first to the hospital, then to the soldier's family. Finally, he called McCord. "Contact Neis's family. Find out if they will need anything. Be certain he receives immediate attention at the hospital."

They rode to the palace in silence, the beauty of the day shattered. Her knees were shaking, but A.J. said nothing, afraid her voice would betray the lingering terror. Damon seemed lost in thought, and she would not add to his concern. The guards ushered them into the palace, and Damon broke off to head toward the Monarch's Suite.

A.J. climbed the stairs, reaction setting in with a vengeance. Teeth chattered, hands quivered as she fumbled to unlock her doors and reset the makeshift alarm she'd installed. She made her way to the bathroom, fighting off nausea. She forced her nerves to settle, and it was nearly fifteen minutes before she remembered. As an ISA agent, she needed to get information on the shooting and report it as soon as possible. Spurred by the thought, and the need to see him, she changed out of her sand-filled clothes and raced downstairs to find Damon.

He was in McCord's office, standing with his hands in his pockets. McCord sat in a deep chair, his voice rumbling over instructions to someone on the phone.

"Damon? What's going on?"

Damon turned at the sound of his name, and A.J. halted on the threshold. Darkly forbidding, he seemed infuriated by her presence.

"I thought you were in your quarters."

"I was. But we have work to do." A.J. came fully into the

office and chose a chair beside McCord's desk. She folded her hands in her lap, and took a steadying breath. "What do we know about the shooters?"

Damon was stunned by her matter-of-factness. Didn't she realize she'd nearly died tonight? "You should be resting, A.J."

"I wasn't hurt." She lifted a pad and pencil from the pile on the desk. "Did your guards give a description?"

Aware of the fragile leash on his temper, Damon said coldly, "The police matters of Jafir are not your concern, Dr. Grayson. Kindly return to your quarters until I send for you."

"Send for me? I'm not one of your servants, Your Highness." The angry retort echoed the recalcitrant tilt of her chin.

Before she could erupt, Damon yanked her from the chair and marched her out of the room. Daily sweeps ensured the sanctity of his offices, and he knew he could speak freely there. Forcing her inside, he slammed the door. In cold, measured tones, he admonished, "You have no right to interrupt a meeting between me and my staff."

"I have every right to be there. It's my job!"

"A job McCord knows nothing about! Do you want to blow your cover?" Damon taunted, "Amateur." Insulting her felt better than the horror replaying itself in his mind. Over and over, he saw her eyes widen with surprise as rock exploded near her feet. She could have been killed by the men who pursued him and the throne.

"I'm sorry. I forgot."

The duly chastened tone only spiked the fear that spread through him. A.J. had no place in this world. She wasn't a spy; she was a scientist. She should be locked safely inside a corporate lab, not sprawled on a beachhead, dodging bullets. In the morning, he would demand that the ISA replace her with someone else. Anyone else.

"I don't care about your apology, Dr. Grayson. You're an obvious security risk. I'll request that you be replaced with a more experienced agent tomorrow." Damon spun on his heel, prepared to leave.

A.J. got to her feet and blocked his path. "I'm not going anywhere."

Anger broke the tether on fear, and he caught her shoulders in his hands. "Do you understand what almost happened tonight? You were almost killed."

"I know that. But I wasn't." She covered his cheek with her hand. "I'm fine."

He pushed her away, and she stumbled slightly. "I don't want you here."

"You can't make me leave," A.J. countered. "Only Robertsi can, and he won't."

Damon glared at her, knowing she was correct. The President had summoned her, and it would be he who sent her away. Damon could try to convince him, but they needed Poppet's theories, now more than ever.

The best he could hope for was to keep her as far away from him as possible.

Satisfied with his plan, Damon spoke. "I'll give you a report tomorrow. Until then, please return to your quarters."

A.J. studied him warily. She wondered at his abrupt about-face, and felt the first stirrings of distrust. "Okay. I'll meet you in the lab tomorrow."

The next morning bore none of the promise of the day before. And, she admitted as she swung bare legs over the four poster's edge, she welcomed the challenge.

She'd always viewed herself as a certain type of person. It puzzled her that others vacillated about career and ambition, when both had forever been clear for her. In her childhood, the objective was to please her aunt and uncle. She'd taken ballet lessons and art lessons and violin lessons, anything one of the older Grayson children considered cool. At seven, she played soccer like Rachel. By ten, it was track with Jonah. Adam, though, had refined her focus. As a teenager, she daydreamed about helming GCI, not about boys or clothes. From that day forward, every aspect of her life had been geared toward a single goal.

A.J. wandered into the bathroom to begin her morning toilette. After her shower, wrapped in thick cotton, she slathered on lotion before a waist-length mirror and contemplated her reflection. Even her appearance was a part of the master plan. The clear, dewy skin and trim athletic body, initially a gift of nature and good genes, were the continued result of a precision beauty regimen and daily runs. The flat midriff benefited from one hundred crunches before bedtime. For the shoulder-length locks, she maintained a standing appointment with Atlanta's leading stylist. From clothes to makeup to shoes, each piece had been carefully selected to reflect smart, conscientious, and driven. Like her life.

Yet, every time Damon entered the picture, the image she'd shaped clouded. At the wedding, she'd been a wanton, a woman guided by passions rather than sensibility. Here, she relished tracking down snipers and saboteurs, no longer content to program her computers.

She thought of the backup flash drive hidden in a secret compartment in an ISA-issue makeup kit that contained in digital the files of people who should have terrified her. Instead, it thrilled. And she was enjoying her evolution too much to halt it now.

So, if she and Damon were to work side by side, one of them had to be the better person and call a truce. Brushing her teeth, she sighed. His destiny made a heavy burden, one that might not accommodate so gracious a gesture, thus she would take on the task herself. It would take all of her energy to be so magnanimous, and would likely require a superb breakfast. The thought of food cheered her immeasurably, and she pushed to the side the unresolved issue of her reaction to Damon Toca. She'd think about it after she'd been fed.

Her toilette completed, and dressed in a slim-fitting maroon pantsuit and a white oxford-style shirt, A.J. headed downstairs. The rooms assigned to her were on the second level of the main building, and she knew from her ISA briefing that the Monarch's Suite lay to the north. Deliberately, she headed south. She required fortification before her next encounter with the King.

"Dr. Grayson?" queried a young guard dressed in pale-yellow and charcoal livery, standing at attention before a sweeping granite archway supported by marble pillars. "May I be of assistance?"

"I'm in search of food. Large, copious amounts." She held up a hand waist high. "At least this much. Mr. McCord told me that today breakfast would be served in the Sahalia Room, which I haven't quite distinguished from the Kholari or Tropez dining rooms."

The newly minted guard, only three days at a coveted post inside the palace, fought against an improper grin and tried not to gawk. The creamy white shirt, with its raised collar and two free buttons, emphasized the slender neck and the gamine features A.J. had highlighted with wine-colored lipstick and black mascara.

She stood right beside him, and he thought her perfume smelled prettier than all the flowers in the Asphodel. Through the heady scent, he struggled to remember his training in the lay of the palace. Passage between the main building and the wings was strictly guarded, and his father would kill him if he lost his job. But then she smiled at him, and he forgot his own name. "Um, the Sahalia Room. It is four doors down on your right," he directed, pointing in the opposite direction, fingers not quite steady.

"Thank you," she answered, pausing for his name. When he failed to fill in the blank, A.J. asked politely, "Are you allowed to tell me your name, or is it a state secret?"

"Madam?" He seemed nonplussed by the question and the notice. His Adam's apple bobbed tremulously as he attempted to swallow. Splotches of color heated his ears, which stood at attention on either side of his head. She had a voice like rose petals, velvet and smooth.

A.J. gently repeated her query. "Your name. It seems only fair, since you know who I am. Are you allowed to reveal that information?"

He had the vaguest suspicion that she was laughing at him, but he didn't care. Now, what was his name? Ah, yes. "Owen, madam. Owen Donley."

"Pleasure to meet you, Mr. Owen Donley." A.J. smiled, and the young man flushed a deep red from pitcher ears to pointed nose.

He stammered incoherently, "My pleasure, Dr. Grayson.

Please, do be of further assistance if I can ask. I mean, please do ask if I can be of further assistance. If you need to know where the gardens are, or—"

"I'm sure someone will be able to assist our guest, Mr. Donley," interjected Damon as he halted beside them. He acknowledged A.J., then turned to face the guard.

The flush paled and the guard snapped to attention. "Yes, sir. I mean, Your Highness."

With a hint of smile invisible to A.J., he offered the freckle-faced boy an escape. "I believe McCord requires aid in the Presidential Suite. I will escort Dr. Grayson to the dining room." When the boy hesitated, Damon prompted, "Now, Mr. Donley."

"Yes, sir. Right away, sir." With a last longing glance, Owen scuttled down the hallway toward the south wing.

The petty curl of jealousy startled Damon, and he turned to A.J. "Would you care to join me for breakfast?" He extended his arm, the question coolly formal.

A.J. paid no attention to the courtly gesture. "Why were you so rude to that nice young man?"

Damon lowered his arm and clasped his hands behind his back, the posture unyielding. "Reminding him of his duty is not rude."

"Humiliating him for being nice to me is."

"You think I humiliated him?"

"Yes, I do." A.J. folded her arms indignantly. "And I think you enjoyed making him scurry away with his tail tucked between his legs."

"Such a high opinion of me."

"And sinking fast. You may not have been to the manor born, but you've acquitted yourself well," she sneered. "I suppose the help is not to mingle with the guests, who are forbidden to consort with royalty."

"You know me better, A.J.," Damon said, his mouth tightening into a thin line.

"What possible reason could you have for your behavior?" A.J. retorted, but she felt a niggling sense of guilt.

Damon glared at her. "Because that nice young man is a new guard, and as such, has not yet learned the decorum or gravity of his post. I was rude to him, as you put it, to preserve his job. If he'd shown such laxity to anyone else, he would have immediately been censured and relieved of duty. He is a military guard, not a tour guide. And after last night, I would think you'd appreciate the difference."

The last sounded suspiciously like a reproach, A.J. thought, and she felt compelled to defend herself. "He was simply being friendly. At my insistence."

Damon agreed wryly. "I realized it was your fault, which is why I removed him from your presence before he began to drool."

Immediately contrite, A.J. apologized. "I'm sorry. I jumped to conclusions. But you were warned."

Accepting the olive branch, Damon replied, "We are not often visited by women of your beauty, Dr. Grayson. Poor mortals must be protected at all costs, and I doubt our guards have received adequate training."

"You flatter me, but you do it quite well, Your Highness." A.J. stuck her elbow out, imitating his earlier gesture, and looked up at him, apology evident. "I'm famished. Shall we dine before I pass out?"

Tucking the slender hand into the crook of his arm, Damon stared down at the upturned face alight with mischief. And desired nothing more than to press hungry lips to the impish mouth. He'd rescued young Owen because he understood the potency of her company. Instead of giving in to impulse, he inclined his head in imperial assent. "Lead on."

As they made their way down the spacious corridors, A.J. stopped them often to examine the portraits hung along the walls. Damon patiently answered myriad questions, calling upon his own recent tutoring. Inquisitive, A.J. ferreted out not only the stories, but his opinions on the artists' renderings. Discussing the play of light and shadow, the intricacy of portraiture, they wandered down the gallery, and Damon hoped they'd never reach the end.

During the night, he'd struggled to find a way to send her home, but he knew they needed her here. He needed her. When they were together, for a brief span of time, he ceased to be King and was simply Damon Toca.

At that moment, A.J. remarked upon a dainty nose obviously disproportionate to the bearer's facial structure. Her quip about ancient cosmetic surgery surprised a laugh from him, and his security attachment vainly attempted to hide their shock. Damon noted the reaction, and knew he had A.J. to thank or blame.

In addition to royalty, the portraits also contained images of past presidents. Confused by the diversity in last names, she asked him, "Why so many ethnic groups? Other than your lineage, I think I heard a name from every country."

"Not quite all," Damon corrected mildly, "but most. In all these weeks, you haven't heard the legend of Jafir?"

"No," A.J. replied in low tones, casting a furtive glance around her. "And my briefings didn't address it. I did learn jujitsu and the ancient art of the deadly stare, though." She fixed her gaze on him and concentrated hard.

Startled, Damon blinked, and she began to laugh merrily.

He lifted a disdainful brow. "Very amusing, Dr. Grayson."

"'The ancient art of the deadly stare'?" she chuckled. She patted his arm sympathetically, burning his flesh through the layers of cloth. Her breath, spiced by mint, blended with the trill of laughter. He was fast growing addicted to the sound.

Uncomfortably aroused, and to save them both from an embarrassing display in the passageway, he muttered, "If you are through with your juvenile humor, I will tell you about Jafir." He launched into the legend and recounted for her the tale of the beloved daughter of the Bantu and the true son of the Yoruba, the island's original inhabitants, who arrived on empty shores.

He explained that later, because of its position between Africa, Europe, and the Middle East in a strategic area of the Mediterranean, conquerors of different stripes had tried to take the island by force. But the landscape of cliffs and stony shoreline as well as the castle's perch at the highest point on the island repelled most invaders. A skillful blend of diplomacy and defense welcomed newcomers and encouraged community. In the end, the Jafirian people had successfully integrated Spanish and French, Italian and Arabian, Jewish and Greek and North African, while maintaining their Yoruban and Bantu core.

"What a lovely story!" A.J. turned with him into the dining room. "How much of it is true? Can I see the ship?"

"It is a legend, A.J."

"Most legends find their origins in fact, usually ones that the elders could not explain. Dracula. The Loch Ness Monster. King Arthur. The Hope Diamond."

Damon recalled the celebrated jewels linked to the Jafirian monarchy. The Kholari Diamond, the Sahalia Ruby, and the

Tropez Sapphire purportedly belonged to a set of stones divided among the original rulers of Jafir. He'd held the Sahalia in the palm of his hand, had felt the tug of history.

"Perhaps," he conceded as he escorted her to a chair, took the seat beside her, and summoned a server. "Any special requests?" he asked as he settled linen across her lap.

A.J. watched the elegant hands arrange the cloth and remembered their touch. She lifted her head and dared, "No. Surprise me."

Damon's lips curved into a slight smile, tinged with danger. "I'll try."

A.J. fought the urge to lean closer, to challenge. He had abandoned the formality between them, and she found herself recalling the man she'd first met.

"You owe me a ball, Damon."

"I'm sorry we had to cancel. However, the Jafirian Dance Society is world renowned, as is the Desira Opera House. If you'd like, I can arrange to have Sarah secure tickets for you."

"Would you join me?"

Damon thought of his decision last night, to create distance between them. Breakfast had been a whim, decided when he saw A.J. leaving her room. He'd succumbed despite his better judgment, but he couldn't afford to capitulate completely. A.J. had almost died trying to help him, and he would not be responsible for a scratch on A.J.

Talking with her, laughing with her was an indulgence, one he could not allow himself too often. The borrowed time with her would end soon, and he'd return to being King Damon. Aloof and solitary. Hunted.

Angered by the reminder, he coolly declined her invitation. "Unfortunately, I will not have time."

"Ever?" A.J. said in disbelief. "I'll be here for three more weeks. Surely, the nation can spare you for a couple of hours?"

"As I said, Dr. Grayson, unfortunately not."

The use of her title raised her hackles, and reminded her of the distance between them. She bit back frustration and derided herself for forgetting. Damon had a job and so did she. "Of course, Your Highness."

They glared at each other, neither willing to break the impasse.

"Good morning, Your Highness. Dr. Grayson." McCord strode inside, and A.J. felt bereft.

This morning, McCord was followed into the room by a striking older woman A.J. had not seen before. The mocha complexion and midnight hair were perfect complements to the high cheekbones and exotic eyes. The two circled from the opposite side of the dining table, and she and Damon rose from their seats in greeting.

"Mr. McCord."

"Dr. Grayson. You made quite an impression on young Master Donley."

A.J. shook her head. "I was trying to be polite." The playful grin received an answering smile from McCord.

Damon looked back and forth between them, intrigued by the exchange. The normally reserved McCord was fairly beaming—for him. It had taken Damon months to crack the stern veneer.

"McCord?"

McCord schooled his expression into one of impassivity but not without a residual hint of mirth. He nodded to the Deputy

Minister, and Damon felt a sudden chagrin at the need to be re-minded of his duties.

"Deputy Minister Isabel Santana, I'd like to present our con-sultant, Dr. A.J. Grayson," Damon introduced. "Minister Santana has been on assignment in Eastern Europe for the past three weeks."

"Deputy Minister," A.J. greeted as she proffered her hand.

"Dr. Grayson," Isabel inclined her head civilly, but did not move to take the offered hand. A.J. pulled her hand back and tucked it into the pocket of her slacks.

Damon noted the frosty reception, and quickly shifted into conversation. "Were you on your way to the suite?"

McCord nodded. "But I heard voices and thought I should investigate."

"Will you join us?" A.J. asked.

"Yes, McCord. Why don't you eat with Dr. Grayson? Minister Santana and I have quite a bit of work ahead of us." Damon took a step back. "We'll be in the office."

A.J. watched Damon murmur to the Deputy Minister, then tore her gaze from his retreating back.

"Nice woman," A.J. remarked blandly after they left the room.

McCord poured tea from a silver carafe on the table as he took Damon's vacated seat. "You must forgive her." He stirred in cream slowly. "She received a demotion before she left."

"I heard. It was to make room for the King's new position as Minister of State. Which would definitely explain hostility to-ward him, but not me."

"Deputy Santana is not the most affable of women at the best of times," McCord replied noncommittally. "But she is a formidable politician."

"Formidable is right," A.J. muttered.

McCord chuckled at the fast agreement.

Soon plates arrived, with an assortment of delicacies A.J. had never seen. She sampled each one, chatting easily with McCord. Overcoming his initial resistance as she had the day before, she soon had him entertaining her with tales of Damon's parents and stories of dignitaries and their mishaps.

In turn, A.J. recounted stories of her scientific failures in the GCI labs. By the time coffee was served, McCord found himself entranced by the sylph of a woman. The mixture of candor and self-deprecation blended nicely with the confidence and imagination. It explained the look in Damon's eyes when he spied them in the dining room. It made him worry.

After the remnants of their meal and coffee had been whisked away, A.J. sighed gustily and closed her eyes. "That was miraculous. Your cook is divine."

"You have a healthy appetite for one so small." McCord watched her with admiration.

A.J. sighed again, and opened one eye. "You are politely calling me a pig."

"Nothing so indelicate." The respectful tone was at odds with the smirk playing around the corners of his mouth. "Though I've rarely witnessed an appreciation of good food in such quantities."

"Waste not, want not," A.J. retorted. "Plus, I require a significant amount of fuel in the morning."

"Of course." McCord slid the chair away from the table and stood. "Shall we join the morning conference?" he asked, offering her a hand.

They left the Sahalia Room, and McCord led her down the corridor toward the Presidential Suite. Guards followed a discreet distance behind. "Most chiefs of staff don't have armed sentries tracking their every move."

"I'm very good at my job" was the bland explanation.

At precisely nine a.m., the Cabinet assembled for the morning debriefing. Sarah had set up A.J.'s presentation, and A.J. launched into her weekly report about the governmental audit.

"I have completed my preliminary analysis, and this week, I will conduct one-hour interviews with each of you. Some of my questions may seem intrusive, but they are quite vital." As she spoke, Sarah passed out questionnaires. "If you will complete these forms and return them to me at your earliest convenience, I can begin the interviews," A.J. finished.

"Why don't we complete them now, so that Dr. Grayson can start the interviews in the morning?" Robertsi suggested, then adjourned the meeting. Banal questions such as date of birth, family history, and recent vacation sites generated grumblings among the members who doubted the relevance of the items.

Sensing their annoyance, A.J. offered, "Feel free to contact me with any questions you have or suggestions."

A couple of Ministers asked why she needed such personal and irrelevant information.

"Personal habits and background affect work and productivity. For instance, the person who skydives on weekends is likely to be more adventurous in approaching tasks, and often more innovative, while a person who prefers rustic cabins in Monaco may pay greater attention to detail. This information will help me assess the combination of skills and outlooks shared by both you and your staff, but again, I warn you, it's only the beginning."

"What will you do with the information?" another Minister queried.

"As I explained, I've developed a program that will combine this data with the other information I've collected to help me detect patterns in output and responsiveness."

More questions followed, and A.J. answered them easily, occasionally fudging her responses. She couldn't tell them that the vacation history would demonstrate travel patterns and correlate to suspected terrorist cells. Or that school tuitions and new cars indicated bribery.

She worked for a few hours, inputting the information provided by the Cabinet. At lunchtime, she sent Sarah off to eat, but continued inputting information. Engrossed in the details, she didn't hear Damon enter.

Damon had instructed the guards to remain in the hallway outside the outer office. Alone, he watched her as she bent over the computer, hair knotted loosely at her nape. She'd removed her jacket, and it lay slung haphazardly across a small table in the corner. Narrow, quick fingers flurried over the keyboard, and he hotly recalled how they'd trailed against his skin. He wanted to feel them again, to know the mad rush of adrenaline as he slid inside the lush haven of her mouth. He wanted to talk with her again, to share stories, position be damned. Longing twisted inside him, tightened his gut.

Torture, he thought, to need what was forbidden.

Memories of holding the soft, lithe body against his own warred with the image of her falling to the ground. He could have lost her yesterday. Damon knew she'd leave in three weeks, that he wouldn't risk her life for futile dreams of a future. Surely, though, he could steal moments to warm him after she'd gone.

Torn between conscience and desire, Damon turned to leave as silently as he had come. But when she giggled at something he could not see, the sound caught him, decided for him. "Position be damned," he muttered as blindly, he closed the door to the office, pressing the lock.

She swiveled in her chair, mouth parted on a gasp at the sudden noise.

"A.J.," he demanded hoarsely. Damon advanced, pulling her up and into his arms. For an instant, she resisted, and he streaked a fervent hand along her arm, over her hair. When he cupped her cheek, forcing her eyes to his own, he felt the yielding. Sunlight, her scent, teased him, and he begged. "Please."

Soundlessly, she closed the distance between them, and Damon resisted the urge to plunge inside. Madness demanded that he take, but the sight of her wide, confused eyes urged patience. Delicately, he tested the satin of skin, the sweetness of lips. Parting the trembling flesh, he eased inside, eager to savor, desperate to taste.

At the heated contact, his control broke and he took wildly, reverently. Liquid softness surrounded him as he dove deeper. Softer moans rose between them, and she clung to him and caressed.

A.J. twisted closer, needing to feel the length of him against her. Without hesitation now, she met the avid foray of his tongue with her own. In his kiss, she tasted despair and sought to replace it with delight. Her body arched in invitation, and he answered by lifting the slight frame into his arms. The seamless kiss continued as he knelt on the sofa, set her among the pillows. When he joined her, she raced reckless hands over the sweep of his chest, the firm hardness of hip. Legs tangled as he lay against her, skimming his mouth down her throat and lower.

She gasped again, this time in celebration, as impatient hands parted her shirt, exposing willing flesh to his ministrations.

"Damon," she whispered.

"Don't speak," he cautioned, aware of his folly. He refused to remember the rules that demanded he leave the warm solace of her arms. Not yet, he thought. Not yet.

He'd imagined having her a thousand times. In his most fevered dream, he danced with her. Bathed in moonlight, he would seduce her into his arms, into his bed.

CHAPTER SIX

D r. Grayson?" Sarah spoke into the intercom as she jiggled the door handle. Damon shifted, breaking off contact and pushing himself away. The haze of arousal dissipated slowly, and he became aware of the impropriety of the moment. He moved to leave the warm, willing body, but A.J. grabbed his arm to hold him still.

"Let me send her away," A.J. urged quietly.

"Dr. Grayson?" This time, the inquiry was more insistent.

A.J. responded, arching beneath him to reach the appropriate button on the phone near the sofa. Damon stifled a groan of pleasure as her breasts brushed exposed skin where she'd released the buttons of his shirt.

She deliberately made her voice groggy when she spoke into the intercom. "Sarah? What is it?"

"Are you alright, Dr. Grayson?"

"Yes. Just a second, I'll unlock the door."

Releasing the button, she looked up at Damon, who braced himself above her, and tried to ignore the places where their bodies remained in intimate contact. With a strangled hope, she asked, "Do I send her away?"

For heaven's sake, yes, he thought hopelessly. Send her away, send them all away. But he said nothing aloud, sanity fully restored.

When he hesitated, she answered for him. "I guess not."

Damon watched desire drain from A.J.'s face, replaced instead with disgust. It mirrored his own self-loathing. What had he been thinking? If a guard or Sarah had barged in, how could he explain a tryst on the consultant's sofa at midday? At the merest hint of a scandal, the press would splay the lurid details across tabloids.

Luckily, his own attachment had been instructed to remain in the outer ring of suites, and they were trained not to reveal his movements or enter without permission. Sarah, a government employee, had no obligation to follow the special military protocol. Thus, he had no choice but to hide from her until he could make a furtive exit. "What will you say?" he asked grimly. "She can't know that I'm here."

"Of course not. Well, rest assured, I won't tell her the truth."

"But if she comes inside—"

"She won't. I'll get rid of her; then you can leave."

"Very good."

Damon freed his arm and levered off the sofa, away from A.J. He swiftly straightened his tie, which had unraveled beneath her hands. The thin strip of silk now carried her scent, and he cursed himself for giving in to temptation. A.J. sat up, and as he watched impassively, she rebuttoned her blouse.

A.J. ran unsteady fingers through her hair, the simple twist undone by Damon's urgency. Satisfied that she'd done all she could to repair the damage, she opened the door. For effect, she yawned widely. "Sarah. I'm sorry. I decided to take a catnap during lunch. I had a rather heavy breakfast."

"Oh. I'm sorry I woke you. Should I return later?"

A.J. smiled apologetically. "Actually, why don't you call it a day? I've got a bit more setting up to do, and it will probably take the rest of the afternoon."

"You won't need me?" Sarah asked, surprised by the change in schedule.

"No. I've got it under control." After Sarah turned away, A.J. shut the door with more force than necessary. She spun on her heel to face him.

"This was a mistake," Damon said before she could speak.

"Which part? Kissing me or pulling away?"

"Does it matter?"

"Yes!" She stormed over to the sofa and plopped down, only to leap to her feet. "Do you have any idea how demeaning it is to have a man apologize for being attracted to you?" Before he could respond, she continued, "Nowhere near as demeaning as having the same man run away every time he touches you!"

"I've explained that." Damon stood rigidly, his back to the window. Shadows moved across the sky, and the room darkened. A.J. saw a similar transformation in him, the countenance flat and dark. Remote.

"To your credit, you have. I just seem to be unable to

remember. The King of Jafir consorting with the Grayson orphan. What would the people think?"

"This has nothing to do with pedigree," Damon snapped.

"It has everything to do with pedigree! Why else do you find it necessary to touch me only when we're hidden away from prying eyes?"

Damon felt fury build, its sensation hot and burning. Anger at her for having such little regard for him flowed like molten lava. Rage made him incautious, and he asked scornfully, "Would you rather I make love to you in public?"

A.J. tossed her head, the sharp chin jutting out in defiance, its menace dulled by the single dimple at its center. "That's not what I meant, and you know it. But time and again, you allow yourself to be with me, and the moment I begin to believe you mean it, you change direction."

Throwing up his hands, he reminded her, "I've kissed you three times. You base a conclusion of my honor on such flimsy evidence? Perhaps you are not the person for such a sensitive job of analysis."

She lifted her hand and began to count on her fingers. "You are capricious and a snob. And you want evidence? One, the kiss in the wine cellar. Two, the aborted attack in President Robertsi's office. Three, the library, not to mention the flirts and feints of the past three weeks. Four, our breakfast this morning. And five, this, whatever it was, just now. One minute, you can't have enough of me, but the instant anyone notices that you've paid me the slightest attention, let alone courtesy, you shut down. And shut me out."

"This morning, I refused an invitation to the opera," he corrected, the tone leaving no doubt what he thought of her theory.

He advanced on her, and lifted a hand to cup her neck, to soothe, to punish. "I realize you hold me in no high regard, but have you so harsh an opinion of yourself?"

A.J. struggled against his grip, but he held her immobile. "Let me go."

Painfully aware he couldn't even if he wished, he instead taunted, "Is this insecurity the result of your position at GCI? Did you get your place only by family ties?" Perhaps the mention of her outsider status there would force her to confront her real anxieties and share them with him.

A.J. took the bait. She stiffened and snarled. "My aunt and uncle have nothing to do with my position at GCI. I've earned every promotion, every post. No one gave me anything."

"So, your obsession with inferiority, it is because you are not one of them? An outsider?"

Pride flashed where doubt had been, and the sharp chin rose higher. "I'm not an outsider. Now, I'm a Grayson."

So complicated, he thought, the acceptance of place and lineage. Did she truly understand how it felt to suddenly lose who you were, to learn that what you knew of your own heritage had been a lie? Perhaps he owed her that.

"Less than a year ago, I was a businessman. I cannot paint or sculpt or build, but I know art. The galleries were my world, and I had two parents I loved more than anything. Then, in one night, my universe crashed. My parents were no longer the people who raised me, but two strangers who died to save me from a madman. Zeben killed my parents, and even worse, he was working with my brother to steal our birthright."

A.J. quietly joined her fingers with his, at their side. "Go on."

"I had to make a choice. To forfeit the life I'd created for myself, or to allow my brother and Zeben to destroy a nation my parents had died to protect."

"You made the only decision you could."

With inexorable pressure, Damon leveled her eyes with his own. "When I came to the wedding, it was simply to complete an errand. But before I could leave, I saw you, and my world shifted again. You were so lovely, so assured. I promised myself a single dance with you. Then one became three; then we were alone, and I couldn't tear myself away."

"But you did."

"Because being with me then was dangerous. And so is being with me now. You could have been shot yesterday."

"I'm in danger simply by working with you," A.J. protested.

"For six weeks. Out of the public eye." Releasing her neck, he traced the bow of her soft, naked mouth, lipstick erased by his kisses. "If I allow myself, I believe I could want you for a lifetime."

"And?"

"And as long as I am King, Zeben will want me dead, and Nelson will want the throne."

"So you intend to isolate yourself for the rest of your life?"

"If I have to. I've made my choice, A.J., and there is no escape."

"You're rejecting me because of something that might happen?" she asked incredulously. "You might fall in love with me or your enemies might kill you?"

"Yes. Or they might kill you."

"Or they might not!" She heard the plea in her voice, and blocked it with scorn. "At least when I thought you were a snob, I gave you credit for moderate intelligence."

Nonplussed by the insult, Damon dropped his hand. This

imp had no respect for the crown or for anything else. She had the audacity to call him *stupid*? "Watch your tongue, *ma fée*."

"Or what?" A.J. shot him a look of contempt. "You'll have me beheaded?"

"You try my patience, A.J."

"As do you mine." She spun around, prepared to stalk away, but Damon tightened his hold on the hand entwined with his own. She half turned, and he tugged on their linked hands.

She fell into his arms, and he held her close. Irritation and curiosity struggled for ascendancy in dark, sultry eyes. To test her, to tempt him, he said smugly, "I did not dismiss you."

"I'm not one of your subjects. Release my hand," she demanded imperiously.

"When I'm ready."

A.J. acknowledged the arrogance as innate, not a product of rank. And she felt the leashed power, where it vibrated between their joined hands. But the power between them belonged to both. For too long, she'd let him have control, pulling her in when he was ready and turning away when he'd had enough.

Now, she'd had enough.

Curling her free hand around his neck, an imitation of his earlier gesture, A.J. lightly scraped her fingers along his nape. When his eyes darkened to golden honey, she tugged at the taut muscles, and dragged his mouth down to meet hers.

Unlike their first kisses, she gave him no space for control. Her tongue slicked over surprised lips, plundered the astonished mouth. Aggressively, she led him into a dance of wills and fought for supremacy. Unable to stop himself, he lifted her into him, and she sank both hands into the silky, brown strands at his nape.

And when he groaned her name aloud, his body tight with need, she wriggled free and dropped to her feet.

Stunned, he watched as she calmly turned, and she knew his eyes did not waver as she marched to the door. She swung the oak on its hinges and dipped into a mocking curtsy. "Good day, Your Highness."

McCord stood on the other side, his hand raised to knock. He glanced at the pair, quickly taking in the tableau of temper and desire. "Ah, Your Highness. I thought you might be here. We have an appointment at the children's hospital."

"I'll be right with you," Damon ground out, his livid gaze never leaving A.J.

"We really must be going," McCord admonished. "The chair of the hospital is waiting for you in the car."

"Alright." He stalked past A.J. and into the hallway. With a feral glare, he warned, "This isn't over."

"I know," she conceded. "But now we both understand the rules."

Closing the door, she leaned weakly against the solid frame. She'd never been so brazen before, she thought, bewildered by her impulse. For that matter, she'd never been so angry before either. And if she were to be honest, she'd never ached so badly for one man.

She smelled once more the scent of sea and forest, the strength of his arms as he'd lifted her high against his chest. What had she been thinking to tempt fate?

Damon was absolutely right about the danger of a relationship between them. If not for the threats to Jafir, then she should stay away because of the ISA's suspicions about him. Raleigh had cautioned her about emotional entanglements, the risks of losing focus. She'd called them the rules of engagement, and A.J. promised her the aberration of one night in the moonlight would remain just that.

Yet at the most inopportune moment, she practically molested her prime suspect. She hadn't stopped to think about what she was doing, intent only on demonstrating that she—not Damon Toca—made her choices for her. And with their hands pressed palm to palm, his beautiful mouth faintly haughty, certain she would submit, she had no clearer thought than to conquer.

At the thought of the tumult of that daring kiss, her lips tingled and her body flushed in an unfamiliar sensation.

Not happiness, but an emotion perilously close.

Don't be a fool, she chastised as she moved away from the door to stand by the bay windows. Below, white-capped waves crested in the gathering tempest. The shadows had turned to storm clouds, black and ominous. What had begun as a glorious cloudless sky now spat rain in fierce columns. And what started between them at the wedding was destined for a bitter end.

Whether Damon admitted it or not, she was painfully aware of the obvious. The differences between them were more than ones of title. A.J. had spent almost twenty years proving herself deserving of the Grayson name. Instinctively, she balked at the notion of trying to live up to the pedigree of a crown.

She pressed a hand to her stomach to quiet the sudden roiling.

Why should the thought of a crown disturb her so? She barely knew Damon, she reminded herself. And, chemistry aside, they had nothing in common.

Nothing except a shared history of surrogate families, an affinity for good literature, and a devotion to duty.

No, A.J. denounced, as images of them together flashed in her wayward mind. They shared nothing sufficient to overcome the distance of status. He was King Damon Toca, and she was—oh, what had he called her—a changeling.

"Damn." She rested her forehead against the thick pane of glass, the cool touch a contrast to her fevered brain.

When another knock sounded at the door, A.J. cursed silently. The laboratory was quickly becoming Grand Central Terminal. She opened the door, and was startled to see Isabel Santana.

"Deputy Minister," A.J. greeted. "I did not expect to see you here."

"May I come in?" Isabel asked. "I would like to speak with you."

"Of course," she said. Pointing to a visitor chair near her desk, she instructed, "Please, have a seat. Can I get you anything?"

The coolly elegant woman balanced on the edge of the seat, and declined. "President Robertsi told me that I should see you about your project."

A.J. didn't have to know Isabel well to sense the contempt. "I can give you the forms now or have them sent to your office."

"I'd prefer to complete them now," she sniffed haughtily.

The thought of the woman finishing the mountain of forms in her office enervated A.J. She'd endured more than her share of calamity today, and being trapped with the Ice Queen was not in the cards. A.J. gathered the forms prepared for Isabel and handed her the thick file. "These will take some time. I can have my assistant get them from you as soon as you're done."

Isabel reclined in the chair, her endless legs stretched out before her, not ready to depart. "What can you tell me about your machine?"

Eager to get rid of her, A.J. gave her a thumbnail description. Undaunted, Isabel asked question after question about schematics and design, as though intentionally holding her hostage.

"Do you want something in particular?" A.J. asked finally, the random questions grating. "I don't think you stopped by for instructions on artificial intelligence. If you did, I can recommend a good book or two."

Isabel stiffened. "I would appreciate you responding to my questions. That is why you're here, is it not?"

"I'm here to perform an audit." A.J. let her irritation show. "However, I don't see how a tutorial in artificial intelligence helps either of us."

Rising, Isabel inclined her head. "I simply wanted to see what the King finds so fascinating about you. I'll return your forms tomorrow." She left quietly, and A.J. stared after her.

Abandoning the attempt to decipher Santana's motive, she returned to her computer, wanly typing in names and facts about the Cabinet. Once the separate files were completed, she'd use Poppet to run an analysis that correlated her gathered information to the data the ISA had on file for the suspected terrorist cells.

The results would be one set of records that she'd transmit to the ISA next Friday. Her designated rendezvous was a fabric stall run by a man named Sashu. She'd transfer the flash drive to him while she purchased material. Hidden in the bolt of cloth would be new instructions for her.

Very cloak-and-dagger, she thought as she prepared to have Poppet run scenarios using last night's attempt. She set the vocal interface.

"Good afternoon, Poppet."

"Good afternoon, Dr. Grayson. How may I assist you?"

"I need a probability scan. Correlate Cabinet Data File with Cell 1. Tell me, who is most likely to be connected with the groups in Cell 1."

"Access code required for Cell 1," Poppet replied.

"Mu iota nu epsilon rho phi alpha."

"Voice frequency print and code confirmed. Next code access rotated."

A.J. had programmed Poppet to accept only voice and code matches, and to change among seven code options. As the sole person aware of the rotations, no one else would be able to access the system.

In minutes, Poppet announced, "Analysis complete."

"Results?"

"Probability ninety-eight percent: Lawrence Robertsi. Probability ninety-two percent: Damon Toca. Probability eighty-one percent: Isabel Santana. Probability seventy-seven percent: Mc-Cord. Probability seventy-seven percent: Teresa Wynn." Poppet continued to list probabilities until it had named the entire Cabinet.

Damon ranked high on the list of suspects, second only to Robertsi. But she'd expected this, given the more extensive travels and contacts they had. However, Damon's high probability concerned her.

"Poppet, did you consider the snipers from last night?"

"Yes, Dr. Grayson. There is a high probability that the attack was feigned. Given the failure of the attack, it may have been a ruse to distract attention."

On the screen, Poppet displayed a list of traits and scenarios, each one ranking Damon's capacity in the areas. The profile Poppet had devised indicated a pattern of subterfuge in their culprit, one that relied on obfuscation rather than plain mendacity. Its analysis concluded that the likelihood of two snipers, whose combined efforts only wounded the guard and never hit its main target, was questionable.

"Poppet, please display background data for analysis of Damon Toca."

Her heart heavy, she read about how Damon had smuggled the obelisk into the U.S. using Alex. He'd thrilled her with charming words; then he'd hidden behind a veil of secrets.

Small teeth chewed worriedly on her bottom lip. Damon should not be as high on the list. His placement would increase ISA trepidations about him, and she had no clue what their reaction might be.

She didn't have to tell them anything yet, A.J. decided, calling up her algorithms. The datasets had been provided by Wynn and the ISA, but she had not yet set a pure baseline to test the accuracy of the results. She would continue to develop the study before she jumped to conclusions.

And she'd glue herself to the King for personal observation.

Content with her decision, A.J. typed in her own information to test the system. When her probability returned at thirty-two percent, she asked for clarification.

"Grayson, A.J. Connection to Caine Simons."

"Who?" she asked, unfamiliar with the name.

"Access to further information denied."

"By whom?"

"Must have security clearance Omega 1," Poppet informed her.

Atlas had hidden information from her as well? Somehow, Poppet had discovered a connection between her and a potential terrorist, a person she'd never met.

That probably explained the error in probability. If she didn't have complete information, she'd continue to receive flawed output. In the morning, she'd have to ask Adam to explain.

For the next six hours, A.J. refined her dataset and finished setting up Poppet. Occasionally, she made adjustments to its matrix, using calculations she'd made during her briefing sessions.

Night fell, evidenced purely by the clock. Beyond the windows, storms continued to rage, and the sky remained a heavy curtain of gray and black. A loud rumble followed by a twinge in her belly reminded her that she'd skipped lunch.

A sharper ache reminded her of why.

She would not think about that anymore. It would only muddy her very clear decision about their situation. Damon Toca was off-limits romantically, but she had to stick very close professionally.

Surely, she could do both?

Slightly fortified by resolve, she left the office and keyed in the security code protecting the office. Only she and Damon had the code; not even Robertsi could enter without her permission. In the event of sabotage, finding a culprit would be easier.

A.J. headed to the main palace, and noticed immediately that she had company.

"How long will you be following me?" she asked conversationally of the woman to her left.

"For the duration of your stay, Dr. Grayson," the sturdy woman replied.

"At whose request?" A.J. already knew the answer.

"His Royal Highness, Dr. Grayson."

"Did His Royal Highness leave any other instructions?"

"No, Dr. Grayson."

A.J. asked the woman her name, and also learned the name of the burly man to her right. She figured since they'd be in close proximity for the next several weeks, they may as well become acquainted. Both politely declined her offer of dinner.

Not feeling in the mood for a State dinner or company, A.J. trudged up the stairs, dutifully ignoring her shadows. She entered her room and yelped.

"What are you doing here?" she demanded.

"It is my house, A.J.," Damon remarked as he rose from the settee to stand in front of her. He'd lit one lamp while he waited, and the dim light played softly with the hollows and curves of her face, the defiant chin raised for battle.

Its single dimple enchanted him, and as it did inevitably in her presence, his normally steady pulse quickened. Blood heated with desire, thudded with longing. Recklessly, he lifted a hand to feather the rebellious mouth.

In the hours since he'd left her, he'd given a great deal of thought to her accusation. He'd thought even more about her insolent kiss. Now, her taste lingered, a companion to the scent that teased and maddened. The eager melding of their mouths had intensified flavors fast growing addictive, heightened fragrances that churned and enraptured. Sweet and piquant, sunlight and storm.

A.J. too was a mass of contradiction, at once bold and insecure.

One moment, she was berating him as a snob, and in the next breath, she belittled her own family background. The puzzle ate at him, and the thought of her insinuated itself deep and refused to be dislodged. He rubbed a hand along a region near his heart. She made him ache to unravel her, thread by glorious, desirable thread, until he found the core.

McCord's lecture after the long, endless series of meetings hit nerves raw from the afternoon. In short order, the older man echoed Damon's logic about the hazards of involvement with A.J. Between the threats to the summit and the rigors of the coronation, Damon could ill afford to indulge himself.

But he found himself compelled as he passed her rooms, heading to his chambers to change for the evening round of appearances. He needed to see her, to talk to her. To simply be near her.

Though he loathed to admit it, she challenged him, and he enjoyed the conflict. Before Jafir, he'd been a man of wealth and privilege, one who used that status to shepherd new artists lacking his good fortune. But there had been a patronizing quality to his good deeds, a vaunted sense of patronage. The significance of rank, of place, associated with the monarchy grated, not simply because it denied him freedom but also because it pleased parts of him he dared not confront. The parts of him that came naturally to his post, like aloofness and detachment.

But A.J. Grayson had no tolerance for protocol, for the distance he could summon with an arched brow with anyone else. With her, the very act of the curtsy was executed with impudence, and she addressed him by his royal title with an ersatz formality. For many months, he'd assumed he fought his new position, and in two weeks, she'd shown him that he also struggled against himself.

The thought of a few more weeks in her company terrified him. Excited him.

Studying her in the lamplight, he balled his fists to keep his hands by his sides. His visit to her chambers had not been prompted by lust, but by necessity.

"We need to come to an agreement." Damon turned away to gaze at the turbulent sea. "What happened this afternoon cannot be repeated."

"Which part?"

"Any of it." He turned back to A.J., tension evident. "Neither of us can afford the consequences."

"Of what? Of a few shared kisses? Damon, don't be melodramatic."

"And don't be coy. We both know this is about more than a few kisses. I am starting to f—" He broke off with an oath, and A.J. took a step forward. Damon raised a hand to ward her off.

She froze in place. "You're starting to what?"

"To lose perspective. The summit, the coronation. These are the reasons you're here. The only reasons," he stressed meaningfully. He wondered if he was warning her or himself. According to McCord, he posed the larger threat. "There can be nothing else between us."

A.J. obviously agreed. With a negligent shrug, she said, "Alright."

The quick response caught him off guard. He'd prepared a litany of reasons for the decision, none of which reflected on her heritage. He did not expect her to take the decision well, and certainly not with that faint look of boredom that crept into her eyes while he watched.

"And we'll work solely as colleagues?" Damon inspected her, searching for an indication that this edict disturbed her at all. Deep brown eyes reflected only placid acceptance, and his fists balled tighter.

"Of course. A mutual cease-fire. Cease everything." A.J. slipped out of her jacket and walked to the closet to place it on a hanger. "No problem," she tossed over her shoulder.

The frustrated look he shot at her bounced harmlessly off her nicely shaped backside. "Fine," he muttered in irritated response.

A.J. turned away from the closet, her hand playing with a button on her shirt. "Was that all?"

"Yes." He shoved the still-clenched fists into his pants pockets. If she had changed her mind this easily, he thought irritably, it was just as well he pulled away.

Mon dieu, she was a baffling woman. One minute incensed at his retreat, the next seducing him with a kiss. And now, calmly undressing as he told her he didn't want her. He'd had a narrow escape, he decided. A.J. Grayson cared nothing for him, and he was well rid of the distraction. "We will meet at seven a.m. I would like to begin the project."

"Oh, I've already started." A.J. perched on the edge of the chaise and removed her heels, massaging the reddened flesh. The narrow feet boasted fire-engine-red nails, an erotic contrast to the chocolate-toned skin. "I'll take you through my analysis in the morning." As she slid onto the chaise, a pant leg rode higher, and exposed the strong curve of her calf.

Damon swallowed hard. What was wrong with him? He'd seen a woman's foot before, had seen shapely legs. Yet, on A.J., both were unbearably alluring. He had to escape before he forgot his well-considered reasons for putting a stop to their flirtation.

"Well then, good night." With a curt bow, he began to walk to the door. The phone rang, and instinct halted him.

A.J. lifted the receiver, pleased by Damon's annoyed tone. If he thought he could dictate the terms of their relationship, even the business end of it, he was sadly mistaken. She had her own mission, and her own agenda. And she'd win.

"Hello."

A mechanized voice, digitally enhanced, spoke slowly. "Dr. Grayson. This will be your only warning. Unless the impostor openly abdicates his stolen throne in two weeks, there will be violent retribution."

"Who is this?" Her question was husky as fear rasped her voice.

"It is the will of the people. We will not tolerate an intruder in our midst. He will not succeed."

"He is the King."

"He is dead."

A.J. motioned frantically for Damon to lift the receiver in the bedroom. She had to keep the caller talking until he got on the other line. There was no way to signal him to get security, so she focused on keeping the man's attention. "Why are you contacting me?"

"Because we know you consort with the fraud. You are a harlot." Vile invective spewed across the phone lines, accusing her of contaminating the sanctity of the monarchy. A.J. felt sick, but she listened as he described their encounters in graphic, sordid terms. "The charlatan will abdicate, and if he does not comply, you will join him in his grave."

"I will find you, and you will pay for your filth," Damon threatened with quiet menace. At the sound of his voice, the caller terminated the connection.

Dropping the phone into its cradle, Damon rushed to A.J.'s side and wrenched the phone from her hand. "A.J.? Who was it? Did he give a name, *ma fée*?" He lifted hands cold as ice, and gently chafed them between his own.

A.J. visibly pulled herself together and said in a low, disbelieving tone, "No. He just said you will die in two weeks unless you abdicate the throne."

CHAPTER SEVEN

We've got to contact Wynn and Robertsi." Damon leapt to his feet and reached down to assist A.J.

She clung to his hand, but not out of fear. Pulling him close, she whispered, "No, we can't."

Damon reared away, infuriated. "Why the devil not? Someone has just called to threaten me, and he used you to do it!" The heat of anger warred with the cold rush of fear he'd felt when he heard the vile words the voice had spewed. "We must report this now." He strode to the door, driven by a fury that rocked him. A.J. had nothing to do with this, with Jafir, and now she too was caught up in its turmoil.

"Damon," A.J. urged, scrambling to her feet, "listen to me. We don't know who's involved."

The threat replayed in his ears, and he knew he had to think, but the walls of the palace closed in around him. "Come with me." Damon waited while she slid her shoes onto her feet.

Taking her hand in his, Damon led her from her rooms down the hallway to his own.

They entered Damon's rooms, and the guards remained outside the chamber. Damon swiftly crossed the expanse of carpet to reach a closet door. At A.J.'s speculative look, he opened the closet and ushered her inside. He grabbed a flashlight from the shelf, and checked the beam.

When he depressed a knob hidden behind a wooden panel, the false wall slid away to reveal a winding staircase. Damon entered first, familiar with the curve of the steps. One hand felt along the wall for purchase, and the other kept A.J. near.

The stairwell ended in a tunnel. Breathing echoed in the granite corridor, and occasional scratching noises signaled the scurrying of mice.

A.J. was more than pleased when they emerged in a wooded field fifteen minutes later.

"How did you know about that tunnel?" she asked immediately.

"McCord. There is a series of them leading into and out of the palace, and there are others in the city. They were designed centuries ago, and we have maps of most. Some are known to the security team; others are not."

"Marvelous." A.J. glanced around her curiously. "I've never seen this section of the estate." Wildflowers grew haphazardly, untamed by a gardener's touch. Nearby, she could hear the trickle of water.

"We're not in the Asphodel," explained Damon. "This is private property, owned by the Toca family."

"You might want to speak to the help."

"I prefer it this way." He gestured to a simple A-frame cabin. "Let's go inside."

The log structure had been recently constructed, A.J. thought as they approached the cabin. The wood had been sealed against the weather, but saws and hammers sat in front of a small storage shed. She looked at Damon. "This is new, isn't it?"

"Yes." He didn't elaborate. Instead, he opened the door and lifted a kerosene lamp from the uncovered floor. With efficient motions, he struck a match from a packet lying beside the lamp, and the room was illuminated.

In one corner, a single mattress lay on a bed hewn from the same wood used to build the cabin. Handwoven rugs covered the floors, and cheerful curtains hung over the windows.

"How charming!" A.J. exclaimed. Eagerly, she traced the edge of an oval dining table, its polished surface carved with an intricate design. It sat in a nook beside the tiny kitchenette, with its pipe stove and gas burners. There was no other furniture besides the two matching chairs, the bed, a cedar trunk, and a craftsman's rocking chair sitting by the fireplace. The single room was less than five hundred square feet, but the overall effect of rustic elegance suggested an openness and a remarkable patience for process.

It should not have surprised her to find both in Damon, but it did. "You made everything in here, didn't you?" she asked in awe. "And you built the cabin."

"I had some free time." Damon carried the lamp to the mantel and trimmed the wick.

A.J. narrowed her eyes at the understatement. "Free time? In my free time, I watch television."

"And develop computer systems."

"We both need more relaxing hobbies," she conceded. While she watched, Damon made coffee for them over the gas stove. The grounds were bitter, and he'd not yet installed a refrigerator for cream.

She gingerly consumed the contents of the cup, grimacing with each sip. Damon choked back a laugh as she shuddered.

"Please, for God's sake, never offer to cook for me," she pleaded.

Damon sniffed arrogantly. "My inability to make coffee doesn't mean I can't cook."

"Can you cook?"

"No," he said instantly. "But thank you for asking."

When she laughed at his easy confession, the light sound filling the room, Damon's answering smile died as desire raced through him. Until A.J., he'd never known laughter could shimmer, could be mindlessly erotic. That the dimpled tilt of a chin or the quickness of a mind could make him ache. Make him need. But now, watching the teasing mouth curve into laughter, hearing forever in such a comfortable sound, he knew that he would have her soon.

Endlessly.

And once he'd sated them both, he would begin anew, until he remembered nothing of before, thought nothing of tomorrow.

"Damon?" A.J. said his name, fascinated and a bit frightened by what she read in his eyes. She knew, without asking, that he was thinking of her. And she understood, without words, what he wanted from her.

"What would Poppet predict that I'm thinking, A.J.?"

The mention of Poppet reminded her of why they'd snuck out of the palace. She sobered and ignored his question, and her own compulsion to hear the answer. "Damon, we can't report the phone call to Robertsi or Wynn. Or anyone else, for that matter."

Damon accepted the change of topic, the seduction in his eyes banked for the time being. "Why not?"

"Think about it. Whoever did this knows us both. There is an intimate cadre of people who fit that description. Robertsi and Wynn are two of them."

"You suspect one of them?" The thought froze him, and he dropped into the seat opposite hers. "Based on what?"

"Tonight, I ran a preliminary analysis of the data I received from the Cabinet. I combined it with the ISA files I'd already been given. Five names showed a high probability for collusion with a terrorist sect. Robertsi and Wynn were two of them."

"And the other three?"

"McCord. Santana."

She debated for a moment, then chose the truth. "It also predicts that you could be involved. It ranks you second."

Damon heard the words, imagined an accusation. For seconds, he stared at her. If she'd suspected him capable of treason, they understood nothing of each other. He stood and asked in a deadly voice, "Me? You believe I could have done this, had someone say those things to you?"

"Of course not, Damon. Let me explain," she sputtered, rising to stand in front of him.

The chair tipped to the ground as he too rose, towering above her. "You wish to explain?"

"I know how this sounds, Damon."

"You will address me as Your Royal Highness. But I believe I'd prefer it if you did not speak to me at all."

A.J. blanched at the cold fury, but she offered, "I had no choice. It was part of the assignment. To study everyone. Including you."

"So you admit it?" He reached out a hand, tilting her face into the lamplight. "Lovely. Brilliant. And you accuse me of duplicity? Yet how easily you fall into my arms at every turn. Is it to uncover the truth about me? Are you the ISA's Mata Hari, here to seduce me into betraying my secrets? Would you sleep with me to uncover the truth?"

The slap reverberated in the cabin, and A.J. dropped her stinging hand to her side. "Go to hell," she spat out, and reined in angry tears that pressed for release. The shocked hurt rippled out in eddies, each fresh wave catching her unawares. But she refused to give him the satisfaction of her pain.

Blindly, she grabbed her bag from the table and sprinted for the door. As before, he caught her there, and caged her against the frame between his arms.

"Ma fée, I'm sorry," he said quietly. "I didn't mean it."

Her eyes downcast, afraid to look and see distrust, she demanded, "Move out of my way, Damon, before I do something we'll both regret."

"More violent than slapping the King?"

She lifted her head, and temper flashed in the guileless brown eyes. "You're a jackass, Damon."

"Yes. But you should forgive me," he rationalized, lifting a cautious hand from the door.

"Why?"

"Because you are the one person on this damned island I can trust, and I could not bear to lose that."

Damon freed her and walked to the table, posture rigid. "But if you'd like, I'll take you to the palace."

A.J. contemplated him and the events of the past hour. Temper aside, she had been sent here for a purpose. "I have a mission to accomplish."

She rejoined him at the table, moving her chair as far away from his as she could. "I was told to investigate the possibility of any member of the Cabinet being the saboteur. You are a member, and therefore a suspect. Anything before or after was personal."

"Was?"

The look she leveled at him was bitter and cold. "Was, Your Highness."

"I've apologized, A.J. I didn't mean what I said. It was that you surprised me. I did not realize I too was held in suspicion." He sighed, a weary sound that seemed dragged from his soul. "I know I am on trial with every person I meet. Citizens and McCord remember my parents and judge. The Cabinet is wary of me. Robertsi hates me. Santana despises me. But you were the one who knew me before, and to hear so baldly that you doubted me too"—he paused—"it threw me. But that is no excuse for hurting you. Especially after tonight." Grief flickered across his lean, gorgeous face, and A.J. relented.

She reached over the table to cover his bunched fist with her hand. The reassuring touch soothed him, quieted the fear of loss that had risen. "I don't believe it was you. If I did, I wouldn't be here with you now."

"Then who thinks me capable of this?"

"The ISA. And Poppet. But neither one knows you."

What hung between them, unspoken, was a declaration neither pursued.

"The ISA? But Atlas worked with me," he snapped, the anger directed not at her. "I cooperated."

A.J. shrugged. "It's his job to suspect. However, you should know, he wants me to eliminate you as a possibility. And Poppet focused on you, because according to its calculations, you could be working with Nelson. Or with Zeben."

With effort, Damon held himself still at the reference to his brother. "I helped put Nelson in prison. I risked my life to capture Zeben. What would I possibly have to gain by destabilizing Jafir?"

"Scimitar is no ordinary terrorist group, Damon. You know as well as I that they have strongholds in all of the Alliance states. Should Scimitar come to power here, the resulting unrest would topple nations. Your family fortunes would increase, and you could wield enormous power."

"That's Nelson's delusion, not mine. My God, I had no contact with international politics before the damned obelisk was brought to me!" Damon pounded a fist into the wood. "I never asked for this!"

A.J. stroked the hand she held captive. "Damon. Look at me."

Warily, he met her eyes, found his control. He would be useless without it.

"I trust you. If I didn't, I wouldn't have told you this." She smiled wanly. "The question is, who else can we trust?"

Damon felt his muscles tense, then deliberately relaxed. A.J. was absolutely right. Their first step had to be figuring out who else they could tell about the phone call. His job was to defend his homeland, and he would.

"McCord. We can tell him." Damon reached inside his jacket for a cell phone. "He knows about the cabin. I'll have him meet us here."

"Damon, no." She disconnected the line. "McCord must be a suspect too. There are too many holes in his past."

Swamped by weariness, but unwilling to concede, Damon tried to refute her conclusions. "McCord served my parents. He has personally guided me through this . . . this morass."

"Which means he could have been in cahoots with Zeben for more than thirty years."

Damon didn't respond, didn't contradict her. McCord may have killed his parents? Reaction set in, and he absorbed the blow.

One more loss.

"Do you have evidence?"

"No. This is all purely speculation. But, Damon, we've got to do this. For every person."

"Of course, you're right," he agreed coolly. Hadn't he learned the first lesson from his brother, the second from his surrogate parents? Trust no one. Believe nothing. Even those who acted for you would betray. "Who's next?"

A.J. frowned at the pallor tinting the light-brown skin, the ice coating his words. "Damon?" she asked hesitantly. "Are you okay?"

"What?" He looked up at her, the hazel eyes flat with banked rage. "Oh, I'm grand. My closest confidant may have killed my parents and threatened my woman. My allies suspect me of collusion. Oh yes, I'm excellent."

His woman? Blood stirred, her pulse jumped, and she flushed at the image that haunted her dreams. To be his, to make him hers, it was too soon to speak the desire aloud.

As much as she wanted to probe that statement—both the machismo and the romance—she reminded herself that they had work to do.

She rummaged through her purse and removed a personal digital assistant. Shaped like a normal PDA, A.J.'s device had a few added enhancements. Ones that would let her share her ISA files with Damon.

She'd be violating the ISA protocol and making a command decision, A.J. realized, but she needed to tell Damon about the ISA's concerns. By sharing segments of the ISA files with him, they could begin to eliminate potential threats. After two weeks with him, and his reaction tonight, A.J. had no choice but to trust him. Their lives were in danger, and she had to figure out from whom before she called in the cavalry.

From beneath her lashes, she studied Damon. The pale skin had shed its pallor, but the revelation that McCord might be a threat etched brackets beside his poet's mouth.

He was an enigma, she thought. For every detail she uncovered, a new layer of complexity appeared.

The man who declared himself a collector of art rather than an artist had constructed a spartanly beautiful sanctuary from the ground up. The handcrafted furniture, with its moldings and designs, demonstrated a yearning for simplicity. A stark contrast, she decided, to the royal arrogance that was innately Damon.

She was fast falling in love with both men.

His dark promise of retribution to their mystery caller had both thrilled and frightened her. In her time at the palace, she'd witnessed a variety of Damon's moods, but never the surety of violence he promised.

In defense of her honor.

"A.J.? What are you doing?" Damon asked, breaking her reverie.

Entering a series of keystrokes with the miniature keyboard she unfolded, she answered quickly, "I've gotten us online with Poppet's database."

Impressed, Damon asked, "You can access the AI from here?"

She glanced up at him, and asked wryly, "Why won't you ever call it by its name? The system is called Poppet."

Aware that she tried to distract him, he managed a snide remark. "It's a silly name."

"It's an acronym, not a name. And I think it's adorable."

How like her to think an inane acronym for a computer to be adorable. He could feel the bands of tension ease further. "Adorable," he repeated, his eyes and heart full of her.

A.J. glanced up, and was sizzled by the heat. With effort, she returned her gaze to the small unit. "This doesn't permit access to the complete system, just selected files I've segregated. But it should get us started." She explained what she hoped to accomplish.

Damon slid his chair next to hers to view the screen. McCord's name appeared at the top of the page, with vital information listed below. "No first name?"

A.J. shook her head. "Nope. Not even the ISA knows. He's always been known as McCord. I've requested more data from Atlas, but I won't receive it until Friday."

"You've also listed Robertsi as a suspect. Why?"

"First of all, he doesn't like you," A.J. acknowledged. "You've taken half of his power and all of his popularity. He's being overshadowed by the young, handsome king who appeared at the stroke of midnight to save the monarchy."

"It wasn't midnight."

"But it was dashing. Television stations around the world carried the story. I saw at least three documentaries about you myself." As soon as she spoke, she stopped.

Damon caught the admission and was intrigued. "Three?"

"They were ubiquitous. And there was nothing else on," she muttered. "But that's not the point."

"And what is the point of watching three documentaries about me?" Damon tilted her chin, causing her eyes up to meet his, and he tucked an errant lock of hair behind her ear. Tracing the graceful shell, he inquired patiently, "You were doing research?"

"I was plotting your demise," she countered breathlessly. "You'd been rude to me."

"It seems I made a bit of an impression." His hand slipped to her shoulder, the flesh warm and soft. For a moment, he thought, he could simply hold her and forget. Forget the possibility of betrayal and the oppressive weight of fear.

Slowly, he leaned in, and lowered his mouth to hers. The touch was a gesture of thanks, a search for comfort. Without pressure, without demand, he took them both under, soft. He felt her hand lightly clasp his shoulder, urging more, but he resisted. For now, he sought only the taste of her, would give no more than tenderness. She drew it from him, like breathing.

And when he felt himself beginning to drown in her, he surfaced with reluctance.

A.J.'s hand fell from his shoulder as he shifted away. "What was that?"

"Necessary."

"Oh" was the only response she could manage. The simple kiss unnerved her, scattered her thoughts. Needs, untutored, raced through her, and she wanted what she could not name. Instead, she turned her attention to the project at hand.

"How well do you know Isabel Santana?"

Damon pushed away from the table to pace. "I met her when I arrived here. She's been unfailingly polite and frigidly unreachable. It is no surprise that she resents her demotion for my benefit." He paused by the fireplace. "What information do you have about her?"

"She's single." A.J. read her birth date and arched her brow. "She's only forty-five, rather young to be a Minister, particularly Minister of State."

"But not as young as thirty-two," Damon reminded her.

"Yes, wunderkind. She started out as a professor at the university before joining the civil service. Before that, she completed a DPhil in international relations at Oxford."

"Any ties to Zeben?"

"Nothing obvious. She did write her dissertation on Middle Eastern conflict, but she was instrumental in the formation of the Alliance. Robertsi promoted her based on her performance." She typed more commands into the PDA, but her connection died.

"May I borrow your cell phone? I need to rig a better connection. We must be more isolated than I realized."

Damon handed her the phone, and she went outside onto the cabin porch, where she would have better reception. She'd download the files, and then they could review them. "I'll just be a minute."

Deep in thought, Damon bent down to start a fire. The evening had grown chilly in the wake of the spring storm. Though the rains had ended, he could hear the wind whipping through the trees. Confident that the smoke would dissipate quickly and keep their hideout a secret, he fed kindling into the blaze until it roared nicely.

The cabin door opened, and he turned. What he saw terrified him.

A.J. stood staring into the flames, arms wrapped tightly around her slender, vibrating frame, eyes wide with panic.

"A.J., honey, what's wrong?" he asked softly, approaching her slowly. "What did you find out?"

"Please, put it out," she whimpered.

"Put what out?" Following her horrified gaze, he saw only the welcoming crackle of the fire. Sparks hissed behind the glass shield, but none of the flames escaped.

In a flurry of motion, A.J. ran out of the cabin. Damon chased after her, perplexed.

"A.J.?"

"Please, put out the fire." Her voice cracked over the plea. "Don't ask me any questions, just put it out."

"Alright," he agreed, rubbing his hands up and down her frozen limbs. "Alright, I'll put it out. Then, will you come inside?"

She nodded shakily, and Damon reluctantly left her on the porch, in the cooling air. Inside, he knelt at the fireplace to smother the flames.

Task accomplished, he returned to the porch to coax her inside. "A.J., it's out. It's safe."

Safe? The word sounded empty, hollow. Fire could never be safe. It ravaged lives, families, stealing everything with its febrile heat.

It had been a long time since her last attack, A.J. thought as she gradually became aware of her surroundings. The phobia about fire had manifested itself during her first Christmas with the Graysons. A ceremonial gathering by the fireplace had sent her into a catatonic state, and from that day forward, the fireplaces in the Grayson mansion remained dormant.

Fixing her eyes on Damon's concerned face, she swallowed thickly. He deserved an explanation for her irrational reaction. The brisk wind died down a little, and she leaned against a railing.

"My parents were killed in a train wreck when I was nine," she started without preamble. "Their car exploded."

"Where were you?" Damon asked tenderly, afraid of the answer.

"I'd been thrown from the car."

"*Mon dieu,*" Damon muttered as he folded her stiff body into his arms.

Wearily, she let her head rest on his shoulder, absorbed the warmth of his embrace. "I hate fire. It terrifies me."

Damon drew her away, tipped her anxious gaze up to meet his determined one. "I put it out. Now, come inside before we freeze."

A.J. trailed behind him, her hand closed in his. He settled her into her vacated chair, and found a throw in the cupboard beneath the bed. Wrapping its warmth around her, he asked as though nothing had happened, "What about Wynn? She's been with the government almost as long as Robertsi."

Appreciating the distraction, she opened Wynn's file. "Fifty-two, married with three children. A decorated officer in the Jafirian Navy. No skeletons in her closet. Married for thirty-five years to the same man. Steady bank account, steady work record."

"You don't think it's her," Damon guessed.

A.J. scrolled through the record. "No. She's the person who first contacted Atlas."

For nearly an hour, they dissected the information contained in each file, and A.J. drew out Damon's impressions of each person. Finally, she called a halt. "Everyone's ties are too circumstantial to draw conclusions. I need more data."

"Which means we need to return to the palace. And report the call," Damon said firmly. Before she could protest, he reasoned, "Regardless of who did it, someone has threatened to kill us both. Precautions must be taken. Also, we will make flight arrangements for you to leave in the morning." Decision made, he crossed to the mantel to retrieve the kerosene lamp.

He didn't see A.J.'s chin lift and her eyes narrow.

"I'm not going anywhere, Damon. I told you yesterday, I have a job to complete."

Damon promised himself he wouldn't insult her, wouldn't argue. But he would protect her. "If you don't get on a plane of your own volition, I'll have you deported," he explained mildly. Brushing his hands free of ash, he rose.

Her gear stored, A.J. slung her bag over her shoulder and stopped in front of him. "Try it, Damon, and I'll go to Robertsi."

Amused by the pugnacious chin and the elfin bravado, Damon ignored the warning flare of temper. "And say what?"

A.J. retorted coldly, "I'll tell him that I suspect you. If he's the culprit, he'll let me stay to implicate you. If he's not, he'll welcome the information."

Amazement at her audacity and the knowledge that she was serious added to his respect for her. Nevertheless, she could not remain in Jafir. If he had to truss her tiny body up like a turkey and store her in a cargo hold, she would be off the island by sundown tomorrow.

Damon understood that he had chosen this life, and its attendant dangers. He'd elected to serve anyway, and to accept the consequences.

A.J. had done neither.

Because he admired her tenacity, he leashed the fear that would spill out like anger. In smooth tones, he reminded her, "You're a scientist, A.J., not a spy. And you do not need to be here to input your data. We can communicate by phone, and I will share what I learn with you."

"For the duration of this mission, I am an agent of the ISA," she replied. "I'm not one of your subjects, and I won't take orders from you."

"You will not remain here, a target of a madman."

"Are you leaving?"

"Of course not!"

"Then neither am I." A.J. turned away, and she flung the cabin door open. "We've got a lot of work ahead of us, Your Highness. Come along."

Forced to lose time by securing the cabin, Damon watched pensively as A.J.'s long legs carried her farther away from him. Moonlight broke through the clouds, and the winds lifted hair that refused to stay confined, streaming ebony strands like a bold pennant behind her.

It dared others to follow, to capture.

Watching her, wanting her, Damon longed to accept the challenge. She was a paradox, this woman he'd once likened to a sprite. A.J. Grayson impressed and infuriated him, equal parts shaky confidence and sheer nerve.

He thought of the unreasonable terror caused by the contained fire, a reaction at absolute odds with her determination in the face of a death threat. Damon started after her, exasperated. She had absolutely no respect for authority. He said sit, she stood. He said leave, she stayed. She entranced him with her fairy looks, the soulful eyes, the elfin features. And she aroused him with her laugh, her brilliance, even the insolence.

With her, he teetered constantly on the edge of the urge to protect and the desire to ravage. Perhaps if he ordered her to stay away from his bed, he'd at least assuage the ache that had become constant and unendurable.

Trampling through foliage, he finally caught her at the edge of the woods. "Damn it, A.J., stop!"

She obeyed, but he should have realized he'd have no easy victory with her. "I'm not going back to America, Damon," she chided as she waited for him to reach her. "You can't make me go."

"I can if I decide to," he argued, not sure if he tried to convince her or himself.

"You need me here, Damon. As you said, I'm the only one here that you can trust." She reset the strap of her bag across her shoulder. "I may not be a super spy, but I am an excellent investigator. I already have access to the necessary files, and with Poppet, I can narrow our list of suspects."

"The caller threatened to kill you too, A.J. I won't keep you here in harm's way," Damon countered stubbornly. "If I have to contact Atlas myself, you're leaving the country."

A.J. smiled complacently. "Try it."

Suspiciously, Damon held out a hand for his phone.

"How do I reach him?"

"You're the King, you figure it out." Resisting the urge to gloat, she patted the hand holding the phone. "Face it, Your Highness, I'm not leaving until the summit. But chin up, that's only a few weeks away."

Damon stopped, spun her toward him, hazel eyes blazing, his voice coldly furious. "This is not a game, A.J.! I've seen what my brother and Zeben are willing to do to gain control of Jafir. And they are not the only ones who want to control this region. I have neither the time nor the inclination to let you play with your toys and try to determine my fate or that of my country."

She tried to wrench her arm from his grasp, without success. His fingers tightened, and he forced her still. Throwing her head back, she grated, "Don't you think I understand the stakes? He wanted to force me to leave, to turn tail and run. I don't know if I've done that before, but I will not do it again. I take my work seriously, Your Highness."

"Your work?" Damon scoffed, the phrase an epithet. "A month ago, you were a modest scientist dreaming up robots and computer games. The ISA sent you to process data, not to protect me." Then, in a desperate attempt to enrage her, to anger her into leaving, he taunted, "What type of protector is afraid of fire?"

"You royal bastard," she cursed in even tones, as the barb sank deep. "Do I seem that easily hurt? Insult me, threaten me, do your worst. I'm not leaving, Damon."

"I won't help you stay," he warned.

A.J. jerked the captured arm free and forced it to her side, clenching her fist to still the urge to retaliate. "Then stay out of my way."

Damon muttered an imprecation and opened the secret door

to the tunnel. Once inside, neither spoke during the journey. A.J. fumed silently.

Damon Toca was an arrogant, self-righteous, supercilious prig! He had no right to bully her, even less right to use her one paranoia against her. And to think she'd worried that she might be falling in love with him.

When demons organized an amateur hockey league.

She had no use for a man who derided her work, who went out of his way to insult and intimidate her.

Who held her when terror froze her into immobility, who comforted her when memories crashed into the present.

A man who could ravage her senses with a kiss, could steal her breath with a look. A man who was so desperate to protect her he was willing to drive her away.

When had she fallen in love? A.J. wondered bleakly. When had flirtation and confrontation transformed themselves into adoration? As she followed his unyielding form through the tunnel, lit by the flashlight he carried, emotions jumbled, conflicted.

What they shared now was merely a passion, but it was one that could consume her if she didn't guard her heart. Perhaps, if she continued to flout his diktats to leave, frustration would conquer the craving that stretched thin between them.

For three more weeks, she could ignore his unexpected sweetness, his compelling ardor, the way he made her feel as though only she existed for him.

And in the process, she would save his life.

Putting aside her turbulent thoughts, she began to plot the next moves. It was, she imagined, what a spy would do.

All in all, she had acquitted herself nicely tonight, she thought morosely. When the caller attempted to terrorize her, she'd motioned Damon to the other receiver. And Damon had the presence of mind to get them out of the palace, away from whomever in the castle might be the culprit.

Still, Damon had the temerity to claim she was inadequate for the job? She may not be a real secret agent like Adam or Raleigh, but she could handle herself. And whether he chose to admit it or not, he needed her.

Robertsi, McCord, Santana, or Wynn, one of them wanted him off the throne. Damon was too close to see it, and she was the optimal candidate to be his eyes for him. Between her own observations and Poppet, she'd eliminate suspects until they found their link, and then she'd summon the ISA.

And then she'd leave, heart and soul intact.

———

D amon stalked through the tunnel, rage and fear dogging his heels. He wanted her gone, needed her away from Jafir, away from him. How could he be expected to concentrate when every other thought turned to her safety?

He wanted her to stay, to listen to him, to talk to him. In three weeks, she'd made herself a part of him, had shown him what was possible. How could he send away what he desired beyond reason?

He called himself a fool for touching her that first night, when she'd captured his eye, bathed in emerald moonlight. Besotted, he'd watched her, and known that he would have her. When she arrived at the palace, the ache he thought had waned redoubled in force.

She'd reentered his life, and he found himself unwilling to let her go. If he did not find a way to remove her, he would surely be the death of her.

Inside the palace, Damon led A.J. to her rooms, and brusquely instructed two of his men to also guard her door. Throughout the night, he wrestled with dreams of her. They stood on a battle-field. Armed to the teeth with troops at the ready, he advanced, sure of victory. Defenseless, alone, she refused to yield. With broadswords, with guns, they clashed, but she held her ground.

Then the field changed, a silk-covered sea. With kisses, with caresses, he pleasured, yet she still would not yield.

CHAPTER EIGHT

Damon woke early the next morning, resolute. Throughout the day, he observed McCord and Robertsi, scrutinized his conversations with Wynn and Isabel. He waited for clues, anticipated mistakes. None materialized.

By nightfall, he'd exhausted himself with doubt, and he made his decision. Ignoring the surprised guards, sans jacket and tie, he sprinted down the steps and strode angrily through the hallways. It was nearly ten p.m., but the person he sought would still be in his office.

With a perfunctory knock, Damon flung the door open. McCord turned and, seeing the King's face, set his half-smoked cigar in an ashtray fashioned from a seashell, which rested on the corner of his desk. The aroma of Cuban cigars, a reminder of earlier times, mingled with the scent of the rain that floated through the open windows.

Damon entered the room and slammed the door behind him. The mixture of accusation and hope in his eyes warned McCord that mistakes of the past refused to stay hidden, despite the best-laid plans. Decisions made in the heat of anger or the cold of grief revisited, seeking their due. Payment was inevitable, but he'd hoped for longer.

McCord came from behind his desk, a gift from Damon's grandfather to the raw young man he'd been, and bowed as custom dictated. "Can I help you, Your Highness?"

"Did you kill my parents?" Damon asked, closing the door behind him.

McCord stood at attention, the boxer's stance a natural posture. "No, Your Highness, I did not."

Eyes so like Jaya's searched the lined, composed face for signs of subterfuge. He had practiced for this moment, and would give nothing away. "Did you threaten to kill me last night?"

"No, Your Highness."

"Why should I believe you?"

"Because I've given you no cause to doubt me." McCord had prepared his answer nearly a year ago, when the past began to come undone. Enough truth would be told this night to satisfy curiosity. With a sincerity that could not be contrived, he permitted age and shame to slump his shoulders. "I traveled with your father and mother to help you come into this world. I held you as a squalling infant, and I convinced your parents that they had to let you go to save you. I broke your mother's heart to protect you."

"You convinced her to give me away?"

"There was no other way. Zeben had grown more powerful

than we'd thought. When Jaya discovered she was pregnant, that there would be an heir, we knew an attack was inevitable."

"And the answer was to send us away? To let my parents die?"

"I loved Jaya as my own daughter, and I grieved with her passing. I failed her, but I swore on her grave I would not fail you." McCord turned to the window, his profile to Damon. Revealing this last would take care, and he could not afford to see Jaya in the face of her son as he told his lie. "I have done nothing to betray that oath."

Damon examined McCord, searching for signs of guilt. He saw only an old man's terrible grief and bitter determination. "You contacted my parents," he surmised. "You're the reason they told me about the obelisk."

McCord sighed. "I waited as long as I could to summon you. Then Zeben escaped from prison, and I knew what he was after."

"If Zeben had not escaped, you would have allowed the monarchy to die?"

"Absolutely." McCord lifted the cigar, dragged deep, the smoke filling lungs weaker with age. "You and your brother were strangers to your homeland. The state was strong, and it did not require a ruler."

"What changed your mind?"

"Zeben had a legitimate claim to the throne. Being a convicted criminal did not change that. And Scimitar had been damaged, but not destroyed."

"If he'd gained the crown, he would have had the funds to rebuild it. And even from prison, the means to control it."

"Very good." McCord nodded approvingly. "The influence of the monarchy, especially over the older generations, would have rallied people to his side. Scimitar manipulates with kindness, not with vengeance. That is the source of its power. Oppression sows dissent, but satiate a population with pleasure, and they will follow you into the sea."

Damon braced himself for the next question. "Do you know who is responsible for the threats now?"

"No, but I have my hunches."

From the tone, Damon understood McCord would say no more. He bit back frustration, and asked instead, "Why did you call in the ISA?"

"I spoke to Wynn and told her that they were too dangerous for us to handle alone, contained too much venom to be from an outsider. I suggested that we call in reinforcements."

"Whom do you suspect?" Damon repeated.

"I will not say. I have no evidence. But I think that Dr. Grayson will help us immensely. An old man's suspicions are not sufficient evidence."

"But you risk the summit with your silence," Damon argued.

Stubbing out the cigar, McCord admitted, "If I think I am, I will speak up. In the meantime, though, why don't you tell me about last night."

Damon paced the length of the room, recounting the phone call and their trip to the cabin. McCord asked dozens of questions and had Damon repeat the conversation several times.

A knock at the door startled them both. Damon stopped, and McCord called out, "Come in?"

Isabel rushed in, skin flushed, eyes bright. "Your Highness, thank God!"

Damon approached her, helped her to a seat. "Isabel? What has happened?"

"Tonight"—her voice trembled, then she leveled it—"I received a call, Your Highness. He said the most horrid things, accused me of—" She stopped, drew in a halting breath.

McCord pressed a glass of water into her hands. "Drink, Isabel."

She gulped the water hastily, but her eyes remained fever bright. "He said you would die, Your Highness. If you do not abdicate the throne. And he warned that if you did not, I would die as well."

The same call A.J. had received last night. Damon exchanged a troubled look with McCord over Isabel's head, but inside, he felt relief. He'd been with McCord the entire time, and although McCord could have arranged for an accomplice to call, he'd seemed as shaken by the report as Damon had been.

Damon summoned Wynn and Robertsi to McCord's office, and Isabel repeated the conversation. Wynn and Robertsi both appeared upset by the report. Watching the four, Damon realized he was no closer to the truth. The meeting soon broke up, and McCord agreed to lead an investigation. Phone calls to the palace would be traced, the grounds would be swept for explosives, and McCord would convene a meeting when he'd found more information.

Drained, Damon sought refuge in the Asphodel. Moonlight shimmered on fragile petals, and he inhaled the fragrance of night-blooming jasmine. He leaned his elbows on his knees, his mind teeming with questions. Were the shots on the beach connected to the threats? He'd asked McCord and Wynn, but no one had an answer.

How could he ensure the safety of his country without succumbing to the tyranny of terrorists? Damon deployed more guards to monitor the estate, and he authorized security details for A.J. and all of his staff. But it did not seem sufficient.

"Wynn told me about Isabel." A.J. sat beside him on the stone bench. "I've added the data to Poppet's analysis."

"Good." Damon shifted a bit, putting greater distance between them. He wasn't quite ready to pretend insouciance, not when madmen threatened her life. He wanted to shake her and force her to leave. To drop to his knees and beg. "Is that all?"

A.J. refused to flinch at the whip of ice. She'd seen him from her windows, the arrogant posture bent by fatigue. She saw how still he sat among the flowers, as though praying for their peace.

"Damon, you must realize why I can't leave."

"You won't leave." Damon glared at her. The tawny eyes were dark with anger. "You prefer to stay and play the hero. All you will do is distract me."

"I can help. I will help. In a few more hours, I should have the initial scenarios from Poppet. Wynn can use them to aid in the investigation."

"In a few more hours, someone could be dead. I don't see Poppet stopping that."

A.J. looked away. Thus far, Poppet had not produced any useful data, only speculation. "I will find the answers, Damon. I swear." She turned to him then, rested her hand on his taut cheek. "Please. Let me help you." Need fisted inside her, its origins not at all sexual. She longed to prove to him that he could rely on someone, on her, to care for him.

His eyes met hers, but she couldn't read their message. Finally, he spoke. "One week, A.J. Then you must go, Summit or no. Agreed?"

A.J. pulled her hand away, folded it in her lap. "Agreed."

When his hand plucked hers up and held tight, she remained silent, watching the sky. And losing her heart.

———

"D ad, now is not a good time for a visit." Damon barely suppressed the alarm in his voice, struggling instead for mild irritation. He'd received a message from McCord that his parents had flown into Jafir. Now, they stood in his offices, beaming with false smiles.

Bill Toca heard the censure and the alarm, and felt the habitual tug of guilt. His sister's son, his son, had been given so much to carry on his young shoulders, and he'd done nothing to prepare him. Of course, he'd always hoped there'd be no need for Damon to learn about his legacy; that Damon would escape the fate that claimed his mother. But destiny cared little for plans and hopes. Now his son was being shot at by the lunatic who killed Bill's sister, and he would not be alone. "Son, your mother and I came as soon as we heard the reports. You should have told us."

Damon countered, "Dad, if you saw the news reports, you know I don't have time to entertain guests. Or to make courtesy calls every time there is a crisis."

Tucker cringed at the term. "Damon, we're not guests. We're your parents."

Damon's hard tone did not waver. "And you should be in Durban."

Bill placed a hand on his son's shoulder, and felt the muscles tense. "We've given you time, Damon. After the trial, we left as you asked. We've seen neither of our sons."

"Nelson is free to have visitors between ten and five. I can arrange for transportation if you'd like."

Tucker threw up her hands in disgust. "What I'd like is for you to forgive us." She gripped the front of his jacket, a mother's fierce love running through her. "We tried to protect you and we failed. We didn't lie to hurt you, Damon. You know that." Relaxing her grip, she stepped away. "We're staying, Damon, until you hear us out."

"Do what you want," Damon said brusquely. "You always have." Damon summoned his secretary. "Please show my parents to a guest suite. Have McCord assign a security detail, and arrange for a car to take them to the prison." Damon flicked a negligent glance over the couple standing in his office. "Felice will show you to your rooms."

Unable to remain in his office, Damon made his way to A.J.'s laboratory.

Just as she had all day, A.J. hunched over the terminal, and matched her wits against the security codes. After exhausting Poppet's resources, she'd tried her hand at hacking into Jafir's security system. She'd never expected to find anything. Level after level, A.J. dodged firewalls, bypassed authentication protocols, evaded detection. Deeper and deeper, she probed logs and databases, downloading files, discarding others. It was a backdoor that caught her eye, one that seemed deceptively easy to open. Hidden in plain sight, she thought as she and Poppet picked the lock.

"It uses steganography," she told Poppet, since Sarah had the day off. "The encrypted file is hidden within this personnel log." When the computer failed to congratulate her on her discovery, she soldiered on. Carefully, she peeled away the layers.

At last, a single file remained. She could tell that someone had attempted to delete it, but it was unclear who had recovered it. Locating the appropriate application, she signaled Poppet to open the file. An image appeared on-screen, and her heart sank.

Shakily, she instructed Poppet to open a second file, one given to her by the ISA. "Enhance Image 1," she requested. "Enlarge Image 2 by fifty percent. Now, side by side." Poppet instantly aligned the images, and the resolution left no doubt. Printing the separate pages, she whispered to no one, "This will destroy him."

A.J. left the system, and prepared to power down Poppet. Her eyes ached from such close reading, and her head pounded from the weight of her decision. Her orders from Atlas were clear. Any incriminating evidence she discovered on her own had to be given to the ISA before she revealed it to anyone else.

Her nature balked at the deception, and her heart cautioned her not to lie to Damon. She'd located other files, ones with information that could prove useful. But this last item, it erased nearly all doubt, and would be damning evidence. Atlas may have an explanation for it, she thought, and she had made a commitment to the ISA.

A.J. thought of Damon's expression in the cabin, and knew that she couldn't tell him. Not until she was certain. It would be Friday soon, and she'd receive the new data from the ISA and clearance from Atlas. After Friday, she thought, she could show him the photo.

Besides, if he'd been curious about her work, he'd have come to see her. Instead, he'd doubled her guard and avoided her offices.

A.J. stared at the pages, wavering.

"A.J." Damon stood in the doorway, watching her.

"Damon," she said coolly, and she quickly stacked the pages together, hiding the photos underneath. "My time isn't up yet."

"My parents are here." The words emerged harsh and unexpected. "They arrived this morning."

A.J. came to him then, closed the door behind him. "Where are they now?"

"Felice is taking them to their rooms." Damon wandered to the window, and began to fiddle with the bud vase that disrupted radio signals. "Did you know my father—no, my uncle—grew up in the palace? He ran off to Paris when he was eighteen to become an artist. My grandfather threatened to disown him, but couldn't. Instead, he helped him buy his first gallery in Senegal."

"Your grandfather must have been very proud of him." A.J. perched on the windowsill beside him, watching both the man and his agitated hands.

Damon tossed the bud vase higher and higher. "He was. Dad used to tell Nelson and me the story all the time. He never mentioned that his father was the King of Jafir."

When the vase somersaulted through the air, A.J. caught it midflight. She removed the Chinese pin securing her bun and gave it to him instead. Dark hair tumbled to her shoulders, but she paid no attention. "Have you asked them why they hid the truth from you?"

"I know why. They wanted to protect me." Damon twisted his fingers around the metal. "They were wrong."

Thinking of the photograph lying on her desk, A.J. protested, "Sometimes, we can't tell the entire truth."

Damon rounded on her then. "You don't lie to someone you love! Not for any reason."

"In a perfect world, of course not!" she countered. "But we don't live there, Damon. In the real world, there is a reason for secrets. You must know that."

"Love means trust, A.J. You can't have one without the other." Damon combed his fingers through her long tresses, tipping her face to his. "Don't you believe that, *ma fée*? You are the most honest person I've ever known. Brutally frank, even."

A.J. winced, closing her eyes over the pain.

Damon kissed her then, light and sweet, seeking comfort. "I don't know how to forgive them, A.J."

Taking a deep breath, A.J. looked at him. "They are your parents, Damon. They loved you. They raised you. And when they could have hidden the truth, sheltered themselves, they gave you a choice." She wrapped her arms around his waist, pressed her cheek to his heart. "We both know the pain of losing parents, Damon. Don't do this to yourself a second time."

Stepping back, A.J. took his hand. "What do you want to do?"

Damon thought of his childhood, of soccer games and art lessons. He recalled the day his parents gave him the deed to the gallery, relinquishing their dreams to his untutored hands. After a year of hurt and rage, he abruptly felt the anger drain, wash away.

He'd been given two sets of parents, the first by birth, the second by sacrifice. Edges were still raw, but at the core, Damon knew he forgave. With a second kiss, as gentle as before, Damon smiled at A.J. "Come meet my parents."

For the next two days, A.J. entertained the Tocas, demonstrating Poppet and answering pointed questions about their son.

"Remind me of how you met?" Tucker asked over tea on Wednesday.

"At my cousin's wedding. Then the government hired GCI for the audit, and we met again."

"How nice for you both." Tucker nibbled on a cookie. "A.J., dear?"

"Yes, Mrs. Toca?"

Tucker watched A.J. carefully. "What are your intentions toward my son?"

The bald question shocked A.J., and she flushed. "My intentions?"

"Yes, dear. He's obviously smitten with you. You aren't toying with him, are you?"

"No, ma'am. I mean, that's really none of your business, Mrs. Toca. With all due respect, what is between me and your son is our business."

"Well said, young lady." Bill settled on the settee beside his wife. "My Tucker can be a bit nosy, but you have the right of it. What happens between you and Damon is none of our damned business." To Tucker, he said, "We've got a flight in an hour, darling. Besides, I'm sure A.J. will be happy to see us go."

Tucker pinched her husband. "Speak for yourself." She smiled warmly at a bemused A.J. "You're good for him, A.J. I don't want him to lose you. He can be stubborn, like his father."

"And meddlesome, like his mother," Bill retorted.

Tucker patted A.J.'s hand, and smiled again. "We both owe you a debt of gratitude. For giving us back our son."

A.J. flushed. "I merely nudged him. He'd already forgiven you."

Bill shook his head, his eyes dark with sadness. "Nelson refuses to see us or his brother. I have very little family left, A.J., and I love Damon dearly. Thank you."

A.J. could think of nothing to say. Instead, she rose and kissed them both. "Thank you too. He needed this." She gathered her bag and slung the strap over her shoulder. "Now, I have to get back to work, and you have a flight to catch."

━━━━━━━━

A cabal with Robertsi and the others broke up near midnight, and Damon found himself passing outside A.J.'s door. Every night, he thought about stopping. She would answer in silk, would welcome him inside. The fantasy grew more elaborate, but the end remained constant and tempting.

But every night, he continued on his way. Tonight, though, he paused. He should thank her for reuniting him with his parents. They'd tried to visit Nelson, but had been rebuffed. Nevertheless, he felt more hopeful than he had in ages.

He wanted to share his day with her, to tell her about his meetings and what they'd discovered from the phone trace and the ground surveillance.

If she opened the door, and welcomed him in, he'd tell her nothing of threats and revelations.

The realization jolted him, stirred him. Then the door swung open, and he knew he'd be with her tonight.

Did she know how lovely she was? Wire-framed reading glasses perched on the edge of her nose. The splendid mass of ebony hair had been gathered atop her head, and leaned haphazardly against its confining pins. A pencil hung from the corner of her mouth, where he noted that she'd chewed off much of the yellow paint. Bare feet curled into pale-gray carpet, and the silk he imagined was actually flannel and cotton. The tank top, suspended by narrow yellow straps, sported a ribald joke, as irreverent as she.

"May I come in?" he asked at last, when rational thought returned.

He saw her weigh her response, noting the curious guards in the hall. She stepped back to admit him.

Clothes draped over chairs; papers covered every free surface. He picked his way through the chaos, and made a space for himself on the sofa. The television muttered quietly, and a laugh track highlighted the important moments. "Have the cleaners not done their job?"

A.J. took the chaise. It amused him to watch her spine stiffen, her mouth curl into the sneer he knew so well. "I gave them the month off."

With a disdainful flick of the hand, he gestured to the pile of newspapers hoarded in the corner. "And it will take them a month to recover."

"Did you come to insult my housekeeping?"

No. To make love to you. "I wanted to report what I've learned from McCord and the others today."

Rising to fix himself a drink, he made his way to the bar, stepping over books and folders. At the bar, Damon dropped ice into a glass and poured himself a scotch. He filled a second glass with a chardonnay he found open in the refrigerator. Handing her the wine, he stood by the cluttered desk and nursed his whiskey. "And what have you been doing?"

"I hacked into Jafir's security files."

"What?" Damon stared at her in angry amazement. "That is a breach of your security clearance."

"And a damned sight smarter than just asking if he's guilty."

Damon inhaled sharply, his grip on temper slippery. "Do you realize, if you'd been caught, I'd have no control over your punishment? You could be imprisoned."

"Or you could be dead."

Because he heard her concern, and something deeper, he decided not to argue. Instead, he declared, "Don't do it again."

"We have to find out who's responsible."

"I will." He stressed the *I*.

A.J. jumped to her feet, dislodging the reading glasses. Prepared for the reaction, Damon absently recovered the hapless frames before she trampled them.

She snatched them from him with her free hand and flung them onto the table. "Are we back to that, Damon? I thought we were partners."

"I didn't come to fight with you, A.J.," he said mildly. "What I do or say is my decision, not yours. You have no say in the matter."

Her eyes flashed insolence, and she fairly glowed with outrage. The impertinence snapped temper, stoked desire. Deliberately, he set his whiskey on the desktop with a thud, snatched the wine from her nerveless fingers, and placed it beside his.

"I think I have had enough." Damon captured her shoulders, his fingers sliding beneath the cotton strings. "I have not had nearly enough," he corrected, as his mouth plunged.

A.J. froze, unable to move, to think. Then his mouth was on hers, searching, igniting. Arousal flared, dark and dangerous. Without thought, her arms rose to lock themselves around his neck, but he would not permit it. Instead, he slid his hands down to cover hers, to lock them to her sides.

Warm, impatient, he strung kisses down her throat, across

her collarbone. Desire rippled through her, and she moaned as he traced a wet line across her skin. A yellow strap slid down, and he dragged her up to him, ready to sample the ripe flesh. A sound, torn from deep in his throat, compelled her to pull her hand free.

She sank her fingers into his hair, gasped at the questing tongue that teased her willing flesh. Enough, he'd said? Could there ever be enough? Could her body feel enough to be sated? Could her heart hold enough to be satisfied?

Yanking her other hand free, A.J. pulled him to the chaise, unwilling to give him dominion. She slanted her mouth across his, feeding the hunger that burgeoned. They sank into the cushions as he ranged himself above her. The second strap fell, and he anointed her with gentle kisses, teasing nips, long slow strokes that hitched her breath, arched her spine.

She ripped at his buttons, felt the disks snap and fall. Twisting, she escaped his hungry mouth, eager to taste, to feel. Strong corded muscles flexed beneath her hands. Heated, salty skin tensed beneath her tongue. Imitating him, she stroked a flat male nipple, pulled his hips into deeper contact with her own. Palm to palm, mouth to mouth, they poured into each other, consumed each other.

Damon wrapped his arms about her naked waist, desperate to merge them. He would take her so high, so deep, she'd never be free of him. The skin, soft and smooth, smelled of sunlight, tasted of rain. Under curves, he discovered pleasure. In hollows, he found delight. He tangled their legs, twined their fingers. Excitement pulsed through him, its message demanding now, now, now.

"*Ma fée.*" He breathed the endearment into her skin, brushed it into her hair. He stood, lifted her. She wound naked arms around his bare shoulders, buried her mouth in his throat.

Damon carried her through the living room, but with her random debris, he bumped a careless hip against the desk, trying to avoid a pile of papers. A folder fell, and a single page spilled to the carpet.

The grainy black-and-white, taken decades earlier, showed a short man with a full head of black hair. Slung around his shoulders was the arm of a taller, thinner man, the face gaunt and familiar. A.J. saw his eyes focus on the image, saw recognition dawn.

"Damon, no," she whispered.

Dumbstruck, he set her down, and A.J. circled to the chaise to retrieve her top. Damon knelt on the carpet, the photo in his hand.

"It's McCord. And Zeben." The identification struck like a fist to his gut. McCord lied to him. And she'd tried to hide it from him.

A.J. stammered out an explanation. "I found it in a deleted file. This photo is fifty years old."

"I can't believe this," Damon muttered. He'd asked him every question. "I spoke with him, watched him."

"Damon, now that we know, we can do something."

"We? You hid this from me," he accused, the pain beginning to settle in his bones. Like a wounded animal, he struck out. "What were you going to do with this? Give it to him? Trade it for secrets?"

"Don't be ridiculous!" A.J. folded her arms, and tried to reason with him. "I was going to tell you, but I had to speak with the ISA first," she pleaded.

He stared through her, unseeing. At each turn, he found fresh evidence of treachery, every conversation a hall of mirrors. Who to believe, what to hold as true, none of it was clear any longer.

Only one truth remained constant, one desire plain.

She stood before him, clad in cotton, lying to him, daring him. Red hazed his vision until he could see only her duplicity.

He fought down anguish, refusing to acknowledge a broken heart. He cloaked agony in revulsion, studied her faithless eyes. "Are you working with him?" he asked coolly.

A.J. felt her stomach churn with anxiety. No matter what her answer, he wouldn't believe. The photo dangled from his fingers as though he could not bear the feel. And the distance between them, mere feet, could have been miles. She took a tentative step forward, and he recoiled, involuntarily. "Damon, please. You have to believe me. I've given you no other reason to doubt me."

The harsh laugh cut off her next words. "Did you practice with him? He said nearly the same words. Same intonation, same façade of sincerity."

She covered her mouth with her hands. "I don't know what McCord said to you. I haven't spoken to him. But I was not working with him."

With care, Damon laid the photo on the desk. "I wonder if Isabel is part of your plan? She had the same story you did. A would-be assassin warning her, accusing her of consorting with the enemy."

"Why would we do that?" A.J. argued.

"To throw me off track, of course." Damon didn't snap, showed no emotion. Instead, he left her and moved to retrieve his ruined shirt. "Only you and McCord knew of my feelings for you, so you had to distract me from that fact. Having your accomplice call Isabel was a master stroke. Tell me, is Poppet providing the vocalization?"

"You know I didn't fake that call, Damon."

"Hmm," he murmured. He slipped into the garment, contemplating the open spaces where she'd torn the buttons. He could feel her mouth against his chest, her quick hands kneading his back, caressing his hips. The way she trembled in his arms, beneath his tongue.

Was it all a mirage? he thought dully. The passion, the vulnerability, a ruse designed to trap him. It fit. She'd been recruited after her liaison with him at the wedding. Whether it was the ISA, who distrusted his motives, or Zeben and Nelson, who wanted him dead, it didn't matter. She was a tool for an enemy, and he'd nearly let them win.

The sudden clapping caught A.J. off guard.

Ice coated her stomach, and for the first time, she knew fear. The layer of calm, of rational, belied the tawny eyes darkened to black, their gold flecks almost invisible. "Applause? Why?"

"For a brilliant performance. Pitch-perfect." He inclined his head toward the chaise. "I would have promised you anything, would have given you everything. If only you were a better housekeeper."

She'd lost him, A.J. realized, whether he accepted the truth or not. Trying to protect him, she'd deceived him, a sin he'd not forgive. "Damon, be reasonable. If I wanted to hide a file from you, why would I leave it on the desk? Wouldn't I find a better spot?"

"Maybe you weren't expecting me. Hadn't had time to conceal the evidence."

"Or maybe I'm telling you the truth. That I found the photo in Jafir's security files and I printed it out. That I didn't want to tell you until I had clearance from the ISA. Maybe I didn't want to hurt you." Listen to me, she entreated silently, but dared not speak aloud. He'd only use it against her, treat it as another lie.

"Don't worry. You didn't. You couldn't." Now, though, the ice in his voice reached his eyes, and she knew she'd failed.

"What proof do you need, Damon?"

"Nothing you can provide." He flicked his eyes over her, the slim form and proud chin. The lying eyes and treacherous mouth. He couldn't turn her in, but he'd keep her from her accomplice. "For the duration of your stay, you are restricted to this room. I'll have the guards come and remove your computer equipment as soon as I leave. If I have any reason to suspect that you've been in contact with McCord or anyone else, I will turn you over to Wynn."

"You can't keep me prisoner," she protested. "I can't help you from in here."

"I know." Damon turned, once more the King. She chased him to the door, pounded the wood as it closed behind him. A check through the door's viewer showed a phalanx of guards, six in all. No longer did they seem friendly, and when Damon pointed to the door, their countenances grew fierce.

A brusque rap presaged the intrusion. In short order, they'd taken her laptop, her PDA, and rummaged through her luggage and bag for more electronic items. Damon stood in the doorway, issuing instructions, avoiding her. He had them carry the equipment out and left A.J. trapped, an unwilling prisoner in a luxurious cage.

CHAPTER NINE

"Did she find it?" Nelson asked his visitor, who lounged by the door.

"Yes, she did. It was difficult, hidden beneath several subroutines, but she's quite good. Better than I might have expected."

Nelson lit a contraband cigarette, a privilege of being the King's brother. "You're impressed? A rare event."

The visitor shrugged negligently. "It does happen. And, as you suspected, when she tried to hide it from him, he found it. According to a guard, he's had her locked in her room with round-the-clock security for the last two days. I don't understand why he doesn't send her away."

Delicately, he sipped fragrant black tea from a Limoges cup, another privilege of royalty. "He's in love with her," Nelson answered, revolted. "My brother has a soft heart. He can't hand over his lover to the authorities, not until he proves her innocence."

"But he doesn't believe her."

"He wants to. Desperately. Just as he wanted to believe I wasn't a smuggler or that our parents didn't throw us away. Damon is weak, and it will be his downfall." Nelson crushed out the cigarette, shredding paper and tobacco half-smoked. The small destruction brought him pleasure.

"I'm not convinced that we need to finish it this way, Nelson. There are more direct methods to eliminate him."

"But none quite so delicious." Nelson flared a match, mesmerized by the swift flame. "It is almost poetic. Damon is isolated. He has no one to trust, no one to call upon. He serves with a Cabinet of liars, and has grave misgivings about his closest advisers. He sees foes in every corner, and will retreat before too long."

"Or he might summon reinforcements."

"From whom? The ISA is his enemy. They sent a spy to trap him, and he fell in love with her. No, Atlas overplayed his hand this time, and Damon will not go to him."

"I still think it is a dangerous plan, Nelson. Too much could go wrong. I tire of the game. I want it finished."

"You want?" Nelson repeated silkily. The tone should have been a warning, but the costly china cup shattering near a face was ample.

The visitor bumped into the doorframe, frightened by the outburst. The volatile temper, shared by both brothers, was less controlled in the younger Toca. Nelson was capable of vicious acts, a demonstration of power or simply on a whim. In the years of their acquaintance, the visitor had seen a man lose his finger-tips for skimming profit, a woman scarred for deceit.

It was too late to end their alliance, and unwise.

And the benefits were more than satisfactory. The tactics may have heaved a stomach or chilled a soul, but the rewards of partnership were innumerable.

―――――

In her now-permanent uniform of a tee and shorts, A.J. paced the length of the sitting room for the hundredth time. The pale-blue carpet would be worn to a nub by month's end, she thought despondently.

It was Friday, the day she was to meet Sashu in the market and get the disks. Instead of traveling into town, she was trapped like Rapunzel in a castle. Without the tower, the hair, or the love of the prince, she thought morosely.

Maddened, she flounced over to the sofa and threw herself onto the cushions. For two days, he'd held her captive. Three times a day, a guard would politely knock at her door and pass her a tray of food. Before she could ask questions or attempt to reason with him or her, the door shut tight and she was alone.

She could open the windows to the sultry air, but the portals offered no hope of escape. The twenty-foot drop would likely shatter every bone in her body, and she probably wouldn't die from the fall.

As long as she remained trapped inside, Damon's life grew more imperiled. She knew he wouldn't ask for help, since she'd effectively convinced him that no one was trustworthy. McCord, Robertsi, Santana, and Wynn all had equal motives to harm him.

Although the guards had confiscated her computers, they'd left her files untouched. For two days, she'd reviewed the materials and developed a disturbing picture.

Robertsi's personal finances had been on record, and she'd tracked a series of payments in equal and steady amounts to a numbered account on the Isle of Man. Too large to be legitimate, the moneys indicated either payments to or from a much richer source. They'd begun a year ago, around the time Damon first learned he would be King.

Isabel Santana had a less suspect file. The gaps between her years at Oxford and her time with the Jafirian civil service worried A.J., but she had no way to find an explanation. Otherwise, the woman was squeaky clean. Perfectly adequate checking account, the requisite level of funds for retirement and a house note that would be settled in a matter of months. What she didn't have, A.J. noticed, was a significant other. Male or female. News clippings of Isabel showed her always alone at state functions. While A.J. didn't cater to the notion that women needed a partner to be happy or content, it was odd that in five years, she'd never brought a date. To anything.

For McCord, her strongest evidence remained the aged photo of him with Zeben. Her briefing file on Zeben explained part of the mystery. Zeben and McCord were contemporaries, both reared in the shadow of the royal family. McCord's family served the throne, and Zeben was a cousin to the heir. Since they had been peers in school, it made sense that they may have once been friends. However, McCord's concealment of his connection to Zeben raised questions she couldn't answer.

Or she could, if only she could get her hands on the records from the ISA. She crossed to the window, and leaned out into the breeze.

"You won't escape that way," Damon said behind her. "The fall would kill you."

"No, it wouldn't. But it would hurt," A.J. replied without turning to face him. The sound of his voice slid into her, its golden tones flat, unsympathetic. She hadn't seen him since Wednesday, when he'd banished her.

"You haven't been eating," he remarked casually. The lunch brought to her at noon sat untouched on the coffee table.

"Haven't been hungry." Her appetite had vanished, for the first time in her life. Daily, she made herself peck at food, but simply to keep up her strength. She wished she'd eaten today, because she was not prepared to deal with Damon. Her traitorous pulse fluttered at the sound of his voice, and her hands clenched the windowsill for support. And clenched harder when he crowded her against the window.

Behind her, his body a furnace that warmed her, he challenged, "Liar." With the mild accusation, he turned her, his grip firm and uncompromising.

She refused to struggle, and instead schooled her expression into blandness. Love, denied, twisted inside her. At the first sign of weakness, he would break her. She'd promise him anything, and he'd send her away. Too far away to save him. "Is that supposed to wound me? You forget, you've called me worse."

"Why don't you tell me what's going on, A.J., so I can free you?"

"Because I'm not finished here," she reminded him, and winced when he shook her once, hard.

"Yes. Yes, you are. You can't contact your collaborators, and you're making yourself ill by not eating. If you won't talk, I can't release you."

A.J. broke his tight hold on her shoulders, skin burned by the touch. "As if you care about my welfare," she berated. "I eat when I'm ready, and I'll leave when I'm ready!"

Damon glared at her, angry at them both, hands shaking. She goaded him, made him want to believe the fiery denial, the self-righteous declaration. "You can't fool me again, A.J.! I saw the photo. I know you've lied to me since the beginning."

"I didn't mean to."

"You did."

"No," she said quietly. "I just didn't know when to tell you the truth."

Damon scanned her face for signs, but he didn't know what he sought. Part of him longed to catch her close, to pretend that he'd never seen the photograph. He yearned to carry her beyond the sitting room, to lay her on the bed and make love with her until the kingdom and its treachery melted away.

"It wasn't the truth that was difficult, A.J., it was pretending to care for me." He hardened his resolve, and carefully stepped away from the temptation of satin skin and ingenuous eyes. "But I must applaud the seduction. That was a heartless performance, priceless. I really believed you wanted me."

Recklessly, A.J. grabbed his wrist, lifting his hand to her heart. "Don't you know I could never pretend?" The beat, rapid and unsteady, knocked against his captive hand.

Damon twisted his hand beneath hers, cupped her breast in an erotic hold. She inhaled sharply, but did not shift away. Deftly, he stroked the nub of flesh that puckered for his attention, the thin cotton of her shirt no barrier to his touch. Frenziedly, he molded her mouth to the shape of his, found the familiar texture of liquid silk and rougher velvet. Frantically, he spun them until her back met the wall, and he wrapped her legs around his waist.

She moaned at the intimate contact, and he exulted in her undoing. Skimming his hand beneath her shorts, he found her ready, waiting. He dove deeper into her mouth, and she met him, chased him.

When she trembled on his hand, beneath his tongue, he whispered, "Never? Then tell me the truth. Who's trying to destroy me?"

Stricken, A.J. scissored her legs to force him away. Sobs wracked her; angry, frustrated gulps of air ripped through her and refilled her lungs. Mortified, she adjusted her clothes, shoved aside by his insincere caresses.

"Get out," she demanded as tears shined wet and bitter. When he stood immobile, waiting, she shoved him hard. He stumbled back, and she pushed again. "Get the hell out of here!"

Damon caught her hands before she was able to do more violence. Shame filled him, but he refused to acknowledge remorse. Grimly, he vowed, "I'll do what I must, A.J. Whatever it takes."

A.J. held herself ramrod straight and said nothing. At last, he closed the door, and like a puppet whose strings were cut, she crumpled to the floor. Humiliation warred with fury, and she reached out for something to throw. From a side table, near the front door, she fumbled for the Tiffany lamp, eager to destroy. She pulled at it, and the table tipped sideways, its legs scraping the wall. A click sounded, and A.J. watched in disbelief as the panel vanished. The table balanced steadily on two legs, and A.J. held the lamp aloft, paralyzed.

"Another tunnel," she whispered, tears forgotten. She scrambled to her feet and peered inside. Like the one in Damon's room, there was a single staircase leading into darkness.

Unlike Damon, she didn't have a flashlight. But she did have candles. Checking the front door's lock, she rushed into the bathroom to retrieve an armful of scented candles arrayed beside the bath. A quick riffle through the drawers produced a book of matches.

She hesitated, then steeled herself. It was a candle, nothing more. A single match, not a conflagration. The tunnel was her only hope of escape, particularly given this last showdown with Damon. He swore he'd give no quarter, and after today, she believed. If the choice was a book of matches or a second match with him, she'd take her chances.

Dumping supplies into her bag, A.J. dragged a chair across the room and forced it beneath the doorknob. Not that it would stop a trained soldier, but it was worth a try.

She'd follow the tunnel to the edge of the palace and make her way into the city. Sashu would give her the disks, and she'd find a way to get to Poppet. And once she exonerated herself, she'd spit in Damon Toca's eye and rid herself of him for good.

A.J. lit the first candle and searched the tunnel for the switch that would let her back inside. Despite her precautions in securing the door, she didn't dare leave the tunnel open. The lever was above her head, but reachable. Armed with her report for the ISA, candles, and matches, she righted the table and lamp.

Descending the stairwell was awkward, one hand guiding her down the wall, the other holding the candle in the air. At the base of the stairs, she traveled the tunnel as it curved beneath the palace grounds. For twenty minutes, she made her way through the tomb-like granite encasement, thankful that her only phobia was of fire and not closed spaces.

Eventually, the tunnel reached a dead end. Kerosene lingered in the air, and briefly, she thought of Damon. Annoyed by the recollection, A.J. hurriedly felt along the wall, seeking a release or a lever of any sort. Finally, near the far wall, she found a pulley. The stiff rope chafed her hands, but she yanked the line until she heard a grating sound, as though a mechanism had engaged. The wall began to separate, and an exit appeared in the granite. Quickly, she raced back to the spot where she'd laid her bag. Near the open gateway, she could hear the waves of the Mediterranean and the squawk of gulls. A.J. leaned out carefully, to confirm her suspicions. She sighed.

The tunnel ended beneath the ridge of a cliff and hundreds of feet above the sea. Below, between the cliffs and the sea, a deserted beach stretched out in rocky welcome.

A.J. scooted back inside the tunnel, swearing. After her repertoire of expletives had been exhausted, she started to consider her options. Obviously, the trick was getting from here to there. Unfortunately, despite her childhood affection for climbing trees, she'd failed to study the art of rock climbing or cliff diving. However, it was implausible that the clever architect of these escape routes neglected vital equipment for scaling a rock face.

Sunlight trickled weakly into the space, but could not provide sufficient light for close examination of the tunnel. Reluctantly, she removed several candles from her bag and lit them one by one. Soon, the flickering candles amplified the milky sunlight. A more thorough search of the space revealed no hidden ladders, no rappelling gear.

"This makes no sense," she muttered, sinking to the ground

in defeat. A tunnel that leads to the middle of a cliff? No way out except down? Suddenly, the solution dawned on her.

She crawled to the edge, grit and sand scraping her knees. At the lip of the entrance, she laid herself flat and steadily inched herself out into the open air.

Above her, dangling within arm's reach, was a rope ladder. Concealed by the overgrowth of bush and brush, the gray material faded into the rock. A.J. also noted that the upper rim of the tunnel curved inward, leaving adequate space for one adult to stand on the lip and climb to a ledge five feet above her head that ran parallel to the beach. Before she could talk herself out of it, she yanked on the ladder, and it dropped down to her level. After pulling on the antiquated contraption several times to test its strength, she eased into the tunnel and extinguished the candles. She slung the bag across her chest and climbed aboard.

Eagerly, she scrambled onto the landing and crouched. The cacophony from the marketplace blended with the sounds of the sea. Unsure of where she would emerge, A.J. remained hunched over as she traversed the length of the path, where it wound upward toward the Desira Plateau. The path ended abruptly, and A.J. ducked behind a row of barrels, standing sentinel in what she assumed to be the refuse area.

"You, there!" a gruff voice shouted. "Get from behind my merchandise. Thief! Thief!"

A.J. raced from her hiding spot, colliding with the barrels and knocking one into the other. As the entire lot prepared to topple, she picked up speed. The shopkeeper shouted for the police, and yelled at her to stop. So much for remaining inconspicuous.

When an officer raised a club and shook it at her, she darted in between stalls, dodged thick knots of shoppers. Finally, reasonably sure she'd evaded her pursuers, she dipped into an open-air café to catch her breath.

"Madam?" inquired a waiter, pen at the ready. "May I help you?"

"Water," A.J. wheezed. "Please."

"Is that all?" The waiter tapped an impatient foot, and skewered her with a look that suggested water was not served alone.

"And a sandwich. Anything. Just please bring water," she managed between gulps of air.

"Very good." The waiter disappeared, and A.J. dragged oxygen into her lungs. Once she'd regained the ability to think, she rummaged through her bag for directions to Sashu's cart.

According to her instructions, she'd find him near the center of the plateau. Blessedly, a glass of water appeared before her, as did a sandwich of indeterminate contents. She drank down the glass and motioned for more. The waiter refilled it twice, since she refused to release his arm as she consumed the second glass.

Replenished, A.J. nibbled at the sandwich, and considered her options. One, she could have Sashu communicate a message to Atlas that she was being held prisoner in the palace. This would likely result in Adam swooping in to rescue her, and blow her cover. Two, she could get the information from Sashu and find a hotel in town. The chances of Damon searching for her were practically nil, but it would jeopardize any hope of ever getting back inside the palace. The third, and only real choice, was to make the exchange with Sashu and return to her captivity. But now that she knew of the tunnels, she could flee if it became necessary.

As it surely would if Damon replayed today's scene, she thought angrily. For weeks, she'd labored away at Poppet, adjusting and fine-tuning, all in an effort to exonerate him and preserve his precious monarchy. And his reaction was doubt, accusation, and humiliation.

Agony built swiftly, and she reeled with the onslaught. The mission began as a lark, a favor to her cousin and a chance to show off her newest tool. Six weeks on a lush tropical island, and hours of analysis.

Four weeks later, she'd been threatened, held captive, and had fallen in love. All because of the same man. Damon Toca. Monarch, lover, sadist.

Though she tried to banish it, love burned fierce and bright. Neither the pain of rejection nor the harshness of denial could quench the flames, but she knew to be wary of its blaze.

Yet, in a matter of weeks, he'd destroyed her plans. In subtle and strong ways, he'd transformed her visions of herself. Fears of inadequacy melted in his arms. Doubts of inferiority evaporated.

Because she paid her debts, she'd finish this. And when it was done, she'd close her heart and return to her life. Jafir would fade, a distant memory of a different time. Love, she had to believe, would be extinguished in time, a victim of neglect.

But if not, if she had to, she'd live with it, just as she'd lived with other disappointments. She had her work, and it would sustain her. Years later, perhaps the pain of loss would be a dull ember.

For now, though, she thought, pushing away the grief, she had a job to complete.

A.J. laid bills on the table, an amount she hoped would cover the cost of water and a sandwich. Without waiting for the surly waiter's return, she grabbed her bag and started moving.

The Desira Plateau contained an open-air marketplace that

attracted citizens and tourists. Similar to the bazaars of Africa and the Middle East, traders plied shoppers with an assortment of goods. A.J. realized that in the tightly packed mass of bodies and shops, her map was less than useless. A glance at her watch revealed that her appointment with Sashu wasn't for thirty minutes, which gave her time to locate him.

Intrigued by the souks, which offered everything from fresh fruits to pirated software, she wandered between the stalls at a more sedate pace. As she sniffed pomegranates and haggled over jewelry, she asked surreptitious questions about Sashu. A young boy heard her query and offered to personally guide her for a small fee. Charmed, A.J. agreed. He slithered between the constantly moving bodies and dragged A.J. behind him.

"There." He pointed to a fabric stall surrounded by customers stroking colorful materials and wrangling over price. A.J. pressed a wad of money into the child's hand. He thanked her and melted into the crowd.

A.J. squeezed her way between the excited shoppers. "Sashu?"

Tall, with a wide, mobile face and inky black hair, Sashu lifted a hand in welcome. "Come. Come." He waved her around to the rear of the stall. Tapping a young woman, he indicated that she should take over. Seamlessly, she began to barter with a stooped old woman intent on securing a bolt of woven cotton in tangerine.

"Welcome to the Desira Plateau." Sashu bent over her hand and smiled broadly.

"It's an extraordinary place. Wall Street seems tame compared to this."

"That old woman could fleece your Wall Street in minutes. She would steal my goods if my daughter could not outrun her."

A.J.'s appreciative smile dimmed. "Speaking of which, I must leave soon."

"Are there problems?"

"Nothing I can't handle, but I need to return to the palace."

"Of course, of course. Well, I have the materials you ordered." Sashu spoke sotto voce for the benefit of any nearby listeners.

They exchanged information, and A.J. shoved the material inside her bag. "You drive a hard bargain," she said as they returned to the front of the stall.

"Ah, but you are a worthy opponent." Sashu lifted a strip of crimson shot through with strands of silver. "I offer this as a token." He leaned forward and draped the scarf around her neck. "I will communicate with Chimera today," he whispered. Aloud, he said, "Perhaps you can take the blood you've stolen and show the world."

A.J. laughed and pressed a kiss to Sashu's weathered cheek.

Damon ran along the deserted beach, feet pounding the sand in time with the crashing surf. He lengthened his stride, increased his pace, and tried to outrun the shame. Though the anger remained cold and clear, doubt pricked his conscience, and he redoubled his speed. It was impossible that he'd misjudged her. Impossible that he'd hurt the woman he could love.

He wanted to go to her, to tell her he believed her, that he would listen to her answers and accept them as truth. Yet, in his mind's eye, he saw the folder tumble from its hiding place. Without explanation, she'd covered herself, her honest face for once a portrait of guilt.

The woman he thought of as A.J. had proven herself to be a mirage. A web of lies and illusions had hidden her from him, and he'd let himself be inveigled by the deception.

Where he'd seen vulnerability, there'd been only cunning. In what he'd welcomed as candor, she'd offered tricks of ambiguity. Could he believe even the beginning? Had even the graceful fairy, a fantasy of time and place, been conjured to mislead?

And what of today? Had he betrayed them both in those last seconds, when passion outraced logic and he'd thought only to take? He'd hurt her, he knew. It wouldn't be possible to forgive himself for such a violation. He'd twisted sex into an ugly, bitter thing and used it to manipulate.

Exactly as he charged A.J.

The pace of his run slowed as he wound along the stretch of land below the Desira Plateau. Because of its proximity to the castle, it was secure territory, accessible only by authorized personnel. Guards had been deployed the length of his run, the three-mile strip a well-used path since his arrival.

White sand, blue surf, and golden sun mocked him, and sea birds called to mates and ridiculed. Driven by instinct, he glanced up at the cliff face, the gray rock covered by bits of lichen and brush. At first, he thought he'd imagined the sight. A ladder bounced into the stone, and long, familiar legs shimmied up its corded length.

Damon stopped his run and, peering up with a hand to shield his eyes, watched in disbelief as A.J. dismounted the rope ladder and landed lightly on the ledge. His breathing stopped as he waited for her to stand, to prove she was unhurt.

When she began to nimbly, furtively, make her way to the

plateau, outrage replaced anxiety. Somehow, she'd found the passage out of the palace from her room.

Damon ran toward the palace, and his guard scrambled to follow. Once he found her, he'd throttle her within an inch of her life, he seethed. Seeing her dangling above the rocky shore, supported by a rope ladder with frayed edges had shaved years from his life. Then, he'd fire the guards who allowed her to escape.

At the palace, he showered and dressed. In minutes, a car whisked him northward to the Desira Plateau marketplace. Pennants attached to the car bonnet whipped sharply in the breeze, the lion crest of the House of Toca on one, the flag of Jafir on the other. Inside the limousine, Damon resembled nothing so much as the great beast.

The mane of dark-brown hair curled itself along his temple and peaked at his forehead. Tawny eyes, narrowed and untamed, stared at the road in search of prey. Though the throng parted to admit the vehicle, the marketplace was too crowded for large vehicles.

Damon found her near a fabric cart. She spoke with the man in hushed tones, and the obvious intimacy of the exchange cut him to the quick. The man, the cart owner he surmised, draped a vivid strip of red fabric around the slender throat. A.J. laughed, and the pain sliced deeper.

He'd been ready to drag her away, to force her into the car. Now, he stood paralyzed, felled by disillusionment. Despite his protestations, he'd held out hope that what connected them, what drew them together across a dance floor and an ocean, had been real. That love, so easily fashioned from a handful of hours, could prove genuine.

He'd been prepared to be wrong.

"A.J." Her name was an oath.

She didn't startle, didn't demonstrate a hint of surprise. Instead, she curtsied, the black shirt and khaki shorts a stained costume. "Your Highness."

Nearby, the whispers began, and old women pointed fingers at the King. Tiny hands tugged at his sleeve, as eager children swarmed. In seconds, the marketplace rustled with news of the King's visit, and customers abandoned their purchases to gain an audience with the King. Damon considered having the guards arrest her, but he wanted to see what she did next. At the very least, he'd alert the ports and airport to deny her passage out of Jafir.

Swallowed in the horde, Damon could only fume silently as A.J. slipped into the masses and disappeared.

CHAPTER TEN

Grateful for the unexpected reprieve, A.J. raced to reach the palace before the irate man she left staring at her. Damon would not be far behind, but the eager public in the marketplace would occupy him for a time. She had Sashu to thank for the warning and the diversion. He'd spotted Damon and formulated a plan to help her escape. Hopefully, Sashu had been able to transmit to Atlas. With any luck, Adam and Raleigh would be on their way in a matter of hours.

She secured the ISA information in her bag and wove through the shoppers. Avoiding the recalcitrant merchant near the barrels, she used the rope ladder to return to the tunnels. The midday sun had dipped behind bleak clouds, and the air grew heavy with the promise of rain. Soon, fat droplets fell from the sky, sheeting off of skin glistening with sweat.

Deep inside the bowels of the tunnel system, A.J. sprinted

along, candles abandoned at the sealed entrance. The tunnel contained several sharp curves, which she would discover by trial and error. However, time was too short to try to keep a flame lit as she dashed through the passage.

Running would shave at least ten minutes off her return trip, and she needed every second. Once in the palace, she had to find a way to get to Poppet and run the new scenarios, without getting caught by Damon or his sentinels.

Too bad none of her training sessions provided for infiltrating the palace.

The part of her that reveled in order and stability screamed for her to abort the mission. Head back to the plateau, and beg Sashu to find her a way home, it cajoled. She wasn't cut out for cloak-and-dagger!

The realm of computers and research was neater. Tidier. Regimented. Equations, with their rational sensibilities. Machines, with their almost faultless logic. Domains where wayward emotion couldn't foul up an investigation or lead to death-defying stunts on antiquated twine hanging out over space and a turbulent sea.

Aloud, she wheezed into the empty tunnel, "I'm a scientist, not a spy. All I want to do is to go home, organize my CD collection, and watch a nice documentary on the three-toed sloth."

Gasping for air, A.J. crouched, hands on her knees, and drew musty oxygen into starving lungs. A hysterical bubble of laughter rose in an already tense chest, but it found no release as she pulled herself together by sheer force of will. Slowly, she sucked in the dank air, and looked into the inky blackness, considering her situation.

Sure, she was running through an ancient hole under the ground of a castle run by saboteurs bent on killing the unpredictable King who thought she was a traitor that was sent to help them steal his throne.

But at least she had her health—if you ignored her psych profile. An image of the single sheet and its harsh words flickered. If she hadn't been hell-bent on proving the assessment wrong, she and Poppet would be safely ensconced in Atlanta, preparing for her new job as head of R&D.

Instead, she was enmeshed in international intrigue and falling in love with a man who wouldn't let himself love her.

As she collided with a wall for the third time and stumbled, A.J. cursed the obstruction. She resumed her pace, one hand trailing the granite, and immediately rammed her hand into a metal rod protruding from the rock. When she finally made it, she'd be battered and bruised. It was her fault for leaving the candles behind.

Actually, she thought with a fierce resentment, this entire fiasco was really all Adam's fault. The shift in blame cheered her immeasurably. Adam Grayson had a great deal to answer for, if she survived to exact her revenge.

But for now, A.J. decided, she had a job to do. Of her listed neuroses, the most accurate one was her commitment to finishing what she started. That's what pushed her through grad school and up the ranks in GCI.

And, if she were to be honest, was why she couldn't ignore Damon, as much as she longed to do so. Something had begun between them at the wedding, and she would know what it was. Maybe it was love, as she feared; and maybe, it was simply an intense chemical reaction that seared her skin and her brain cells whenever they were in the same room. Either way, by week's end, she'd discover the answer to both problems.

Hopefully, by the time Damon returned to the palace, she'd have confirmed her suspicions. Options for getting to Poppet played out in varying scenarios, none of which had a prayer of working. A few seconds later, she stubbed her toe on the bottom step.

With stealth and relief, she crept inside her room and closed the passageway. The mechanism closed on a whisper, and A.J. marveled at the craftsmanship. Centuries, perhaps, had passed since the first use of the tunnels, and they continued to perform their task admirably. She tossed her bag on the desk and removed a small device. Courtesy of Adam.

The handheld resembled a remote control, sleek and black. Above the keypad, a series of lights blinked red, green, and yellow. Red, she knew from her instructions, meant that the room was indeed under audio surveillance. A.J. stood in the center of the room and entered a series of codes into its keypad. The lights flashed yellow; then a steady green glow appeared. A signal jammer, the device emitted a low frequency that would scramble all audio receivers in the main room. She set it on the desk and pulled out the flash drive.

The next task was to get to Poppet. By now, Damon had likely extricated himself from the crowd and was on his way to the palace. Sashu had promised to keep him busy for an hour, and a glance at the slim silver watch on her wrist told her she had thirty minutes remaining. A.J. racked her brain for options; then inspiration struck. In the bedroom, she grabbed some items and bundled them with the flash drive.

A.J. reopened the tunnel, candle in hand. Retracing her steps, she stopped fifty feet inside the walls. The metal rod that had scraped her flesh stuck out from the wall at an odd angle. Acting on a hunch, she stood on her toes and grasped the aging metal. She pulled down, and another false wall disappeared. Given the direction of the tunnel, and its relational position, she could extrapolate where the tunnel would lead. If she was correct, the new tunnel would connect with the one Damon had used to spirit her out of the palace.

She jogged down the path, unconcerned about the flickering flame. When she reached the familiar staircase, she scrambled up to the door. At first, she fumbled around searching for the opener, but finally, the door skated open on a soft hiss. Inside Damon's closet, A.J. rejoiced. She was becoming quite adept at this spy game.

A.J. surveyed the bedroom, which they'd passed through so hurriedly before. Her eyes encountered then slid away from the indigo-silk-covered bed, with its wrought iron, that dominated the center of the room. Unbidden, unwanted images flashed, and she dismissed them as nonsense. "Focus," she ordered.

Using precious time, she shimmied out of her shorts and T-shirt, replacing them with a brief black skirt and violet top that crisscrossed her torso in a daring V. A rapid French bath, and she was ready.

A.J. approached the door, the flash drive concealed in the waist of the skirt and covered by the top. Her shorts and shirt were hidden in Damon's closet. Steeling herself with a deep breath, she twisted the knob. Outside in the hallway, the guards immediately came to attention.

"Has the King returned yet?" she asked in a husky, sleepy voice. To punctuate her deception, she yawned coquettishly.

The man she assumed to be the leader of the attachment shook his head, eyes wide with curiosity. "Um, no."

When he did not immediately seize her, A.J. had her suspicion confirmed. Damon had placed a special contingent of guards on her door, but not everyone had been informed about the informal house arrest.

Nice going, Agent Grayson, she congratulated. Now, the next trick would be to make it down to the office without passing her own room and alerting that security detail.

She looked to the two men standing sentry with the first guard. One shrugged, and A.J. nearly danced for joy when she recognized the third.

"Mr. Donley, isn't it?"

Deep red slid up the young soldier's neck and suffused his freckled face. "Ah, yes, yes," he stuttered.

"Can you help me? I need to get to my office, but I would prefer not to encounter anyone on my way downstairs." A.J. allowed herself to look chagrined and slightly embarrassed. "It would be better to not be seen by anyone who may gossip."

Donley bobbed his head in agreement, as did the other guards. Protecting the reputation of the King was paramount, and which of them would not have succumbed to temptation? "Dr. Grayson. There is a private stairway the King occasionally uses. If you'll follow me?"

Triumphant, A.J. smiled sweetly at the guards and shadowed Donley down to the first level. When he offered to escort her to the office, she declined, but pressed a swift, heartfelt kiss to his cheek.

"Thank you," she gushed. While Owen struggled to control his color, A.J. keyed in the code and opened the door to the office.

"Phase three," she announced as she ran a loving hand over Poppet's frame and powered it on using the combination of passwords and voice print identification.

Its soothing voice announced, "Hello, Dr. Grayson. I have completed the analysis you requested."

"Thank you, Poppet. Please review your findings while I input new data. Run a Level II analysis and report your suppositions."

"What is the proposition, Dr. Grayson?"

"Given the parameters already explored, and in light of the new data, who is most likely responsible for the attempt on Damon Toca? Also, what is the most probable alliance between the culprit and known terrorist organizations? And, Poppet, please anticipate the next attack scenario."

"Working," Poppet responded. "I will require eleven minutes, forty-three seconds to complete my analysis."

<hr>

Damon found her there, hunched over the keyboard, staring at the blue glow of the terminal, conversing with the computer. Hair piled chaotically atop her head in a loose mass, so contrary to order and precision central to her nature.

But hadn't he learned that he understood nothing about A.J. Grayson?

"Did you want me to catch you?" he asked caustically. Standing behind her, close enough to touch, he saw the bare shoulders tense, the slender neck stiffen. "If you'd hidden in your room, I would have been none the wiser. Still, you return to the scene of the crime. Are you taunting me, Dr. Grayson? Trying to force me to have you arrested?"

"Cease report, Poppet." A.J. straightened, but did not turn to face him. "Not really, no. I don't think I'd like prison very much. And I didn't intend to flout your orders, but it was necessary."

Gripping the leather arm of the chair, Damon spun her around to face him. Betrayal slicked sickly inside him, and he grated out, "Necessary? Like lying to me was necessary?"

"I never lied to you."

The denial, though impassioned, was subdued by the pallor he suddenly noticed. Her skin was sallow, her eyes shadowed. She looked beaten, but he refused to succumb to pity.

Anxious about her and irritated by the emotion, Damon leaned over her threateningly. "What's wrong? Are you worried about your punishment? The penalty for treason and conspiracy?"

Concern warred with ire. "What's the matter with you? Fight back, damn you."

The listlessness he saw in her face colored her voice, thinned her words. "I don't want to fight with you, Damon."

A.J. twisted to face the computer terminal, but Damon refused to allow her to shut him out. Not before he got an explanation. For nearly two months, he'd been a dupe of the Jafirian government and the ISA. In one week, he'd be officially crowned the monarch of this godforsaken place he wished he'd never heard of. And one way or another, today, he'd have answers.

"What the devil is going on? Who were you meeting with, and how did you get out of your rooms? Who are you working for? And who is working with you?" The stream of questions was cold, flat, at odds with the storm building inside him.

Damon shoved fisted hands into his pockets, afraid he might be tempted to touch her. Because he could not be certain of calm, he did not risk contact. "Answer me," he demanded harshly.

A.J. raised a hand. "I know I have no right to ask, but give me a moment, please." She returned to the keyboard, tapped in a series of commands.

"Analysis verified," Poppet intoned. "Scenario within ninety-seven percent accuracy given established parameters. I do not detect a more probable suspect, Dr. Grayson. According to protocol, you should take appropriate steps immediately. The Minister of State should be alerted, as should King Damon."

Surprised by the announcement, Damon inquired, "Tell me what?" Though he directed the query at A.J., it was Poppet who responded.

"Voice print identified," greeted Poppet. "Hello, Your Highness."

"Be quiet, Poppet." A.J. dropped her face into her hands. "Give me a second to think."

For a brief spate, Poppet was silent. "Time has elapsed, Dr. Grayson."

Not amused, A.J. snapped, "Shut up, Poppet!"

Damon, patience gone, commanded, "Someone or something had better explain what is going on. Now!"

Out of options, A.J. rolled away from the terminal, without regard to Damon's proximity. He stepped aside, and A.J. jumped to her feet to pace.

"A.J."

"Shut up, and give me a second to think, will you?" she muttered.

"To whom do you refer, Dr. Grayson?"

"Yes, Dr. Grayson. Was that command directed at the computer or at me?"

"At this point, both of you are getting on my nerves."

"I am nowhere near your nerves, Dr. Grayson," Poppet corrected. "As that is a physical impossibility, I must inform you that King Damon could also not be responsible."

With a fulminating glare at Poppet, she ignored its logic and instructed, "Poppet, please move into suspended mode." In suspension, Poppet would no longer monitor their conversation.

Taking a deep breath, A.J. searched for the right words. She accepted that she had no other choice than to tell Damon what she'd learned.

"Damon. Your Highness. I know who the saboteur is." She risked a sidelong glance, but his face remained impassive.

"When I was in the marketplace today, I received information from an ISA informant."

"The man in the market?"

To protect Sashu, she lied easily. "No, not him. I saw you arrive and thought I needed to create a diversion. I told him that you were on the plateau. It worked."

"What did your informant give you?"

"Financial records. Wire transfers. For the last few years, a member of the Jafirian government has received large sums, which have been deposited in accounts around the world. The deposits correlate to transactions initiated by the ISA through a mole they'd planted in Scimitar."

She paused, gathering the courage to tell him a story he wouldn't believe.

"And?" Damon prompted.

"The transfers, the deposits, all went to one man."

"McCord?" The name slid out, the sound desperate and disbelieving.

"No, Damon. Not McCord. Robertsi. President Lawrence Robertsi."

The explosion, as she'd expected, was immediate and fierce. "You expect me to believe that Robertsi is the traitor? The President of Jafir?"

"I'm so sorry, Damon." A.J. reached out to comfort, but Damon moved away, as though scalded.

While she watched with troubled fascination, Damon drew himself in, shuttered his emotions until only the hazel eyes flickered with a banked fire.

"Turn the computer off, A.J." Damon pointed imperiously to Poppet. "Now." His voice, like his eyes, was wintry, but for the flare of irritation.

Uneasy, A.J. complied. She engaged her security protocols, powered down the computer. "It's off."

"Come with me," he instructed.

A.J. searched his inscrutable face for a sign of what he'd planned, but she saw only deliberate intent. Fear, real and potent, churned in her stomach, clutched at her heart. If he didn't believe her analysis, he could be taking her to the guards for incarceration. She'd have no way of warning the ISA, no way to escape.

A.J. climbed the private stairway, her mind racing for options. When she hesitated at the landing, Damon took her arm in a merciless grip.

"Don't speak and don't try to run away. They'll catch you," he warned.

When they reached his door, Damon dismissed the guards. A single attempt at protest was immediately quelled by his deadly stare.

Damon ushered A.J. inside and locked the door.

Annoyance joined the fear, and A.J. welcomed the new emotion. "Either take me into custody or release me, Damon. I've had enough of this."

"You've had enough?" Damon shrugged out of his jacket, which he tossed carelessly over a divan. Next, the strip of blue silk knotted at his neck landed beside it. A.J. watched with growing anxiety as he removed his cuff links and unbuttoned the collar of his shirt.

"Yes," A.J. ventured. "I have spent the past two days locked in my room, because of your suspicions. And when I exonerate myself, you drag me back to your cave like some Neanderthal. I demand to know what you intend to do with the information about Robertsi."

"What happens in the internal affairs of Jafir are no concern of yours." Damon cocked his head. "Would you like a drink?"

"No, I don't want a drink. I want to know what's going on. Are you alright? Should I call McCord?"

"Call McCord?" The harsh laughter should have warned her. "Am I alright? According to you, the President is a traitor who wants me dead. And my allies—my trusted aide and the ISA agent sent to help me—are collaborating to deceive me."

"Damon—"

"In one year, A.J., I've lost everything. My parents, the people who raised me to be honest, had hidden my past from me. My brother, for years my best friend, had stolen and looted priceless treasures for greed. Then, I'm told that I'm the heir to a heritage people died to protect for me. And if I don't want their sacrifice to have been in vain, I must leave my home and travel to some godforsaken island plagued by thieves and criminals."

A.J. stumbled over her response. No axioms of trust would

appease the ache born of betrayal. No platitudes about haste or regret could satisfy the bloodlust simmering in his eyes. She stepped toward him, drawn by the need to soothe.

When Damon shifted beyond her reach, she tried not to cringe. She understood how pain inflamed, making even the gentlest touch unbearable.

He continued, relentlessly. "I come to Jafir, leaving everything else behind. I learn, I study, and I act the part. The President treats me like a pariah, and his Cabinet thinks me beneath contempt. But I do my duty. Then you arrive, and I find out that I'm the target of a madman, who might be my brother. You're threatened, I'm shot at, and still I remain. Only to discover that the mastermind has inside help from one of the people I trust."

Damon glared at her then, acid revulsion searing her skin. "Is it the man who made himself my confidant? The President who accused me of being a traitor to Jafir? Or the woman I thought I might be in love with?"

A.J. flinched at the tense, at the accusation. "I explained why I didn't show you the photograph. The ISA gave me orders, and I had to obey them. But I've never betrayed you. I wouldn't." Warily, urgently she approached him again, hands outstretched in supplication.

The tenuous hold Damon had maintained over temper broke. Lies met him on every side, and in the center stood the woman he'd thought he loved. Innocently, she gazed up at him, her face wreathed in earnest confusion. Tempted to believe, he again saw her with the man in the market. She'd eluded her guards twice, once to reach the plateau and a second time to break into the lab.

Had she been born a liar or learned it in training? he wondered. "Did you plan it?"

"Plan what?"

"Our first meeting at the wedding. The way you circled around me, luring me in, making sure I noticed you."

"I did no such thing. You were standing with my family."

How convincingly she feigned hurt. Damon nodded in appreciation. "Perhaps that's when they corrupted you. When they saw us together."

"You're being irrational, Damon! There was no conspiracy. I've done nothing wrong."

"You lied to me, A.J."

"I tried to protect you."

"From whom?"

"From your enemies," she snapped.

"And you're not my enemy," Damon repeated her claim, struggling for calm, for reason.

A.J. approached him, crossing the pale gray carpet. "No. I am not your enemy." The narrow hand caressed his cheek. "You know me."

Sunlight, even in the gathering darkness, filled his senses. Yet, he watched her through a miasma of distrust. Scenes flickered, a reel of conflicting images. Of laughter, anger, desire, and regret. Faster and faster, they played in his head until he could decipher honesty in a single moment. The first moment. When passion had held its own truth.

Everything before, everything after, Damon acknowledged as false. But that bright evening in Atlanta, he had to believe it had been genuine, unsullied by lies and subterfuge. The feel of her, the taste of her, had to be real.

Like a drowning man, he clung to the thought, to the slender wrist that his hand had circled unknowingly.

"I don't know what you are, and I don't care." Damon dragged her close, his arm coming around her taut frame to band them together. "What I do know is that tonight, you belong to me."

A.J. twisted in his unyielding grip, chin angled in rebellion. "I belong to no one."

"In this"—he streaked a hard hand over her, reveling in A.J.'s involuntary gasp of pleasure—"you are mine."

Blood stirred, heated, but still she resisted. "I won't be taken by you," she warned.

Damon laughed again, the sound softer, assured. "Yes, you will. And you'll take me." He lifted her into his arms, carried her into the bedroom.

Storms raged beyond the windows; rain cascaded in violent sheets against the panes. The blues and lighter shades dimmed, melded in the murky light of the tempest. White flashed in brief relief against the sky, then vanished.

Understanding the urgency of the lightning, the dark command of thunder, Damon set A.J. on unsteady legs beside the bed. When she turned to escape, he caught her, spinning her to face him. Passion, rebellion, alarm shuddered on her skin, trembled on sultry lips.

"When I look at you, I can't see the truth," he whispered, brushing ebony strands away from wide, uncertain eyes. "And when I touch you, I can't seem to care."

"Damon, please, let me go." Her voice shook with need and trepidation. "It shouldn't be like this. Not if you can't trust me."

"I'm not sure there can be anything else." Damon cupped her chin in his hand, drew her mouth to his. Lowering his head, he claimed her mouth in a questing kiss. Blindly, he hunted for the complex flavor he remembered, for an answer to the doubts.

The sharp, sweet taste flooded his system, the breathless moan ravaged his soul.

She met the foray silently, sadly, and their tongues dueled for supremacy. Slick, hot, wet mouths angled in discovery, seeking dominion. Unbidden, bare arms circled strong, trembling shoulders, her hands sinking into the silky brown hair, tugging. When Damon complied and met her challenging gaze, A.J. paused, gathered her breath.

"You have to trust me. If you can't, none of this is real."

"What I feel for you is real. So real it's destroying me." He slid a strong thigh between her legs, forcing her closer. "I want you, A.J. More than I've ever wanted anything. I'd do anything to have you." Damon yanked her closer, marauding her mouth in plea.

Lost, she succumbed, then pulled away, their hips in volatile contact. "Can you believe in me?" The question, ragged and uneven, tore from her on a sob.

Damon looked at her. Love, powerful and damning, flowed through him. Despite the evidence, despite the past, he'd gone beyond truth and lies with her, beyond right and wrong. Now, he could see only A.J., could feel only love. And if it demanded trust, he would give. If only for one night.

"I believe in what's between us," he equivocated. "Can you accept that?"

She met his clouded gaze, the mixture of love and despair. For tonight, she would accept the possibility, would refuse to hide behind frenzied desire or mindless capitulation. Between them, at least for tonight, there would be no more deception.

"I want you," she whispered.

"Then have me," he groaned, and swept her into a maelstrom of sensation.

The roughened hands of a builder tore down hesitation, dismantled lingering fear. He stripped the slight top from her, lifting it over her head and tossing it to the floor. Midnight locks framed the gamine face, and Damon wondered at her beauty. They curled around her in riotous glory. Taut globes, the shade of caramel, the shape of fantasy, beckoned him, but he resisted the urge to sample, the compulsion to linger. Instead, the swathe of skirt slithered down naked limbs, and he traced the journey with a damp, ravaging trail that shattered her.

In soulful cries, he heard a promise of forever, and yearned to believe. Trickery had no place, and he vowed they would never leave.

Delirious, A.J. undressed him, skimming her tongue over the sweep of muscles, dipping into the hollow of his navel. When his knees threatened to buckle, after she bared tumid flesh to purposeful ministrations, she rose in triumph, more goddess than fairy.

With her touch, she'd prove her loyalty. With her love, she'd win his trust. In each other's arms, they'd find peace.

They tumbled onto the bedding, a tangle of arms, legs, and desire. To torment, he molded her breasts to his touch, lifted them for his kiss. She writhed in pleasure, in delightful agony, when his teeth abraded then soothed the vulnerable flesh.

A.J. straddled lean hips, driven to stroke, to savor. Where muscle curved into muscle, tiny wet licks of flame discovered the essence of man. She nipped at the length of his waist, marauded the mouth urging her to explore.

Desperate, he forced her beneath him. The banquet of soft and supple called to him. Lovingly, he lifted her to his mouth, where tongue and lips and teeth worshipped the curve of breast, the crease of thigh.

Over, under, hot, and wet. Kisses met sighs. Bites fueled moans. Driven, each battled to bring the other unbearable pleasure.

Damon brought her shuddering body to a peak, and she cried in wonder.

A.J. raked callous, careful fingers over skin taut to bursting, and Damon groaned in ecstasy, his hand flung out to seek protection. Fumbling in a single drawer, he closed grateful fingers around the sliver of foil.

Humid flesh beckoned, and he arched to take. She covered him with hurried strokes, urged him with whispered pleas.

"Now," she demanded, her breath, her body shuddering with need.

"Forever," he replied, sinking inside her, taking her into him.

In the joining, he fought for tenderness. She refused it, compelling strength. As one, they plunged and rose, skin sliding against skin, need slanted against need. Thrusting, rocking, taking, giving, each straining to taste, to know.

"Ma fée."

"My love."

Control shattered, and Damon caught her hips, desperate to have all of her now. A.J. tangled her legs with his, determined to make them one.

Thunder shook the palace, toppled trees, tossed branches, but they paid the destruction no heed. They came together, into each other, ignoring all that separated them. In unison, beyond

awareness, they accepted their fate, wrapped together against
the storm.

———

Night had fallen, and the moon shone through the dissipating
clouds. A.J. wearily opened heavy lids, and remained mo-
tionless. Damon lay beside her, watching with the quiet stillness
that unnerved and enthralled her. Sometime during the night,
he'd drawn the covers over them. Limbs, torpid from their lovemaking, draped over skin still slick with desire. Want crested
unexpectedly.

She didn't know the proper words for what she wanted,
needed. What did one say to the man she loved, when he believed her to be a traitor and a liar? When words weren't an option, could she show Damon her heart and make him accept?
Leaning past him, she rifled through the bedside table and found
another foil-wrapped disk. She'd refused to allow him to take
her, but she'd made no promises about seduction.

Wordlessly, she ranged herself above him and peppered his
face, his throat, with gentle kisses. Hands that attempted to draw
her closer were pinned to his sides. Slowly, inexorably, she lathed
salty skin with wet caresses, satin strokes of tongue that cajoled
and excited. Tenderly, she sampled flat male nipples, sinewy bi-
ceps, the moist cavern of mouth. To arouse, to inflame, A.J. wriggled beneath the comforter to explore the textures and varieties
of skin.

Damon lay quiescent, tormented and thrilled by the sensu-
ous investigation. For hours, he'd watched her as she slept, unable to fathom the complicated truth. In repose, black hair fanned

out in abandon, A.J. resembled the fairy he likened her to in passion. He heard her whispered declaration, when she'd called him her love. Throughout the night, he'd fought the urge to wake her and repeat the words to her.

He loved.

As surely as the storm's lightning, love had pierced the cynicism, eroding the doubt. Though he knew better than to rely on his notoriously faulty analysis of others, he thought he could trust her. She risked her life to find evidence to protect, hadn't balked when he confronted her. Would the guilty return to the scene? She'd found a chance to escape, but instead, she returned to him. For him.

In the tumult of the past weeks, she'd been his lodestar, a beacon that guided him through suspicion and expectation. He'd wondered if he dared to trust her. Now, his heart challenged, could he dare not to and lose A.J. forever?

Reaching out, he yanked the covers away. Naked, exposed, A.J. stared up at him, questions wrestling with desire. He drew her to him, under him, as he initiated his own sensual assault on her silky skin. The narrow waist, rounded bottom, slender throat, nothing escaped his attentions. Hard and soft, slow and fast, he readied her, readied himself, their fingers surrounding him, protecting her.

With urgency, she opened to him, welcomed him. With reverence, he entered her, cherished her.

Pleasured sighs became ragged moans became cries of rapture. Passion consumed them, and eagerly they sank into the oblivion of release, the declaration complete.

CHAPTER ELEVEN

Midnight had come and gone. Hunger woke A.J. around three a.m., and she complained about the need for fuel. Pleasantly exhausted, A.J. wandered into the bathroom, eager to regroup before facing the aftermath. Shedding her makeshift robe, the shirt she'd torn from him, she stepped beneath the scalding water. She braced herself against the tile, and let the panic wash over her.

In her prior relationships, the morning after had always followed a logical discussion of parameters the night before. She hadn't sought out the tepid relationships, but until Damon, her choices had been careful, considered. Men with whom she could share her mind and body, but somehow, never her heart. They were like-minded, career-driven men. Comfortable relationships that didn't tempt her to excess.

Not men who lured her into trysts in wine cellars or

seduction in the King's quarters. With Damon, careful romance vanished, obviated by a torrent of emotions destined to leave her edgy and off-balance.

She hated being edgy and off-balance, A.J. reminded herself, as the water sluiced through spiced foam. Hadn't she always been a faithful adherent of self-control? Not that she didn't fully enjoy her life, but in moderation.

Spontaneity, on the other hand, resulted in dangling from cliffs and seducing a king. In mere weeks, she'd become a woman she'd scarcely recognized. Equanimity and caution merged with the audacity and temper she typically held in check.

Now, both women were necessary if she intended to save Damon. And both women were vital if she planned to save herself.

The shower door slid open, and fragrant steam billowed into the bath.

"I ordered one of everything I know you like." Damon entered the stall, which had space for a family of five. "I plan to ensure that you require copious amounts of energy." Covetous eyes slid over the swell of her breasts, the long expanse of leg. "Lots of energy."

"Already?" A.J. thought for a second to shield herself, but a thread of boldness made her stand open to his admiring gaze. "We haven't gotten much sleep tonight."

"Is that a complaint?" Damon murmured as he stalked her beneath the heated spray.

A.J. bumped into the slippery tiles, then stepped forward with a sly grin. "Merely an observation."

"Good," Damon warned darkly, and his mouth swooped to claim hers. "Very good."

Later, a polite tattoo on the door signaled the arrival of food and dragged them from the lovely stupor where they lay entwined on the dressing room floor. They ate seated at the sitting room table, and light conversation turned abruptly serious.

"Have you told anyone else about what you've found?" Damon ran negligent fingers through still-damp hair. "I need to know everything you've done."

A.J. sipped from her orange juice and frowned at the accusatory tone. "I told you. I met my ISA contact at the Desira Plateau, got the new data. I snuck back into the palace and down to the lab." She decided leaving out the assistance of Owen the guard wouldn't qualify as a lie. "I didn't confirm my theory until yesterday, when you walked into the lab. Poppet crunched the latest records, ran multiple models. The evidence points directly to Robertsi. The bank accounts are routed through several channels and linked to legitimate investments. But they're his."

"A set of bank accounts is your proof? Anyone could have established them to implicate him."

A.J. inched forward on her chair, sorrow wreathing her face. Robertsi had been kind to her, had shown her every courtesy. And she could tell that the thought of another betrayal ate at Damon, burning inside him, a living thing.

How well she'd come to know him, she thought. The balled fist. The clenched jaw. And less obvious signs, like the quick speech and the brighter flecks of gold in his narrowed eyes. In passion or distress, the gold flared, dominating the tawny brown.

She'd have given anything to alter the facts, but a lie would aid only the guilty. Steeling herself, she answered calmly, "I thought of that. The accounts required fingerprints and signature cards. Poppet detected an exact match on all of them."

The balled fist pounded the glass table, and the base rocked under the pressure. "It doesn't make sense! If he wished to have me killed, why not do it here? The assassination attempt on the beach was incompetent. The phone threats were crude."

A.J. shrugged. "Maybe to deflect suspicion. Maybe because security inside the palace is too tight."

"Obviously not, since you were able to escape with ease." Damon gave her a pointed look. "How did you discover the tunnels from your room?"

A.J. recalled the furious attempt to destroy the lamp, and the humiliating events that preceded her rage. "I knocked over the table in the foyer and triggered the mechanism."

Damon shook his head in contradiction, his gaze speculative. "Merely shifting the table won't work. The lamp must be removed first."

"Well," A.J. grumbled, "I might have been throwing the lamp."

"At what?"

"At you, Your Highness," she snapped. "And I think it is in your best interest to drop this interrogation."

Raising his hands in mock surrender, Damon returned to his earlier line of thought. "What does Robertsi have to gain by my demise? Nelson becomes the monarch then. Or Zeben."

"Poppet's supposition is that Robertsi intends to quash the monarchy. With Nelson and Zeben incarcerated, he consolidates his power."

"Then why would either of them help him?" was the dogged response. "If Robertsi wants them eliminated, why would either one trust him?"

"Evil makes strange bedfellows. Perhaps Robertsi intends to

double-cross his partner. And Poppet did suggest that there may be a third enemy that we aren't aware of yet. But none of the usual suspects seemed promising."

"Any theories?"

A.J. ticked off the list she'd compiled. "A dissident agent of the Mossad has made overtures to Hezbollah leaders about destabilizing the summit and the Alliance. But that predates the earliest payment. A new group no one knows about. Maybe one of the Alliance members."

"So Robertsi could be working with anyone."

And she'd failed at her mission, A.J. added. Aloud, she concurred. "I have Poppet rechecking its assumptions. The information from the ISA might open a new line of inquiry. I didn't get very far yesterday, once I pinpointed Robertsi's guilt. But I'll keep working on it."

"And you trust this contact? The one who gave you the files?" Damon pressed.

"Yes."

Damon nodded. "I'll need you to meet with Wynn and me at seven. If she's convinced, I will instruct her to take Robertsi into custody today." The weight of the decision seemed to rest heavily, and Damon shoved away from the table. He flung open the balcony doors, and walked out to the dew-dampened railing. In the wake of the storm, debris littered the ground, but already the maintenance staff gathered and tidied.

Standing in the half light, the tall, rangy figure appeared to slip beyond her reach into shadows.

A.J. refused to let him go. "This isn't your fault, Damon. You have no choice," A.J. whispered behind him. Taking a chance, she slipped comforting arms about the firm waist, the open shirt billowing in the morning breeze. A.J. pressed a cheek to the tense back, rigid and stiff. "But you have me."

———

Robertsi has received millions in payment, hidden in off-shore accounts," Damon explained to Wynn an hour later. "Dr. Grayson has the account numbers and the transaction dates."

Wynn nodded wearily after she reviewed the printouts. "I will have him placed under arrest immediately."

Damon roamed the expanse of the spacious office. He'd wrestled with the decision since dawn, once he accepted A.J.'s analysis as correct. Strain ringed his mouth with lines, darkened his eyes. The almost complete lack of sleep added to stress, but he could not regret the reasons.

He risked a look at A.J., who had returned to her rooms at dawn. After sating themselves one last time, he escorted her to her quarters and issued orders restoring her access to the palace. The speculative looks from the guards raised color on A.J.'s cheeks, but Damon had not cared.

The day before, she'd been his prisoner. Now, because of her conclusions, he would seize power from the duly elected president. A bloodless coup worthy of Nelson. The comparison chilled him, and he spoke brusquely. "I would prefer that he be placed under house arrest, with communication from the mansion restricted. Remove his security detail and replace them with officers he will not know."

"Why not take him into custody?" Wynn questioned. "He poses a threat to national security."

Damon glanced at A.J., who'd stiffened at his pronounce-ment, then he faced Wynn, shutting A.J. out. "Until we have verified this information ourselves," he emphasized *ourselves*, "I will not humiliate the man publicly." Damon saw no need to em-barrass the President, despite A.J.'s certitude.

Accusing the Head of State of treason a week before the sum-mit would erode Jafir's position and undermine the conference. He explained this to A.J. and Wynn. "Too much is at stake. And we do not yet know if he's working with Nelson or Zeben or both. We must keep him in play until one of them shows his hand."

"You're risking your life," A.J. argued fiercely. "He has at-tempted to have you shot once already. Why in the world would you give him another chance to kill you?"

Damon bristled at the tone of rebuke. "Because I have a greater duty, Dr. Grayson." He deliberately used her title to lengthen the distance between them. When he thought of her as A.J., he found it impossible to keep his focus, to ignore how her scent clung to his skin. If he allowed himself to feel, he'd whisk her off to safety and leave the turmoil behind. Luxuries he could ill afford.

"Jafir and the summit are my priorities. Until we know who Robertsi's accomplice is, I can't risk tipping our hand."

To Wynn, he said, "Arrange the house arrest and notify me when they are ready. And share this information with no one."

"Has McCord been informed?" Wynn queried.

"No. You know because you are the head of security. Dr. Grayson is the ISA operative. That is sufficient."

"And what shall I tell the guard? This will test their loyalty." Wynn rolled her shoulders and rubbed at a headache brewing at her temples. "I am a member of President Robertsi's Cabinet. I've served with him for five years, as have most of the regiment. They will require an explanation."

"Tell them Robertsi's life has been threatened and that he refused to take precautions."

"And if they resist?"

Damon stopped pacing and spun on his heel to face Wynn. Power shone in cold hazel eyes. Command eased the lines of strain, stiffened resolve. In low tones, firm and uncompromising, Damon answered, "You can tell them that they will obey or they will be replaced. By order of the King."

Wynn lifted a green phone, its buttons removed. Immediately, she was connected to her second-in-command, the admiral of the navy. "Assemble fifteen members of the First Battalion. Have them meet me outside the presidential mansion." She paused briefly, then said, "Yes, in full armor."

When she stood, Damon informed her, "I will accompany you to see the President."

"That's not necessary," Wynn protested.

Damon heard the loyalty, and the desire to protect Robertsi from him. Perhaps, he thought wistfully, there was also an inclination to spare him the bitter quarrel that would inevitably come. "I issued the order, Minister Wynn. Robertsi's ire will have one target. Me."

"Yes, sir." Returning to the phone, Wynn recalled the on-site guard, gave instructions for the switch to occur in thirty minutes. Damon and Wynn headed to the mansion, and A.J. accepted the tacit order to stay behind.

A peremptory knock on Robertsi's study door was welcomed with a curt invitation to enter. Damon walked inside alone.

Wynn stood sentry outside, alerted to the possibility that Robertsi might try to escape.

At the sight of Damon, Robertsi stood and bowed. "Your Highness. I was not aware you were coming. Shall I have coffee brought in?"

Damon studied him, searching for signs of deception. Instinct screeched at him to share his findings with Robertsi, to seek his counsel. But the file he carried quelled the impulse and fortified his determination. "This isn't a social call."

"Has there been another threat?" Robertsi asked. He clasped his hands in a military pose, legs braced.

"Not directly. However, Dr. Grayson has completed her analysis of the Cabinet." Damon offered him the leather portfolio. "There is a disturbing conclusion."

Robertsi accepted the file, and quickly skimmed its contents. "You believe that I am the culprit?" The question was bland, as was Robertsi's expression.

Startled by the tone, Damon responded, "The evidence points directly to you. I don't know of another plausible explanation."

"I suppose you wouldn't believe that I've never seen these accounts," Robertsi replied conversationally. He walked around the desk, its pristine surface identical to the one in his office. Seated, he riffled through the documents, scrutinizing each carefully.

"These are my signatures," he conceded. "But I did not sign these bank cards. Nor did I authorize the reported transfers."

"Can you offer an explanation?" Damon sat opposite, hands lying open on the desk. "Who would want to frame you?"

Robertsi laughed, a hollow sound. "My only guess would be you, Damon. But you're not likely to confess, now are you?"

"I didn't do this, Lawrence. And I pray to God that you didn't either." He stared at the older man, his eyes troubled. "But until I have an alternate theory, I'll have to place you under arrest."

For the first time, Robertsi showed frustration. "The summit is in seven days. Dodi Hannah, the Israeli attaché, comes tomorrow."

"I know. An open arrest will derail the summit. That's why I've arranged for a house arrest, pending a full investigation."

"And Hannah, what will you tell her?"

"That you are indisposed due to illness. Santana and I will meet with her and the delegates as they arrive. In the interim, I have removed your personal guard. Members from the First Battalion will be stationed inside the mansion. I understand Mrs. Robertsi returns from her visit to Bolivia tomorrow. She will be met at the airport and brought here. After Wynn has interviewed her, she may be able to move freely, but under close supervision."

"You've thought of almost everything," Robertsi congratulated Damon. "Clever boy. If I were you, and eager to strengthen my position, I'd do exactly the same."

Ignoring the insinuation, Damon stood. Robertsi rose, in custom, as Damon took his leave. He dropped heavily into the chair, and Damon turned at the door. During the interview, the President had aged. The proud frame stooped, and fatigue dulled the piercing gray eyes. "That's what I'm afraid of, sir," he murmured as he left the room.

Damon strode through the phalanx of guards, greeting each one in turn. The fifteen-member team would be under the control of Damon's chief of security. He motioned to Wynn, who broke away from a conversation with the chief.

"Stay here and secure the mansion. I want a tactical report by ten a.m."

"Yes, Your Highness." Wynn held her tongue, then asked, "Where are you heading?"

"Back to the palace. I will update McCord on the situation, give him the same report we issued to the guards."

"Begging your pardon, sir, but McCord has a greater understanding of the personnel than your chief of security. And he is McCord's subordinate. Is it wise to leave both outside the informational loop?"

Despite the photo, Damon remained unwilling to share his doubts about McCord. Instead, he explained, "Robertsi may have been collaborating with any number of Jafirian officials. Until I say otherwise, Minister Wynn, it is our policy that no one else needs to know."

On the ride to the palace, Damon replayed his discussion with President Robertsi. The man had not chafed at the accusation, except to offer a simple denial of the charges. Was it possible Robertsi was innocent, a dupe in a game he never agreed to play?

If so, Damon had to wonder who was actually moving the pieces around. Against his will, his thoughts turned to A.J. She'd produced evidence unknown to anyone, after a clandestine meeting with the ISA.

And she'd explained how, his heart countered.

Trust wrestled with doubt. Everything he knew about her, everything he felt, shouted that she was as honest, as frank, as he'd sworn to believe. She'd escaped, yes, but she'd returned to him. In her own way, she tried to protect him. To love him.

As soon as the car stopped, he bounded out and rushed to her office, where he knew she'd be huddled with Poppet, searching for more clues.

Three lines would furrow between her brows, and locks of hair would hang loosely from her makeshift bun. A.J. would smell like sunlight and feel like heaven. And she'd heal the broken places inside him, help him learn to trust again. In turn, he would love her so fully, so completely, she'd never doubt again.

Damon brushed past the guard standing sentry outside the office. Necessity demanded that he tell her now, before another crisis rent his world.

He swung through the outer office and past Felice at the front desk. "Your Highness," she called out anxiously, but Damon paid no attention. He keyed in his code, and pushed the door open.

McCord sat on the corner of the computer table, and A.J. giggled at something he'd said. Then, inexorably, his attention was drawn to McCord's hands. In the gnarled grip was the photo of him and Zeben.

Doubt returned, redoubled, and fury threatened to explode. Beneath it, jagged pain lanced through him, and he fought not to buckle where he stood. Instead, he reached for the cynicism that had sustained him. "What a cozy picture," he gritted out. "Not quite as interesting as the one in McCord's hands, but just as telling, I suppose."

"Damon," A.J. greeted cautiously, aware of the violent tension in Damon. She watched in disbelief as suspicion twisted his beautiful mouth in a sneer. When she glanced at McCord, she remembered the photo and knew Damon had imagined the worst. "Uh, McCord stopped by to check on my progress. I told him I'd been sick most of the week, but that things were moving apace."

"And you shared a nice laugh over my mission to see Robertsi?"

"Of course not, Damon," A.J. corrected faintly, as sorrow arrowed through her. She'd deceived herself, she acknowledged. Damon had warned her of his distrust, but she hadn't listened. The illusion she'd demanded in the night had not survived the morning. Tears pricked, clawed at her throat, but she swallowed the anguish.

As instructed, she hadn't shared the purpose of Damon's visit with McCord. Trying to forestall the angry denunciation brewing inside him and to forget about the vicious pain of loss, A.J. cautioned numbly, "McCord decided it was time to reveal a secret he'd been keeping for decades. He brought me this photo."

By this time, McCord had risen from his perch. He walked to Damon, and extended the aged photo, with its creased edges. "I decided Dr. Grayson would find it eventually, so I thought I'd save her the trouble. I should have told you first, but you've been difficult to speak with this week."

Damon accepted the photograph, and looked at McCord in confused dismay. "So it's real. You were friends with Zeben?"

"Years ago. Nearly half a century ago." McCord sighed deeply. "I grew up in the palace. My father was the King's Chief of Security. My mother was companion to your grandmother, then governess to Queen Jaya. When this photo was taken, I was nearly twenty-five." Walking to the opposite side of the room, McCord continued. "I wanted to leave the palace and Jafir. My best friend was a distant cousin to the King, Kadifir el Zeben. We attended university together, and served a stint in the navy at the same time."

McCord opened a window and lit a cigar. Smoke wisped into

the morning air. "After our discharge, Zeben came into an inheritance. He wanted to travel the world, and he asked me to join him. Against my parents' wishes, I agreed. We hiked across Europe, learned Swahili in Kenya. At Zeben's insistence, we mined diamonds in South Africa and emeralds in Columbia. Zeben became fascinated by the gemstones, obsessed."

"That's when he started searching for the Kholari."

"Yes. I decided it was time to return home, but Zeben refused to join me, and we parted ways—and not on good terms. He'd already formed the basis of Scimitar." He took a deep drag from the cigar, coughing lightly as the fumes filled his lungs.

"I assumed my father's position, became your mother's chief of security and more. When Zeben began to grow infamous for Scimitar, I couldn't bear the thought of losing her esteem. So I hid my past."

"How could you hide it so thoroughly?" Damon wondered. "A.J. said that the ISA had no record of you, yet you attended prestigious schools and lived here."

McCord smiled and glanced at A.J. "That's what we were laughing about when you entered. The difference in documentation fifty years ago and today is the moral equivalent of stone tablets and electronic mail." He shifted bulky shoulders arrogantly. "I was responsible for recordkeeping, and I decided what would and would not be kept. I destroyed my birth certificate and purged the university files using my contacts."

A.J. pointed to the photo. "We assume Zeben planted the photograph to focus attention on McCord and to deflect it from his accomplice." She pulled up a screen on Poppet. "I checked the link that led me to it, and the photo wasn't uploaded until a month ago."

"Can you tell who did it?" McCord asked, moving to stand over A.J.'s shoulder. "It could focus our investigation."

A.J. and Damon exchanged a meaningful glance, and A.J. held her tongue. Obviously, since he had yet to mention Robertsi, Damon wasn't ready to accept McCord's version of events. Not that it surprised her. He obviously trusted no one, not even the woman he'd made love to last night.

Perhaps there was some comfort in his universal lack of trust, A.J. thought wanly, and when she could feel again, she'd search for it.

For now, though, she'd concentrate on making it through the next sixty seconds. Then sixty more, until the week came to an end and she could go home. How naïve to think that one night of loving would make a difference, she taunted herself scornfully. Did she really imagine passion and tenderness would be an adequate substitute for love and trust?

No, all their lovemaking did was lay bare the distance between what he could offer and what she needed from him. And she needed forever.

Submerging the sharp pain, A.J. fiercely tapped the keyboard. "I'll start tracking the link," she explained to McCord. "I can retrace Poppet's information sources, check to see where the file was uploaded."

"I appreciate it," McCord said gruffly. He faced Damon, head held high. "I never betrayed your mother or you, Damon. I was ashamed, but I am not a traitor."

Damon hesitated, then extended his hand to McCord. "You've served me well, McCord. I won't forget that."

Realizing it was all the reassurance he would receive, McCord shook the offered hand briskly. "I'll return to my offices.

Perhaps I can locate additional clues as to who could be assisting Zeben."

"Good," Damon concurred. "I'll meet you when I've finished here."

The door whispered shut behind McCord, and A.J. continued to enter keystrokes furiously. Damon watched, waiting for her to say something. From the tense line of her neck, he easily divined that she was angry. He traced a fingertip along the fragile nape, and she jerked convulsively. When she still refused to turn, he asked, "Are you mad at me?"

A.J. stiffened slightly, but kept her back to him. "Should I be?"

"What you should do is look at me." Annoyed, Damon took up McCord's vacated position on the corner of the desk. "You *are* angry," he said.

"A brilliant political mind at work," sniped A.J. "The country is in good hands."

Damon scowled at the derision. "Perhaps you'll leave your snit long enough to tell me why you're so mad at me."

The keystrokes grew louder and harder. "I don't plan to tell you anything, Your Highness. Unless, of course, it's how you can go straight to—"

"Condemning the King to hell isn't very cordial, A.J." Damon leaned forward, vaguely amused by the fury that flagged her cheeks with red. "I assumed that after last night, we'd have greater honesty between us."

"And trust?" A.J. spat. "I thought that after everything, I'd finally earned that. It seems we were both wrong about what last night meant."

Fear prickled along his spine, and Damon caught the nape of her neck fully in his hand. He forced her livid brown eyes to his own fuming gaze, alarmed by the sheen of tears. "Am I not allowed any concern when I see you giggling over a damning photograph with the man who's lied to my family for decades?" he argued defensively.

A.J. arched away from his hand because the contact eroded her conviction, tempted her to accept whatever he could give.

She clung to her indignation with Herculean effort, knowing that if she didn't, she'd be lost. "Concern, yes," she lashed out. "But you immediately suspected the worst. That I was somehow collaborating with McCord to hurt you. I saw it in the way you looked at me. I know that look."

A.J. met his eyes directly now, and hers were bitterly dry, the urge to weep burned away by brutal disappointment. She'd gambled last night, and she'd lost. What remained was the stubborn pride that had always driven her. Bleakly, she told him, "I deserve more, Damon. And I won't settle for less."

"Won't settle?" Damon thrust an impatient hand through his hair. He asked warily, "What does that mean?"

A.J. answered coldly, her decision clear. "It means that as soon as I've found Robertsi's accomplice, I'm on the next plane to Atlanta."

Damon tried to process the words through the wild rush in his ears. She would leave him, he thought urgently, and he'd lose his heart, before he had the chance to tell her she held it. His chest tightened with despair, and he knew the savage grip of fear.

Damon explained huskily, "I doubted you, yes. I'm sorry for that. Give me time, A.J. Please." Damon laid a pleading hand over hers on the keyboard. The skin, warm and soft, shifted beneath his palm as she pulled away to stand.

A.J. wrapped slender arms around her waist, and Damon

ached at the grief reflected in her eyes. Then the words came, and his heart broke.

"I don't want to hear your explanations, Damon," A.J. said contemptuously. "If it's not mistrust, it's protocol. Or danger. It will always be something. The only time you trust me completely is when we make love." She smiled sadly, the curve of lips a mockery. "You warned me once that there was too much distance between us. I didn't want to listen. But I hear you now. I can't keep loving you, waiting for the day you decide I can have your full heart, trust and all. You can't give me that, Damon."

"And you won't let me try?" Damon asked, his voice ragged. He could see her slipping away. With minced steps, he advanced toward her, but she recoiled.

Lifting her hands to ward him off, A.J. promised, "I'll find Robertsi's source of funds. And I'll prove to you that you can trust McCord and your Cabinet. I can give you that. But nothing more. I won't love a man who only has use for me in bed. I'm better than that."

Damon watched her, and he realized she spoke the truth. Only in passion did he allow himself to show her what he held in his heart. In all else, he kept himself apart. Part of his isolation was necessary, a defense against the treachery he'd come to realize surrounded him. But a greater part was fear. Fear that he'd find what he needed in A.J., and that he'd never be able to let go.

What words could he give her to prove he could change? That he could trust when it mattered most? Because she mattered most?

"A.J. Listen to me," he began. He took another step toward her, and the thin control she held over her emotions snapped.

"Don't touch me, Damon. Please." A dry sob wracked through her, and the clear brown eyes filled with tears. "I will help you save your kingdom, but that's all I can give you, Damon. Anything else would destroy me."

Torn by the need to comfort and her distressed plea, Damon hesitated, hand outstretched. *"Ma fée?"*

For a final time, she drew away from him. Sunlight pooled around her, highlighting the tension that vibrated through her. "Just go," she asked in a hoarse whisper. "Let me finish my work. Please."

The anguish decided for him.

"Are you sure that's what you want, A.J.?"

She spun away, unable to look at him. Damon accepted the decision. "Then I won't touch you again," he vowed.

He clenched his fists, then made himself turn and leave her. Crushed by the growing weight of emptiness, he walked down the corridor and up the private stairs to his rooms. Without a word to the guards, he slammed the door, bolted it shut. With halting, tired motions, he gathered the flashlight and entered the tunnels.

He emerged at the forest, birds trilling song, creatures calling to their mates. Stumbling through the fallen limbs, he tried not to collapse beneath the agony. Damon fumbled to open the cabin, and he barricaded himself inside until he was as he'd always been in this treacherous kingdom, as he would forever be.

Alone.

CHAPTER TWELVE

A.J. hunted through files and formulated decryption codes throughout the day and into the night, driven by demons to bring this torment to an end. At six, Sarah tried to coax her away for dinner, but A.J. refused tersely, and told Sarah that she wouldn't be needed. Sarah skittered away, warning all comers of her boss's truculent mood.

At a quarter past ten, McCord rapped on the door, and A.J. grudgingly stepped aside to admit him.

Gingerly, McCord poked his head inside, having received the admonition from Sarah. "I'm looking for Damon."

Irritated by the interruption, A.J. gestured to the empty room. "Obviously, he's not here," she sniped.

McCord frowned at the churlish dismissal. Sleepless night or no, the girl really was a bad-tempered brat sometimes. "Do you know where he is? The security team reported that he left here hours ago."

"No, I don't know where His Highness is," A.J. replied, returning to her computer. Out of propriety, she neglected to tell how she'd driven Damon away. Nevertheless, she rationalized, she'd answered honestly that she didn't know where he'd gone; but she had a clue. He'd probably retreated to his sanctuary, the cabin.

Where he had first claimed to care for her. As long as caring didn't require faith. The caveat ripped through her, wounding her anew.

Hadn't she earned his confidence, shown her allegiance? A.J. understood his reluctance to believe in her, given his recent past. Nelson had lied to him and used him to smuggle. His parents, as nice as the Tocas were, had kept his heritage from him. Though their prevarications were well-intentioned, on the heels of learning of his brother's duplicity, the blow must have been doubly hard to take.

Indignation slid away as she thought of the life he'd been forced to lead. Hunted by madmen, Damon had accepted the challenge of serving a country whose leaders suspected his every move. Could she fault him for a moment of reservation, when they'd had less than two months between them, when decades of trust had proven worthless?

Dismissing the wisp of doubt, A.J. reminded herself sternly that she'd been right to break it off. Right to refuse his apology. Right to be enraged by his continued skepticism.

But the wisp of doubt billowed, filling her head with contrary questions. Was she right to cast away the only man to make her feel truly alive? her heart argued. Right to end a miracle because an embattled man saw her laughing with his enemy and wondered? Right to deny love out of pride?

"A.J.? Are you listening to me?"

A.J. blinked, jolted from her reverie. "I told you, I don't know where he is," she snapped.

McCord gave her a quizzical look. "Yes, you did. And then I said that Damon won't respond to calls to his rooms. And when you were still not listening, I told you that I've also been unable to reach President Robertsi. I went to the mansion, but I was rebuffed by naval officers." McCord watched A.J. closely, certain she was withholding information. "So, to repeat my earlier question, would you happen to know why?"

"You'll have to speak with Damon," demurred A.J., embarrassed by her lack of attention and her boorish attitude. McCord had done nothing to her, except be her friend. Unwilling to lie to him about Robertsi, she equivocated, "Don't ask me about affairs of state, McCord. I'm just the hired help."

The bitter tone alarmed McCord, and he studied the shadowed eyes, the drawn features.

"Did you and Damon have another fight?"

If shattering your own heart counted, then yes, A.J. thought mutely. Aloud, she said, "We had a disagreement about my role here. But everything is settled now." He was gone, and in a week, she would be too.

"A.J., listen to me," McCord began, the words quiet but firm. "Damon is a difficult man to know."

"I realize that." A.J. scrolled through a screen filled with numbers and names. Finding a promising entry, she instructed Poppet to search for connections. "He carries a great burden."

"Alone. Completely alone."

A.J. stared blankly at the bank registry, stunned by the simple analysis, her hands moving idly over the keys. She protested, "He has you. And his parents."

"He has no one. Damon is isolated from family and friends by a duty few can grasp."

"Damon chose to accept this life." But she understood that, at his core, he'd had no choice. What made Damon extraordinary was his strength of conviction, and his refusal to shirk responsibility. Loyalty to his parents' legacy had drawn him across a continent and chained him to its shores. Though A.J. refused to face McCord, her tapping stilled.

Into the sudden silence, he said, "You understand him better than anyone else, A.J. You refuse to be awed by his power or held at bay by his aloofness. You challenge him, and he welcomes the contest."

A.J. linked her fingers, propped her elbows on the table. "So you think I'm contentious? Not a flattering description, McCord."

"I don't intend to flatter you, dear. You probably get enough of that at home. I want to warn you not to let love slip away."

"I know you mean well, McCord, but the differences between Damon and me aren't simple ones smoothed over by easy comparisons. We are fundamentally poles apart, and nothing will alter that. It simply wouldn't work."

McCord snorted. "I've seen more in my seven decades than you and Damon could conceive of. And I've learned from that time how precious love could be, if you're willing to fight to hold it. Young people picture romance as a game, an adventure where two hearts find each other and frolic in bliss." He sneered at the imagery. "My dear, nothing that lightweight will weather life.

The only love that lasts is forged in arguments and recrimination and forgiveness."

He thought wistfully of his beloved Louise. For forty-seven years, they'd been inseparable, despite his secretive ways and her insatiable curiosity. More than once, he'd found himself sleeping alone, but all he remembered was the feel of her in his arms. Cancer had stolen her body, but he carried her soul with him.

It infuriated him that these children would squander so easily what he realized was so rare. He scowled and continued, "Despite your supposed brilliance, neither you nor Damon have good sense. You're both too arrogant to fight for it, but I'll be damned if I sit silently by and watch you throw it away."

A.J. checked a smile at the curmudgeonly defense of love, and reminded him, "Not a month ago, you were warning me away from him. So what are you talking about?"

"I'm talking about how well you two fit together." McCord bit the end from a cigar, spat the tip into the receptacle. Flicking a match, he harangued, "I'm talking about how you are daring where Damon is cautious. That you are driven when he can be discursive. And Damon can match your wit, your determination, and unlike most men, I suspect, he can stir you and disturb you."

Nonplussed by the shrewd analysis and the gruff delivery, A.J. bristled. "I annoy him. He irritates me. I don't like him, and he doesn't trust me."

McCord smiled kindly. "But he does love you. As much as you love him."

Defeated, A.J. sighed and dropped her chin onto her linked hands. She shut her eyes, remembering their last row. "I wish that were true. I wish he believed that I can be his partner, his confidant."

"He will. Give him time."

"I can't." A.J. shook her head mournfully. "I love him too much. I'm afraid if I stay, if I accept less than everything, we'll only hurt each other. Eventually, somehow, I'd disappoint him, and there'd be nothing left."

"So you'll run away first? Or push him away?" he summarized with stern accuracy. "Not only did I tell you to steer clear of Damon, I warned Damon to stay away from you, but he didn't listen. He told me that you were unique. For a while, I thought so too. But you're a coward, Dr. Grayson. Not worthy of the love you two could share."

"You know nothing about us!" A.J. railed, stung by the tart denunciation. "I've done everything I can think of to show him he can trust me, but it's never enough. There's one more hurdle, one more mistake I can make. I won't live my life being tested by his doubts."

"Then live it erasing them. He has put his faith in you, and that's a dangerous gamble for Damon. Don't prove him wrong." McCord stroked her bowed head gently, father to daughter. "Give him another chance, A.J. He won't disappoint."

As McCord stubbed out his cigar, and prepared to leave the room, Poppet beeped shrilly. McCord halted at the door. "What's wrong?"

At a loss, A.J. turned to the computer screen and froze. "McCord, find Damon. Now."

McCord hurried from the room, and A.J. followed behind and secured the door. First, she printed out the records, then she stalked the twisted trail of funds until she reached the same conclusion Poppet had.

Satisfied that she'd verified her evidence sufficiently, she used the computer to place a transmission to Atlas, and waited impatiently for his face to appear on the screen.

"Cipher? Report," Atlas barked.

"Poppet has discovered a new link to Robertsi." A.J. glanced down at her report. "Does the name Stephen Frame mean anything to you?"

Atlas drummed his fingers on the desk, which filled the bottom of the monitor. "Where did you see that name?"

"It appears that the funds siphoned into Robertsi's accounts came from Frame. Over the course of three years, nearly half a billion was drained from other financial institutions, public and private, and laundered on behalf of another set of accounts."

"And do we know whose accounts were targeted?"

A.J. shivered as she confirmed the decryption, knowing what it would mean to Damon. "The source of the funds was Jubalani. And there's more. Poppet located several wire transfers in the past eight weeks, sizable amounts. I've programmed it to initiate a trace, to find the expenditures. I think it will tell us how the attack on the summit is planned."

Atlas absorbed the report impassively. Muting his end of the transmission, he lifted a device that resembled a cellular phone from the corner of his desk. Flipping it open, he issued curt instructions, the words unintelligible to A.J. He placed a second call, then disconnected the phone.

Atlas released the mute button, and asked, "Have you told anyone else what you've found?"

Shaking her head, A.J. explained, "Not yet. McCord was here, but I sent him to find Damon."

"Good." Atlas motioned to someone beyond her line of sight. A folder was placed in his hands, and Atlas quickly skimmed the contents. "The Iota team will assemble at your location by oh seven hundred Monday morning. In the interim, do not reveal what you've learned to anyone," he instructed.

A.J. knew that the Iota team referred to Adam and Raleigh, and other agents assigned to Jafir. They'd explained the procedure in Washington, and she easily recalled their cover story. At the thought of seeing her family, A.J. was swamped with incredible relief.

Then, the last part of Atlas's edict penetrated. She couldn't tell Damon about Jubalani? A.J. gathered her courage and said abruptly, "I can't obey the silence order."

Startled, Atlas lifted his head from the notes he was making and pinned her with a grave look. "This is not a democracy, Cipher. You do as I tell you. End of story."

A.J. shook her head again, bolstering her confidence. In this exchange, at least, she held the cards. Damon deserved full disclosure, and he would have it. "I'm sorry, Atlas. But I will not conceal this information from Damon Toca. He needs to know."

"He needs to know what I instruct you to tell him," Atlas countered, thrown by the apparent beginning of an argument. Not since Raleigh Foster took off on her own to avenge her partner's murder had he been faced with such insubordination. Unless, he thought unhappily, he counted Phillip's tirade last year when Alex was kidnapped. Smothering an irritated sigh, Atlas decided that as soon as the matter was settled, he'd require that all field agents stationed in Jafir undergo basic training again. Obviously, Jafir eroded their recognition of the chain of command, and his role as the top of the heap. Maybe it was something in the water.

To A.J., he said softly, "This is not a negotiation, Cipher. I've issued a direct order. You are to tell no one about this information. Do you understand me?"

"Yes, sir."

Atlas nodded, the reins firmly in his hands once more.

"But I will inform the King of the threat from Jubalani. As the Head of State, he has a right to know. And I have an obligation to tell him," A.J. finished firmly.

Atlas felt the top of his head grow hot, and struggled not to yell. A.J. Grayson wasn't a trained operative, thus he'd make allowances for the stubbornness. With great effort, he sucked in air and repeated to himself that she didn't know any better. "Cipher. I understand that you feel an obligation to Damon Toca. Given your history, it's understandable. But Damon will jeopardize this mission if he confronts Nelson before the summit, and we can't risk it. Therefore, if you dare reveal this information to him—"

A.J. cut him off. "If I disobey you, you'll do nothing. You can't terminate me or reprimand me. You could extract me, but I'm too close to an answer for you to risk it. So, when it seems appropriate to share information with Damon, I will."

"Now listen here, young lady!" Atlas roared, all attempts at coaxing forgotten. "I can have you locked up so fast your head'll be doing the two-step. Don't test my patience!"

A.J. leaned forward, her set expression an uncanny replica of her cousin's. "I'm not trying to undermine you, Atlas, or countermand your orders. But I will not deceive Damon. He has too few people he can rely on, and I won't become someone he can't depend on."

While Atlas processed her speech, A.J. lifted the report. "I found this information, and you need me to find the rest. Plus, there's still the matter of the threat to the summit, which begins in seven days. You won't pull me out and you won't cut me off." A.J. smirked, a crafty smile that warned Atlas he wasn't going to like what came next.

"You're worried that Damon and I will become vigilantes. Well, as much fun as being a spy may be, I'd just as soon not be shot again anytime soon. So here's the compromise. I'll brief Damon on everything that I know, on the condition that he stay away from the prison. And I will swear him to secrecy. When the others arrive, they can help us apprehend Nelson's accomplice. In the meantime, I'll compile enough evidence against Nelson Toca to ensure that he never sees the light of day. And if Robertsi is his collaborator, he'll regret it. I swear."

"You're a damned nuisance, Cipher," Atlas bit out, impressed against his will. "And you'd make a good agent if you decide you want to come on board full-time. After some reconditioning on command structures."

A.J. grinned, a genuine one this time. "I think I'll stick to computers, if you don't mind."

For the next few minutes, Atlas briefed her on who else should be informed of the Iota team's arrival, and had her recount their cover stories. To her surprise, she learned that Phillip would accompany Adam and Raleigh, as would his new wife, Alex.

She logged off the transmission, and returned to her digging. Finally, the pieces were falling into place, and Poppet could begin constructing scenarios. By Monday, she and the Iota team would be able to complete the mission, and by next Friday, she'd be at home.

And if the thought of home rang hollow, she studiously ignored the ache.

Saturday melted into Sunday, and dawn tinged the sky with rose and amber. Yawning widely, A.J. wearily ordered Poppet to continue tracking the wire transfers. Thus far, she'd determined four of the recipients—Brooks Civelli, David Kronnberg, Reena Cortes, and an outfit called the Triad, the latter two secured with Omega 1 blockouts. Poppet found records of Civelli, an Ethiopian expatriate hired for his access to contraband computer hardware, with a sideline in gathering information. Kronnberg was ex-Mossad, suspected of ties to Hezbollah. His specialty in the Mossad had been covert assassinations, and A.J. deduced that they'd found their shooter.

However, attempts to uncover even minute bits of data on Cortes or Triad consistently bumped into the blackouts. Now, she had a list of names whose ties to Nelson were forbidden: Caine Simons, Stephen Frame, Cortes, and Triad. Until Atlas responded to her queries and released the blocks, she was stymied. A brief message informed her that she'd have clearance in twelve hours. To continue the investigation, she programmed Poppet to begin running scenarios involving Civelli, Kronnberg, and the summit.

She arched her back, stretching muscles tired and cramped from her hunched position over the keyboard. Sleep weighted her eyelids. McCord had not yet returned with Damon, and they'd need to move quickly once they got back. Worry had prompted her to ask Wynn if Damon had been seen, and she'd told A.J. that he was safely in his room. More than likely, McCord had taken the tunnels to the cabin to retrieve him, A.J. decided.

Lethargy was slowly dissolving her brain, A.J. thought

groggily. Since coming to Jafir, she slept less and worried more than she ever had. When she made it back to Atlanta, she was crawling beneath the bed, and didn't plan to emerge until they dragged her out. She could lick her wounds and catch up on sleep, both in the fetal position.

It maddened her that twice Poppet had to prompt her for directions or correct ones she'd given. Too tired to continue with programming, she printed out reams of information and curled onto the sofa to read. Seconds later, she drifted into sleep.

A.J. woke with a start, and blinked sleepily in the streaming sunlight. A heady dream faded slowly, and she struggled to recapture its gauzy, sensual edges. The rustle of papers replaced the patter of rain. Alarmed, disoriented, she angled her head toward the sound. Damon sat at her desk, printouts in hand.

"Good morning, Sleeping Beauty," Damon greeted, alerted by the yawn she couldn't stifle.

"When did you get here?" A.J. questioned groggily, instantly recalling how she'd been awakened the day before. Stifling a blush at the memory, she bombarded him with questions. "What time is it? Where's McCord? Why didn't you wake me?"

Damon smiled at the litany, the tender one that ravaged her senses as surely as a kiss. In his eyes, she saw no hint of yesterday's rancor, but she refused to relax.

As though he read her mind, Damon said, "A.J., let us hold the inquisition until you've had the coffee and Danish on the side table. You are always feistier when you're fed."

Ignoring the double entendre, A.J. perked up at the thought of food. She fairly pounced on the Wedgwood carafe and china set, particularly the breakfast plate holding a pastry filled with an anonymous fruit. Unconcerned by the mystery, A.J. gobbled it down. She'd skipped dinner last night, after missing lunch as well. Besides, the impromptu meal gave her an opportunity to marshal her defenses against the sensual voice and the charming smile. With the six days that lay ahead of them, she'd need every guard she could muster.

She reached for the last bit of Danish, only to realize it had disappeared. Regretfully, A.J. delicately licked the crumbs from her fingertips and barely restrained a sigh. With exaggerated motions, she prepared a cup of coffee, adding copious amounts of sugar. It had tons of calories, didn't it? And it allowed her to avoid Damon for a few extra minutes.

"Take this."

Or maybe not, she thought when Damon spoke from above her, his voice hoarse. When she peeked up from the pewter-blue cup and saucer, a second Danish lay on a similar plate held by the clever, beautiful hands she coveted.

"Thank you," she murmured, accepting the proffered treat. Silently, she admonished herself for the wayward thoughts, and refused to dwell on the sizzling look Damon aimed at her as she consumed the second pastry.

When she lifted her fingers to her mouth to savor the remnants of frosting, an intense, questing look from Damon convinced her to use a napkin instead.

Despite McCord's commentary, she had no intention of changing her mind about Damon. He was too complicated, too hard.

Too kind. Too generous.

Too suspicious. Too arrogant.

Too loyal. Too thoughtful.

"Too much," she griped aloud. Damon fixed her with a

puzzled stare, and A.J. stammered in embarrassment. "Too much sugar," she covered lamely, and bobbled the cup. Dark liquid sloshed dangerously close to the rim, and A.J. hastily set the cup down.

Amused by her drowsy confusion, Damon nudged her shapely, bare leg where it extended the length of the wide sofa. The skirt had traveled up during her nap, and she had mercifully failed to readjust the hem. Desire flared, higher, hotter than even seconds before. Yet, he'd made her a promise not to touch, and he would honor that vow.

Through the long evening in the cabin, Damon had replayed the past month in his head, a cacophony of emotion that raged and tortured. To have lost with one look what he'd spent an eternity in search of slashed through him, leaving him weak. To know he could never tell her he loved her, and have her believe, burned into him, leaving him empty.

He could not recall the time before A.J., and who cared for after? In the shadows of his heart, where love lay rejected, he could remember only the sweep of the moment when he saw and knew love. The low, sultry voice, and the agile mind, he so admired. The elfin beauty of a face, so incongruously and artfully paired with the gorgeous, strong body, long and mythical like the nymph he'd called her.

He knew then the power of that first night, in the moonlight of a wedding party, when he looked and saw and fell. Now he understood that the why meant less and the where meant less, but trust meant all.

He would spend a lifetime regretting and wishing for a second chance that was never to be. So he would cling to what remained, to his duty to Jafir and the safety of his people.

Taking a seat beside her, Damon waited while she languorously stirred cream into the coffee. The sleep-shadowed eyes continued to blink heavily, a habit she would continue for at least ten minutes, as he'd learned.

Her wake-up ritual fascinated him, seduced him. One more lesson to unlearn. As she explained yesterday when he'd teased her, A.J. would intermittently stretch in exaggerated and non-sanctioned yoga poses. The lithe frame would twist and turn, arching and releasing until his blood heated and he hardened in uncontrollable response.

But unlike yesterday, he would not be able to drag her to the floor and sate them both, with frenzied strokes and devastating rhythm that left them a damp mass of limbs and release. He would hold to his vow and honor her request.

"You had some questions," Damon began, his throat closing when she rose from the couch and started her daily contortions.

When she bowed at the waist, dark hair in a cascade around her, the thin blouse slid silkily to pool at her breasts, the shirttails having come untucked during the night.

The expanse of creamy-brown skin beckoned his hands, tested his will. "Please," he groaned desperately, "sit down!"

A.J. wrestled the blouse into place, furiously shoving the fabric deeper into the waist of her skirt. After the third pass, Damon cautioned, "Any deeper and it will reach your knees."

"Oh, shut up," she growled. She gave the offending shirt one final push, then dropped onto the sofa. Pulling her legs beneath her, A.J. lifted her cup and took a hasty gulp.

Damon smothered a grin at the surly tone, and settled into his end of the sofa. "I believe you had some questions. *What time is it? Where's McCord? Why didn't I wake you?*"

"You forgot *when did you get here?*" A.J. added waspishly.

"Tsk, tsk." Damon reveled in the narrowed eyes, the curl of her lip. "You do have a temper in the morning, don't you?"

"Keep pushing me, and you'll find out." A.J. stared pointedly at the half-full carafe.

Duly warned, Damon draped an arm along the back of the sofa. His fingers rested millimeters away from A.J., close enough that he could sense the warmth of her skin. Dragging his mind from that forbidden path, he launched into his responses. "I got here around five. You were nearly comatose, despite our not-so-quiet entrance. Since I knew you'd gotten precious little sleep last night, I wasn't ready to wake you, so I told McCord we needed to speak alone. It's now a few minutes before six."

Damon lifted the stack of papers from the floor beside his feet. "Is this why I was summoned?"

"No. I needed to tell you that Atlas is sending Adam, Raleigh, and Phillip to Jafir. They should be here Monday morning." With resignation, A.J. moved to the file cabinet. She keyed in its passcode, and slid open the drawer. Clutching the file to her chest, she crouched near Damon, her deep eyes studying his face worriedly.

"What is it?" Damon demanded, unnerved by the scrutiny. He held out his hand for the file.

"Last night, I found confirmation of the payments to Robertsi. I also located expenditures from Robertsi's accounts to two known terrorists. I've requested clearance to learn more about two other suspects, but it will be several hours before I can try to construct a complete scenario." A.J. laid the thin folder in his outstretched hand, laid a comforting one on his thigh. Beneath her touch, the muscles bunched, from trepidation, not desire, she realized. Her heart screamed for her to hold the truth back, but she disregarded its pleas. "Damon, I also found the originator of the payments. It's Nelson. The organizer is your brother."

Braced for the revelation, the news still struck him like a fisted blow to the gut. Damon doubled over, the enormity of his brother's hatred for him stealing his breath. Not only did Nelson want to steal the throne, he wanted Damon dead. The threats, the shootings, messages from the twin who shared the very beginning of life with him. He'd pathetically assumed himself prepared for this ultimate betrayal, but how could he have been?

Like a lost child, he longed to call his parents, but he understood the dual obligations that would render him silent. As King, he couldn't risk the breach in intelligence. As a son, he couldn't risk demolishing their fantasy about the children they raised. That one would kill the other for power, money, revenge.

Ashen, Damon tried to shove the knowledge away, his psyche unwilling to process the depth of his anguish. When he knocked A.J.'s hand aside, a futile gesture to ward off reality, she refused to go. Instead, she crawled into his lap, her arms circling his painfully set shoulders. She held on helplessly as tremors wracked the proud body. In a stiff, aborted movement, his arms lifted to hold her, then dropped to his sides, the knuckles showing white.

"Damon?" she whispered, perplexed.

"Please," he rasped. "Go away." When she did not immediately comply, he grated out, "For the love of God, A.J., please. If you don't move, I'll break my promise."

A.J. tilted his chin up, her eyes wide with confusion. "Your promise?"

Tension vibrated through him, amplified by a grief that

threatened to consume him, and he fought not to seek the comfort he so desperately needed. Honor was all he had left, and he would not be forsworn. "I promised I wouldn't touch you. Please, move."

"Oh, Damon," A.J. cried out. "I never meant this." With care, she lifted one strong arm, then the other, encircling her frame. She tucked her head beneath his chin, pressed a reassuring kiss to the rigid jawline. "Let me hold you, Damon," she asked, as she gently sheltered his arms with hers.

Wrapped together, they sat, while shock settled around him, sank into him. Time slowed to the choppy gasps of air, the dry sobs that found no release.

After an eternity, the shudders stopped, and Damon broke their embrace. Rising to his feet, he cleared his throat once, then twice. "Thank you for the information. I appreciate your hard work."

A.J. curled restraining fingers around the bunched muscles of his arm to halt the quick movement toward the door. This time, as his world tilted on its axis, he would have an anchor. "Where are you going?"

"To my rooms. There's nothing more we can do for now. I expect you to get some rest as well." The edict was clipped, and he jerked his arm from her grasp. "Good night."

"Good morning," A.J. corrected as she sidled in front of him, blocking his path. She searched hooded eyes for a hint of his thoughts, without success. "You don't have to do this by yourself. Damn it, Damon. Talk to me."

"Why?" he ground out, the golden eyes turbulent, his head lifted proudly. "You've made your position quite clear."

In spite of the imperious posture, the suffering in the tawny depths cleared any lingering doubt. A.J. inhaled sharply. "I still care about you," she declared. "You don't have to go through this alone."

Laughter, harsh and biting, echoed in the lab. "Of course I do, A.J., I can't depend on my family. What would I tell them? That they raised a murderous, lying son? I still can't bring myself to trust McCord. And by God, I will not give you more to—"

"To what?" A.J. slid her hands up his heaving chest, along his enraged face.

"To push me away with," he finished, and he shoved her hands aside. "I've given you who I am, A.J., and it wasn't what you wanted. And you've shown me what you can offer." He gestured angrily to the sofa. "I don't want your pity."

"This isn't pity, Damon," she corrected quietly.

Striding to the door, he jammed the code into the keypad. "The hell it isn't."

On instinct, A.J. reached past him and canceled the exit sequence. "Do you remember this, Damon? Crowding me here, forcing me to face how you made me feel?"

"Get out of my way, A.J.," Damon ordered testily. "I'm not in the mood for games."

"I'm not playing." Confidence flooded her, filled her with power. "McCord lectured me yesterday, and in typical crotchety fashion, he made sense. Will we let ourselves be lost in the battle, and lose the war? I almost did." A.J. stroked the slant of mouth, her fingertips outlining the stern, masculine lips. "I demanded your trust, but refused to give you my own. I'm sorry."

Damon swallowed once, hard. "What are you telling me?"

"Exactly what I told you before. I will not allow you to survive this alone. That's not pity, Damon. It's love." A.J. pressed them together, hip to hip, and reveled in his reaction. "I love you, Damon Toca. I love the arrogance and the condescension. I love the loyalty and the commitment. And I will not abandon you, no matter how you feel about me."

"How I feel?" Damon corded steel arms around her, lifting her into him. The words crowded in his throat, begging for voice, but he could not give them air. Instead, he vowed silently to show her what he could not say.

With savagely restrained motions, he captured her stunned mouth in an infinite, enervating kiss, until her knees buckled and the unfocused brown orbs slid closed. He caught her, carried her to the sofa, and settled her across his length, the endless legs encasing his hips. Wordlessly, he peeled the clothes from her taut, slender body. He marked the chocolate satin flesh with delicate nips, tantalized with insistent caresses. Perfectly rounded, her breasts invited his tongue, his teeth to taste and delight in. Where skin creased into hidden curves, he lathed the vulnerable flesh until she quivered. At the indentation of her navel and below, he reveled in drawing broken sobs, and the quivers turned to shudders and to a keening climax.

Turning them, A.J. undressed Damon in a flurry of motion. Her avid tongue licked along his chest, his stomach, his thighs as she imitated his every caress. When moist heat surrounded him, he arched in tormented delight. A.J. shivered with triumph.

Sated, hungry, he fumbled for his wallet, and she sheathed him with ardent strokes. Relentless, he dove into her, and she captured the rhythm with undulating hips. Remorseless, she drove him, and he strained to hold the moment for an eternity. Senseless, they tumbled into release, clinging to each other, love wrung from their lips, tossed into forever.

CHAPTER THIRTEEN

amon, how wonderful to see you!" Alex exclaimed as they embraced. She leaned back, cupped his cheek. "I have missed you dearly."

"And I, you," he responded warmly. Damon turned to the trio standing in the drawing room, and clasped each hand in turn. "Phillip, Adam, Raleigh. Thank you for coming. I had hoped that your next visit to our country would be for pleasure." He brushed a courtly kiss to Raleigh's cheek, and bowed slightly. "Jafir *is* more than a site for intrigue, I can assure you."

Raleigh smiled. "We know. During our next visit, we will do nothing but bask on the shores and relax."

"However, I must say it's a clever ploy to secure repeat trips," Adam quipped. He glanced around the opulent space, its rich leathers and silk-covered walls. "Will A.J. be joining us?"

"Yes. She was resting, but she'll be down shortly." Hopefully with her temper in check, Damon hoped fatalistically. They had spent the twelve-hour respite in his bed, slaking a hunger for each other that never seemed to cease. When a guard contacted him on his private line to inform him of visitors, he'd left a heavy-eyed A.J. sprawled naked across knotted sheets, with a coverlet over her and a mumbled explanation of "state matters."

After nearly three days of nonstop activity, he made the command decision that she required rest, and he knew her well enough to know she wouldn't agree. A short note propped on the pillow would alert her to their presence. Already, he prepared for the argument that would surely come when she realized he hadn't awakened her.

But a single look at the shadowed eyes and tousled hair had left him no choice. As a peace offering, the obscenely strong coffee and treacly pastries she favored waited in the sitting room on a warming tray, as well as fresh clothing he'd collected from her closet.

"Please, have a seat." He led them into the main area. Coffee and tea lay ready on the center table. "A.J. thought you'd arrive in the morning."

Phillip answered, "Alex had a show in Rome. Raleigh and Adam were on, um, business in Athens. We met up and caught the earliest flights we could." In fact, after A.J.'s second transmission, Atlas commandeered an Interpol jet to hop from Rome to the tiny village of Scado on Náxos, where Raleigh and Adam had been completing high-level negotiations with a dissident faction of the Tamil rebels of Sri Lanka. Phillip, for his part, had been working with the Vatican to plug a funds leak that led to a burgeoning insurgency in Brazil, while Alex showed watercolors in the Olympia Galleries. Try as he might, he'd been unable to convince Alex to remain behind. As usual, her convoluted plan of acting as their decoy, given her tenuous connection to the King, had immediately convinced Atlas and eventually tired Phillip into complacency.

When Alex passed him a cup, she leaned forward to press a soft kiss to his mouth. As though she'd read his mind, she teased, "Let it go, Phillip. I won. You lost. And you love me anyway." She shifted away, gloating at her victory.

Phillip stopped her retreat and fused his mouth to hers, leaving her breathless. "I let you win," he amended. "And you love me too."

An exaggerated cough from Raleigh reminded them they were in public. "Sorry. We'll be more circumspect once we're married," Phillip apologized ruefully.

Staring at where his fingers twined familiarly with his wife's, Adam replied, "If you say so."

"Adam! Raleigh!" A.J. rushed into the room, arms outstretched. She painstakingly ignored Damon, still incensed by his high-handed decision.

Adam swung her into a ferocious hug, lifting her feet from the ground. "Mom and Dad send their love, and Rachel said you're in trouble for not calling. Jonah, of course, said to tell you he hadn't noticed you were gone."

"Adam, put her down," Raleigh scolded. She hugged A.J., then held her at arm's length. "How are you? You look, um, tired."

"I'm fine. Really." A.J. greeted Phillip and Alex, and the group stood together, a tight knot of family. A glance over Phillip's shoulder revealed Damon standing beyond the circle, his expression impassive.

Instantly contrite, A.J. held out a hand in welcome. After a brief hesitation, their hands touched, clung, and Damon joined them.

Everyone saw the easy intimacy, and Adam scowled. Hearing the quick inhalation, Raleigh elbowed him in the ribs, and he yelped.

"Stop being a baby," she muttered. "And don't say a word."

Settling for a fulminating glare, Adam held back the threatening diatribe he'd used for years on A.J.'s suitors. Though, he thought darkly as he examined her, none had ever made her glow before. Eager to move on with their mission, Adam took control.

"A.J., we should review your audit data."

All business, A.J. nodded briskly. "Right now. It should have completed its last set of directives. I was planning to check before you landed in Jafir, but"—she flushed brightly—"I got distracted."

"Oh man," Adam groaned beneath his breath, and Raleigh patted his shoulder sympathetically.

"If you can show us the way," she said warningly, "we'd better get started."

A.J. keyed the group into the empty outer office, having given Sarah the week off. The level of classification made her presence an increased security risk. Damon secured the door, while A.J. admitted them into the laboratory. Poppet whirred companionably, and issued intermittent beeps.

"It found something," A.J. explained. "It receives constant updates for its database from the military as well as private security details and controlled ISA feeds. Poppet?"

"Yes, Dr. Grayson?"

"Please report."

The computer hummed as it accessed its latest report. "Dr. Grayson, you requested probable scenarios extracted from data regarding the African-Arab Alliance and its Summit meeting with the Israeli delegation. I correlated the selected financial records, wire transfers, and known associates Civelli and Kronnberg. I then cross-referenced past events with Nelson Toca, also known as Jubalani."

"And?" Phillip prompted.

Poppet buzzed softly. "I do not recognize the voice pattern. Please verify."

"In a minute," A.J. interjected. "Poppet, display scenario on supplemental screen." On one section of the wide projection screen, photos of Civelli, Kronnberg, and Nelson appeared, with rows of dates and events listed below each picture.

Poppet added a map to the second quadrant. "In 1996, Civelli brokered an illegal deal with Kronnberg to transfer two kilotons of Semtex from Romania after the collapse, which led to his discharge from the Mossad. In 1999, Kronnberg acquired antipersonnel mines, surface-to-air missiles, and cooperation from Reena Cortes from Jubalani for forty million dollars."

"The name Stephen Frame is indicated, but I can locate no records of his existence, and details on Cortes are also unavailable. However, according to my analysis, Civelli, Kronnberg, and Nelson will likely utilize explosives to target the summit."

Damon noted with interest the shared look between the trio of spies. Cortes and Frame were names he intended to have by day's end.

Poppet displayed a third map on the screen, one of the island. "It is a reasonable hypothesis that three detonations will occur in the next forty-eight hours. Contraband shipments have been detected by the ISA. Operatives suspected weapons or drugs. Prison officials reported a blackout yesterday, and reconnaissance indicates unauthorized surveillance of the palace and grounds. Likely targets are the palace, the Jafirian prison, and the presidential mansion."

Damon spoke first. "Why forty-eight hours, Poppet? The summit is not until Friday."

"Probability is ninety-two percent that Nelson Toca will attempt to kill Damon Toca and replace him on the throne. Because the first delegate arrives today, an attack is imminent. The explosions will create confusion and offer sufficient chaos to affect the switch. The Triad mission to disrupt the government and destroy the Alliance will succeed. Probability is sixty-seven percent that Nelson Toca will attempt to kill Damon Toca and flee the country; however, the psychiatric profile indicates a narcissistic nature, which will mandate that he assume the throne. Probability is fifty-two percent that Nelson—"

Damon cut off the recitation. "Have Civelli and Kronnberg been linked to other attacks?"

"Yes, Your Highness. December 1997, Kronnberg is connected to a coup d'état in Armenia, and Semtex residue was in the debris. August 1999, Azali seized power on the island of Comoros, with the assistance of Civelli. Civelli sold computer equipment to the rightful government, but rigged the hardware with C-4, possibly remnants of the Semtex sale."

A.J. examined the map closely, then inquired, "Why would they target the presidential mansion, Poppet? Robertsi is the accomplice, is he not?"

"Unable to confirm, using additional information."

"What additional information?"

Poppet beeped, and placed the photo of Robertsi in the lower right-hand corner, with two silhouetted graphics. "The classified logs referring to Frame and Cortes may have direct bearing on the selected financial records. Probability that Robertsi is collaborator has decreased to forty-seven percent."

Adam laid a hand on A.J.'s shoulder, and shifted to include Damon in his range of vision. "We have the additional information that will verify Poppet's conclusions. Phillip?"

With a heavy sigh, Phillip began to speak. "During my time with Zeben, I was responsible for funneling money to various accounts controlled by Zeben and his henchmen. Including Nelson. I did so as Stephen Frame. One of my clients is a counterintelligence operation known as the Triad. Their agenda, as we understand it, is to foment dissension among governments and factions."

"To what end?" asked A.J.

"So they can broker the services of terrorist cells like Scimitar or disgraced operatives. They start the war and force you to pay them to clean it up." He crossed to the computer to stand beside Adam. "If I may?"

Fascinated, A.J. gave him access to Poppet's core memory and added his voice print. Phillip uploaded data, then typed in a series of codes. The display was replaced with a central dot surrounded by four satellites. White lines extended from the dots and fanned across a background of blue.

"We've been battling the Triad for nearly a decade, but if you cut off one head, two more spring up, and spawn a dozen. Their agents are placed in positions of importance throughout the world. Poppet, overlay diagram with wire transfers to selected financial records." A series of yellow lines crisscrossed, all leading from one of the satellites to another on the other side of the central icon. "I've been on inactive status since Damon's return to Jafir, and agreed to return to active duty a week ago, but during my stint here, I rarely encountered any Jafirian officials other than Robertsi. I met Reena Cortes only once, and that was during my brief encounter with

Nelson. Yesterday, I reviewed the files you transmitted, A.J. Poppet, now, map data regarding Reena Cortes and the Triad."

Suddenly, red lines connected the second dot to multiple transfers. "Add Kronnberg and Civelli." The transfers flashed in steady succession.

Phillip pointed to the display. "This is not a Scimitar ploy. They don't have the capacity, and that's why I was such an asset. I believe Reena Cortes is your spy, and she is an employee of the President. Unless Robertsi is now a leggy brunette with killer eyes, he's not your man."

"Gray eyes?" Damon asked harshly.

"Possibly," Phillip concurred. "Blue and green and violet. But the color is inconsequential. Cortes's eyes are cold, soulless. You'd recognize them if they were orange."

"Isabel Santana is Reena Cortes," A.J. summarized. With a stricken look, she turned to Damon. "And she's with the President as we speak."

Damon stood swiftly, reaching for the phone. "No, she's not. I sent her to greet Dodi Hannah, the Israeli attaché."

"What time is her plane arriving?" Raleigh questioned as she removed her communicator. "I'll arrange for an intercept at the airport."

"Seven p.m. from Jerusalem." Damon waited for the connection. In a brisk tone, he issued orders. "McCord? I need to see you in A.J.'s laboratory immediately. Bring weapons." He dropped the receiver, and looked at Adam. "We must evacuate the prison. I'll arrange for brigs at the naval base. Can your agents assist with security?"

"Of course." Adam stood as well and moved to the window to begin making calls.

"I'll dispatch Wynn to the prison to begin the process." To Phillip, he said, "I'd like to have you coordinate with McCord. We'll need to empty the palace without raising any alarms. I know you have friends in the community who would be willing to shelter the dignitaries. Perhaps a hotel not formerly controlled by Scimitar?" At Phillip's curious expression, Damon explained simply, "I do not know who to trust. You do."

Nodding, Phillip walked across the room to an unattended phone and prepared to reconnect with allies.

Anxious to help, A.J. stepped forward. "What should I do?"

Damon hesitated, afraid she would agree to his request. "I'd like for you and Alex to stay with the President. Go to the mansion and move him to the cabin. Use the tunnels to avoid detection." Damon glanced around the room, wishing he didn't have to utilize the novices. "Damn it, I need the others here, and I can't risk alerting Isabel if she's compromised the guards at the mansion."

"I realize I'm not an expert, but I did have some training. Like you said, you can't spare Adam or Phillip or Raleigh. McCord has to coordinate the evacuation. You're running out of options."

Alex spoke up. "I've used the tunnels, Damon. We'll be safe."

"Don't forget, McCord is a former naval officer. We're not being asked to guard his life, just sneak him out of the house. Teenagers could do this job, Damon." A.J. tapped her watch. "Time's running out."

Acceding to the lack of options, Damon finally agreed. "I'll have my guards drive you to the mansion. Get the President and leave as quickly as possible. Do you understand?"

A.J. nodded briskly. "Yes. Where are the tunnels connected to the mansion?"

"In the President's study, check the wall behind the door. The mechanism is under the middle hinge. Left, left, right will lead you to the clearing. The key is under the mat."

Despite the gravity of the situation, A.J. smirked. "You leave the key to your cabin under the mat?"

Damon shrugged, an impudent grin erasing the serious furrow for an instant. "Who'd break into the King's log cabin?" But just as quickly, he sobered and stared at both women. "Are you sure you want to do this? I can send Raleigh, and you two can be evacuated with the staff."

A.J. shook her head vehemently, a movement echoed by Alex. "You need Raleigh to disarm the explosives, if they're already in place. She's the chemist. Poppet and I have done all we can from here."

Alex added, "I know the tunnels too, and two nonspies are better than one."

Gratitude and affection swamped him, and he kissed Alex on both cheeks. "You are a true friend, Alexandra." Alex squeezed his arm in support, and left to join Phillip.

Damon grabbed A.J.'s arm, pulled her into the last free corner. "I don't want you to do this," he whispered urgently, his forehead pressed to hers. "I'd rather tuck you into a hotel or put you on a plane to Atlanta."

Stroking the tense line of his neck, A.J. murmured, "I wouldn't go. You know that. My place is here with you." She let the brown hair at his nape slip through her fingers, the texture smooth and calming. "I woke up and looked for you. When I read your note, I called you a variety of unflattering names, and I planned several inventive tortures. First, I was going to set termites loose in your cabin, and then I would reprogram your phones to make prank calls to heads of state. Next, I was going to—"

"I love you." Damon spoke the words softly, intently. "*Ma fée,* you have stolen my heart."

"Damon," A.J. whispered tremulously. "I never thought— I mean, I knew, but, you wouldn't—"

"I was afraid, of what, I don't know. I didn't realize that you were everything I've longed for. The only thing." Dipping his head, he feathered the parted lips with a tender kiss. In soft forays, he sank into her, drew her into him, their mouths and bodies a seamless unit, united by heart.

A discreet tap on the shoulder from Alex separated them. Damon left to admit McCord and brief him on the situation. Adam motioned for A.J. to join him.

"Let him send the soldiers to get Robertsi. You're not trained for fieldwork, A.J."

"Neither is Alex. However, according to your report, she acquitted herself well." A.J. patted his cheek. "Damon can't risk revealing the tunnels to the soldiers. It would undermine the security of the entire estate. Besides, you taught me everything I know."

Adam frowned. "If you're doing this because you have feelings for Toca—"

Indignant, she retorted, "I'm doing this because it must be done. We don't know who Isabel Santana may have corrupted."

"Surely there is a guard, a naval officer. Someone."

Aware of the sincerity of his concern, she softened. "I know the tunnels, Adam, and I know Robertsi. He'll trust me. You and everyone else can contribute best from here. I'll take Robertsi and Alex to a safe place." Suddenly, it occurred to her why Damon would hide Robertsi away, but stay behind. She whirled around to locate him, but Adam stopped her with a restraining hand.

"I wondered if you'd noticed. He's clearing out everyone but himself."

"Then you have to make him come with me. He'll listen to you," she declared rashly.

Adam shook his head in denial. "No, he won't. He shouldn't. His place is here."

"Robertsi is the President."

"But Damon is the King."

Beaten, A.J. watched Damon consulting with McCord. "He won't let anyone else confront Nelson. This is his fight."

"He's a good man." Adam wrestled with admiration and annoyance. "I suppose you could do worse."

A.J. beamed, her eyes luminescent. "You'll learn to accept it, I promise."

Soon, each member of the team had an assignment. They'd decided it was smarter to send Phillip to the airport, where the authorities agreed to detain Santana. Raleigh would work with McCord's staff to evacuate the palace and to coordinate bomb squads for deployment. Adam was headed to the prison to monitor the prisoner transfer, particularly Zeben and Nelson. As a precaution, A.J. authorized Adam as one of Poppet's users.

After changing into close-fitting black pants and a tee, A.J. joined Alex and received firearms to take to the mansion. The five-day crash course she'd received in DC seemed like ages ago. At Adam's directive, McCord outfitted her with a .22, the gun she'd used during training. Daunted by the heavy pistol, Alex opted for a small revolver.

"It will not be as effective long-range, but it will take out close targets," McCord explained.

Handling the gun gingerly, recalling her last encounter with the cool, hard metal, Alex decided, "Next time, I'm taking lessons."

The team dispersed, with quick goodbyes to loved ones. A.J. loitered in the outer office, wanting one final moment. Damon walked through the office accompanied by McCord, and he sent him ahead.

"What's wrong?" he asked, catching her hands in his.

"Nothing," A.J. replied, feeling silly. "I just wanted to, you know . . ." Her words trailed off.

"I know. We have all the time in the world, as soon as this is over."

McCord's radio shrilled, and he connected. "McCord."

A frantic voice reported over the din. "This is Wynn. The prison has been attacked. I repeat, the prison has been attacked."

Damon snatched the radio from McCord. "What about Zeben? Nelson?"

"Zeben had been moved to the naval base as per your orders. Sir, the second explosion occurred in the transport vehicle carrying your brother."

Damon breathed in harshly, then steadied himself. "Did you find any remains?"

Wynn was silent, then reported, "Not yet, sir. The fire is too high. We should have it under control in seven to ten minutes."

"Find the body, Wynn," Damon ordered. Turning to A.J., he said unnecessarily, "Go get Robertsi."

At a run, A.J. grabbed Alex, and they commandeered a vehicle from the auto bay. Luckily, Owen was on duty, and drove them to the mansion. Sensing their urgency, he zipped across the palace grounds, crushing grass and fauna beneath the jeep's wheels.

At the mansion, A.J. and Alex rushed inside. Damon had

warned the officer on duty to grant them access, and A.J. found Robertsi in the study.

"Dr. Grayson," Robertsi greeted politely, rising from his desk. Though he was obviously surprised by their appearance, he merely added, "Ms. Walton, an unexpected pleasure."

"President Robertsi, I don't have time to explain, but you must come with us." A.J. felt along the doorjamb, counting the hinges. Behind the third one, a small button bulged almost imperceptibly. She pressed it, and the faux wall slid away.

Robertsi stared at the opening in amazement. "How did you know it was there?"

Alex nudged him forward, her arm linked with his. "Mr. President, people are trying to kill you. We'll explain everything on the way."

A.J. removed the wide-beamed flashlight from her satchel. Alex started to do the same, but A.J. stopped her. "We may need the extra power later." Quickly, she located the closing mechanism, and the door swung closed.

Robertsi followed noiselessly as they jogged through the tunnel. At the first fork, A.J. guided her band left, and took the second turn as instructed. After a quarter of a mile, the last fork appeared, and she directed them to the right. As a precaution, she told them both how to take the tunnels to the palace.

A.J. signaled the group to a stop and searched for the release. The tunnel opened, and she ushered them into the clearing. Winded, the trio hiked to the cabin and gratefully collapsed once inside. Alex settled beneath the window, and A.J. and Robertsi sat against the opposite wall. An intruder would see them first, giving Alex time to disable him or escape and run for help.

In accordance with Adam's instructions, she sent a coded

message to his communicator, which Adam had rigged to bounce the intelligence to Poppet's server. "Decoy secured."

"President Robertsi, thank you for not asking questions. We were unsure of the security status of your mansion. Your home may have been compromised." A.J. dug into her satchel for the tube of papers inside and the second gun. She handed both to Robertsi. "First of all, Damon sends his regrets for the wrongful imprisonment. He was acting in good faith."

Robertsi nodded. "I know. I saw the wire transfers and the forged signatures. They were excellent."

"They weren't forgeries, sir. You signed those cards. Five years ago, you opened a series of accounts throughout the world. Grand Cayman, the Isle of Man, Antigua. Money from drug rings, smuggled artifacts, every source you can imagine."

"How?"

A.J. took a deep breath. "We have reason to believe that Isabel Santana is a member of a covert group known as the Triad."

"The Triad? Nonsense. I've worked with her for nearly ten years." Robertsi waved away the papers. "Admit it, Dr. Grayson, your Poppet has no clue who is trying to undermine the summit."

"Please, President Robertsi, listen to me. Before Alex and I came to retrieve you, an explosion occurred at the prison. Nelson Toca was being transported from the facility, and the van exploded. Poppet predicted the event. It also predicted that the mansion would be the next target."

"My people—" Robertsi scrambled to his feet, but A.J. unceremoniously jerked him back down.

"Snipers," she reminded him. "Damon is evacuating the mansion and the palace grounds. The ISA is providing agents to support the military complement already on-site."

"He should alert the navy," Robertsi demanded. "Do we have radio communication?"

"Only essential contact. We don't know how badly the infrastructure has been compromised." She met the concerned leader's tight expression with a level gaze. "Damon has anticipated the worst, Mr. President. He'll mobilize the First Battalion, if necessary, but his first priority is your safety. If Nelson is alive, and finds him . . ."

Gently, Robertsi patted her hand. "Don't worry, my dear. He'll be fine."

The splintering of wood shocked them all, and they jumped to their feet. Remembering the black-and-white mob flicks she loved, A.J. tucked her gun into the back of her waistband. The bad guys always made the good guys drop their weapons, but if Robertsi gave them his, she could use hers when they least expected it. She crouched, imitating Robertsi. Near the rapidly disintegrating door, Alex tried to roll aside, but the door opened before she could escape.

"No, no, no," said the disdainful voice of Nelson Toca as he grabbed Alex by the arm and yanked her close. Recognition occurred immediately. "Ms. Walton? What a surprise. I thought my brother's consort was more petite." He rubbed the barrel of the gun along her temple. "Have you returned to reclaim Damon's affections?"

"Prison treating you well?" Alex inquired caustically.

Growling, Nelson shoved Alex into the center of the room, his hand manacled around her wrist, and Alex stumbled from the force of the blow.

When she righted herself, Nelson caught the gleam of metal in her hand. "Your weapon, please?" he requested politely, and reluctantly, Alex handed him the tiny revolver. He tucked it into his waistband.

Then, he locked eyes with A.J., and the feral grin widened. "Ah, now you must be the formidable Dr. Grayson. Your weapon as well."

Paralyzed, A.J. hunted for the proper response. Her priority was keeping Robertsi alive. Once she didn't check in at the appointed hour, Adam would send help. Assuming they weren't all dead.

Dismissing the morbid thought, she managed, "In the interest of safety, they decided not to arm me." She raised her hands and twirled, the gun safely disguised beneath the black. For good measure, she skimmed her hands down her shirt. "I'm the scientist, not the secret agent, Mr. Toca."

Apparently satisfied, Nelson brandished the pistol, trailing the steel along Alex's sallow cheek. "Call me Nelson, please. Mr. Toca is my father. Or, truth be told, my uncle. I think of it as musical parents."

While he chortled at his joke, Alex tried to inch away. Abruptly, Nelson broke off the chuckle and draped his arm across the fragile neck. "Don't move, Ms. Walton. Or may I call you Alexandra?" Tightening his hold, he continued, "I have not forgotten how you helped Damon steal the throne from me. I'd rather not kill you before he arrives, so be very, very still. Mr. President, your gun. Now."

Robertsi stepped forward, but halted as Alex began to gasp for air. Cautiously, he set the gun on the floor, kicked it to Nelson, and held up his hands in a truce. "Release Ms. Walton, Nelson, and let these women go. Your fight is with me."

"Actually, I don't like any of you," Nelson corrected with dire menace. "You've all conspired to shield my sainted brother, who is determined to squander our legacy." Nelson casually checked the watch on his wrist, the broad chrome face outfitted with unusual buttons.

Noting the movement, A.J. presumed he was waiting for something. A signal or perhaps the arrival of Santana and the Israeli attaché. Either way, she realized time was running out.

With a gun to Alex's head and her limited training, a direct attack was not feasible. Like water, plans and schemes sloshed around in her brain, none of which she could accomplish without helicopter support and an extra sixty pounds of heft.

If she couldn't fight him, she'd have to outthink him, she decided. She focused on his mental weaknesses. Quickly, she replayed the psych profile from her research. Narcissistic, competitive, and greedy. Basically, he was a ten-year-old boy. If she could goad him, A.J. figured, perhaps he'd loosen his hold on Alex long enough for her to escape. Alternatively, she could move in front of Robertsi, giving him access to her gun.

Summoning courage she thought spent during her trip up the cliff, A.J. jeered, "You believe *you* should be King?" Hands held out, palms forward, A.J. moved nearer and, simultaneously, took a step closer to Robertsi.

"You find that laughable, Dr. Grayson?" Hazel bored into brown, and A.J. readied herself for the outburst.

Which never came. Nelson applauded, one hand further constricting Alex's windpipe. "A nice ploy, Doctor, but a bit cliché. I'm not a madman, despite my brother's testimony to the contrary. I won't be distracted by idle banter, while the heroine makes her way to the palace to bring the guards." In emphasis, he set the barrel of the gun under Alex's chin. "A single shot will kill her instantly. Don't risk it, Doctor."

A.J. took a second step, again moving forward and to the side. Keep him talking, she prodded herself, while she prayed that Robertsi would catch on to her backup plan. "I'm confused, Damon. I mean, Nelson. What is it you hope to gain by holding us hostage?" She cast dubious eyes toward the shattered door. "Almost no one is aware of the cabin, so they're not likely to come in search of us for a while."

"Don't worry your pretty head, Dr. Grayson," Nelson assured her silkily, and again, he glanced at his watch. "Everything is moving right on schedule. Though I didn't expect to find you all here. A bonus, I guess. I wonder if Damon realizes I've captured his lover? That is what you are, isn't it?"

Looking bored, A.J. retorted, "Didn't your reconnaissance fill you in?" Inside, she grew nauseous at the thought that Nelson had spied on them, a voyeur to her most personal moments.

"It informed me of your nocturnal visit to the King's boudoir. Quite cozy."

A.J. cocked a hip, and balanced her fist on it. With the fingers of her hand, she surreptitiously indicated the gun to Robertsi. A few more steps, and he'd be able to grab it. "Spying on your brother's bedroom, Nelson? Are you that lonely for company?"

"Naughty, naughty, Dr. Grayson," Nelson lectured.

A.J. froze, terrified he'd figured out her plan. She held her breath and waited for him to demand the firearm.

Instead, though, he continued, "Still trying to distract me with taunts? I expected a more original attempt to overwhelm me."

Robertsi leapt forward, snatching the gun from A.J.'s waist. Prepared for the sudden action, A.J. shouted for Alex to duck and run.

Startled by the turn of events, Nelson loosened his grip, and

Alex stomped on his instep, a replay of her last escape from him. She broke his hold and sprinted for the door.

"Left, left, right," A.J. screamed as Alex dove through the splintered frame, giving her directions to the palace again. In the next second, she regained her footing and flashed a thumbs-up sign. Soon, she disappeared into the dense foliage.

At the same time, Robertsi tackled Nelson, and Alex's purloined weapon skated across the polished floors. A.J. heard the sound and raced to retrieve it. Enraged, Nelson drove his elbow into Robertsi's jaw, delivered a chop to his throat, and the older man dropped like a stone.

Hard, biting fingers grabbed her ankle as she scuttled toward the gun. She kicked out, aiming for his face, but Nelson twisted away. Scrabbling for purchase on the slick wood, A.J. felt herself losing ground. Her right hand skimmed the cool, dull metal, but she couldn't form a solid grip.

Nelson launched himself over her, and a booted foot glanced off the side of her head. Dazed, A.J. struggled for the gun, but Nelson proved stronger. Third gun in hand, he propped himself against the wall and trained the larger weapon on Robertsi's prone form and A.J.'s bruised face.

"Do you think you've saved him?" Nelson gasped.

"I think I thwarted you, and that's half the battle," A.J. rejoined, furiously dragging air into burning lungs. Indifferent to the threat Nelson posed with all three guns, she crawled over to Robertsi and checked his pulse. The beat was there, but his breath was shallow. "Alex will bring the cavalry, Nelson," she taunted.

CHAPTER FOURTEEN

Raleigh bent over the block of C-4, studying the timer. "Remote device," she concluded. "There's no timer, but a wireless transceiver can emit a pulse detonating the bombs after it receives instructions from the main site."

Bomb-squad dogs had found the stash in the Presidential Suite, in Santana's office. A second bomb had been discovered in the mansion. Raleigh squatted near the device, impressed despite herself. "The detonation frequency could come from anywhere within a thousand yards or hundreds of acres."

Damon crouched beside her, staring at the metal container and its deadly contents. "Can you disarm it?"

"Of course, just as I did with the one at the mansion. The dogs haven't located any other stashes, but I want to do another sweep." She opened her toolkit and began to sever wires. "What concerns me is this infrared pulse. Whoever holds the controls has gone through a lot of trouble. If it were me, I'd have a backup plan."

Warily, Damon asked, "Like what?"

In her element, Raleigh ticked off options. "A cache on the roof, which we've checked. Or maybe a delay that would arm itself after the primary system is severed." Before Damon could ask, she replied, "I've eliminated that possibility as well."

"So what's left?" Damon demanded as he began to pace. "If the purpose behind Triad is to destabilize the government by killing Robertsi and me, and installing Nelson as my doppel-gänger, how would you ensure that we both died?"

The answer struck them at the same time. "The cabin!" Da-mon exclaimed.

"But how would he know?" Raleigh asked, cutting the final wire. "I thought the cabin was recently constructed on private, secluded land?"

"I built one exactly like it in Durban. If Santana has been do-ing satellite recon for Nelson, he'll know that's where I'd retreat to if the palace were damaged." Damon grabbed the radio, fear pulsing through him. A.J. and Alex were in the cabin, and Nelson was headed their way.

"McCord? I need weapons," Damon ordered. "Have someone bring them to the Presidential Suite."

"What are you going to do?" The question was tinny, anxious.

"Just send the weapons. Now." Damon cut off transmission.

Raleigh came to stand next to him, her eyes filled with con-cern. "Damon, wait. You can't just charge out to the cabin. We don't know what Nelson has planned."

"He plans to kill me and anyone close to me. Including your

best friend." Damon threw up his hands, guilt slicing through aggravation. "I sent them there, Raleigh. Two novices. If he harms them—"

"Call in Adam and Phillip. Take them with you."

"No time. Nelson's body is missing, and Phillip apprehended Kronnberg, not Santana. They're probably going to meet up at the cabin, and she'll tell him they've been discovered." Damon's hand fisted over the radio, his eyes cold and deliberate. "If he harms her, I'll kill him."

"Nelson won't have a chance." Raleigh knelt by her toolkit, removed a palm-sized cylinder. Handing it to him, she explained, "I call it *war in a bottle*. You shake it vigorously, then toss it against a hard surface. Once the glass breaks, the chemical reaction to oxygen and carbon dioxide sounds like gunfire, with a nice smoky effect. It should buy you thirty seconds before he notices he's not dead."

Damon accepted the vial, and Raleigh passed him her field backpack, which contained binoculars and a flashlight. He nestled the concoction in the cushioned pocket. "Thanks."

"Hold on," Raleigh said as she rummaged through the lower compartment of the toolkit. This time, she emerged with a blob of gray putty. "Damon," she warned, "I've only tested this a few times."

Damon stared at the globule. "Tested it how?"

"It's an explosive, detonated like a grenade, but without fumbling for a pin. The trigger is inside, so you'd squeeze the putty to ignite. Then you throw it and run like hell."

"Damage?"

"It would destroy a small studio apartment."

"Or the cabin." Extending his hand, Damon took the bomb

from Raleigh. She opened a small box, and he cautiously set it inside.

"Reinforced titanium with lead filler," Raleigh explained proudly. "If it goes off in here, you might lose a hand, but that's all."

"You frighten me," Damon muttered as he added the bomb to his bag. A guard tapped him on the shoulder, and Damon turned. The .22 he received was identical to A.J.'s gun, and his eyes glittered with determination.

"When Adam and Phillip return, you all can come after me." Leaving Raleigh to finish the bomb sweep, Damon headed for the tunnels. Guided by the narrow beam, he raced along, sure of his path. Scents, sounds, all flew past him as he pumped his legs harder, desperate to reach A.J. in time.

The collision toppled Damon, and a body lay crushed beneath his. Light bounced along the ceiling, and steadied on a mass of hair spread on the ground. Muffled shrieks convinced him to lever away, certain he recognized the voice.

"Alexandra? What are you doing here?" he asked as he pulled them to their feet. "Where's A.J. and President Robertsi?"

"Back at the cabin," she panted. "Nelson is holding them hostage. I escaped and came to find you, but I got lost. No flashlight."

"Are they hurt? Is Nelson alone?" The questions poured out on a wave of terror.

Alex shook her head wearily. "I don't know if they're hurt. Everything happened so fast. But Nelson was alone when I left them. I didn't notice any other vehicles approaching either."

Grateful for the information, Damon thanked Alex, gave her his light, and resumed his run. Long, steady strides ate up the distance, and he soon emerged in the clearing. Stooped behind a fallen tree, Damon removed the binoculars to survey the landscape. Near the cabin, a small jeep stood in a copse of trees, the greenery an adequate but penetrable camouflage. He adjusted the lenses and trained the glasses upon the window of the cabin. Nelson stood near the left wall, and on the right, A.J. curled over an unconscious Robertsi. Increasing the magnitude, Damon saw the livid bruise blooming red on her cheek, the scraped knuckles on her slender hands.

Nelson would pay for every mark, every scratch. Focused by a rage so deep it chilled him, Damon removed the vial and crept to the cabin. He'd target the destroyed front door and enter through the side window closest to A.J.

In position, Damon lobbed the vial skyward, and it struck the doorframe. Nelson dashed toward the racket, bent down to avoid a spray of bullets. The fumes rose, and Damon scented the acrid stench of spent ammunition. Satisfied that Nelson believed the cabin under attack from soldiers in the bushes, Damon circled around to the side window. A quick check verified that Nelson had taken up post beside the broken door, firing shots in at random. Noxious gas drifted through the opening, and Nelson coughed heavily.

Damon lifted the window, which he habitually left unlocked. He pulled himself inside, and dropped soundlessly to the floor. Stealthily, he moved to A.J., who tended to a confused Robertsi. Covering her mouth with one hand, he whispered into her ear, "Don't make a sound. When I give the signal, you and Robertsi run for the door. Can you do that for me?"

She nodded once in assent, and pressed a salutary kiss to the calloused palm covering her mouth. Reluctantly, Damon released her and hid behind the cedar trunk. As the fake attack died down, Nelson stayed by the window, firing rounds. When the chamber clicked empty, Damon removed his weapon, and aimed it at his brother. A.J. helped Robertsi to sit up and both shifted, ready to flee.

"Nelson!" Damon shouted. "Behind you!"

Nelson turned, reaching for the second gun. A.J. grabbed Robertsi and dragged him toward the door. The heavier man stumbled, then regained his balance, and they burst through the leftover planks. A.J. forced Robertsi into a jog and, turning, saw the jeep.

Arrogantly certain of victory, Nelson had left the keys in the ignition. A.J. hissed at Robertsi, "Are you well enough to drive?"

"Yes. Get in." Robertsi rubbed his eyes to clear his vision. "Come on."

"I can't leave him here." A.J. backed away from the door. "Go and get help."

"Damn it, A.J., there's nothing you can do!" Robertsi argued, and he reached for her arm.

A.J. flung the hand off. "I won't abandon him, Robertsi. Never." Before Robertsi could protest further, she headed in the direction of the cabin.

The roar of the engine signaled the truck's departure, and Damon sagged with relief. Inside the cabin, Nelson and he were in a standoff, weapons aimed.

Nelson spoke first, the drawling voice a lighter timbre than his brother's. "Nice decoy. I constantly underestimate you."

"Is Santana your accomplice?" Damon interrogated, certain it was his last opportunity to learn the truth.

Apparently, Nelson agreed. He sat on the floor, gun braced

between his thighs where his wrists rested on his knees. "Isabel is my partner. In everything."

"You're lovers?"

An oily smile curved the elegant mouth. "Of course. Since I first began my business in Jafir. I find older women, um, imminently more satisfying. It helps if they have connections."

"She introduced you to Triad."

Nelson nodded appreciatively. "You've been doing your homework. Or your computer geek girlfriend has. Few people know about Triad. Even Zeben is just one of their pawns."

"They must have been delighted to learn you were almost heir to the throne," Damon goaded, hoping to trick his brother into revealing more. Nelson chafed at any hint of inferiority, and Damon prodded the sore spot. "I guess they were also furious when you failed to take it from me."

Riled, Nelson glanced at his watch and fingered the shiny device. "I will have the monarchy," he vowed in a tone perilously close to a pout.

"I don't think so," Damon retorted coldly. "For example, there was your plan to destroy the palace. Was that the transceiver for the bombs, Nelson?"

The astonished look confirmed Damon's hypothesis. He continued smugly, "We've dismantled the Semtex. There's nothing more you can do. You lose. Again."

The clatter of helicopter blades erased the amazement, and Nelson regained his cocksure expression. "No, you lose, big brother."

Outside, Isabel set the helicopter down in the clearing and scanned the area for signs of Nelson. In a matter of hours, the recent King of Jafir would be dead, and Nelson would take the throne in his place. Nelson's charred remains would be found in the wreckage from the prison explosion, and the counterfeit Damon would take the throne.

For fifteen years, she'd plotted with her partners in Triad, trying to accomplish what the feebleminded Zeben never had. Whoever controlled Jafir would control the region. Jafir dominated the Alliance, had ties to the U.S. that matched those of Israel. Like Scimitar, Triad had no religious zealots or ideological mission. It simply existed to foment war and reap the profits. Isabel could scarcely imagine a more noble calling.

The basic idea for Triad had been born during her studies at Oxford. International relations too often tried to unite dichotomous factions, to mend fatal rifts in culture and religion. But she'd seen something different and entirely less idealistic. There was money to be made in brokering war rather than peace. Together with colleagues from the computer-science department and economics, she'd convened the inaugural meeting of Triad. The name appealed, as much for its unity of three as for its musical connotation. Rather than harmony, Triad would be known for sowing discordance throughout the world.

Isabel chuckled at the memory and began to survey the landscape again, irritated by Nelson's delay. She never saw the fist that caught her beneath the jaw.

A.J. pulled the lax body from the aircraft and searched for a piece of cord to bind her hands. Merely stunned, Isabel tackled A.J., and they tumbled across the earth.

Isabel contorted her body, reaching for her boots. A.J. followed the movement and grabbed the handle of the knife before Isabel could. Panting, she jabbed at the taller woman, forcing her to scoot back along the ground to a tree that allowed her to keep an eye on the cabin. She made Isabel sit on her hands. "If you're waiting for Nelson," A.J. said as she dragged air into her lungs, "he's inside with Damon. Security is on its way."

Leaning against the rough bark, Isabel examined A.J., noting the reddening bruise. "Did Nelson do that?"

"Small talk, Isabel? I don't think so."

Isabel shrugged and adjusted her torn sleeve. "Isn't this *de rigueur* for captives? You foil my plans, and I explain how I almost won?"

Willing her breathing to slow, A.J. gasped out, "Fine. Have it your way. How did you almost win?"

Isabel almost snarled at the tone of contempt, but she held herself together. If she could lull the girl into conversation, she might be able to overpower her. Plus, someone should be able to appreciate her brilliance, and if not another woman, then who? "I met Nelson when he was a fourth year at Oxford. I seduced him."

"Quite a coup," A.J. noted. "As I understand it, Nelson was quite the wastrel. Not much of a bookworm."

Nostrils flared, Isabel said, "I didn't want him for his mind any more than you want Damon for his."

"You have no idea what I see in Damon."

"A means to an end, just like Nelson. At first, he was good for stealing items from his fellow students. He was a first-rate fence, with connections with all the lower beings. Later, he grew more adventurous, and provided a lovely supply of baubles for me."

"Pimp to your prostitute?" Isabel lunged, and A.J. pressed her back with the knife. With obvious insincerity, A.J. apologized. "Sorry. Please, continue with your story."

Isabel sucked at her teeth, then glanced at the cabin, but saw no movement. "When Nelson learned about the monarchy, I decided to tell him about my other endeavors."

"Triad?"

"I don't know what you're talking about." Isabel stared at a point beyond A.J.'s shoulder, but A.J. didn't turn. "I meant my embezzlement scheme with President Robertsi. I started when I became his aide, and he took me with him everywhere he went."

"Until Damon usurped your position?"

The exotic eyes flared with heat. "Until Damon stole yet another person's birthright. He and Robertsi had to pay."

"But why frame McCord? I know you sent the photograph."

Isabel laughed. "Not to frame McCord. To distract Damon. And it worked. He didn't know who to trust. Not until it was too late."

Inside the cabin, Nelson launched himself at Damon, throwing him off-balance. They rolled along the floor, and both guns were knocked aside during the struggle. Damon slammed his fist into Nelson's nose, and blood spurted violently.

Nelson countered with a vicious jab to the kidneys. He flipped Damon over his head, and Damon crashed into the trunk. Nelson slithered toward the gun, and Damon closed his hand over the satchel. The guns were too far away to reach them before Nelson did. And he had no guarantee Raleigh had dismantled all the bombs. One way or another, this ended here.

Opening the box, Damon removed the putty bomb. "Stop, Nelson!" he warned. "Don't make me hurt you."

Nelson ignored the edict and closed desperate fingers around the handle. "Hurt me? I've got the gun, Damon. I've got the power."

"I won't let you win, Nelson. You and Isabel, you're caught. Surrender now, and I promise I'll be sure you get a fair trial." Damon pleaded with his twin, terribly saddened. Unable to contain it, he asked quietly, "Why do you hate me? Our entire lives, I thought we were best friends, but you've always hated me. I loved you."

Nelson spat at the sentiment. "You're weak, Damon. Always doing as you were bid, never seizing control. You let our parents control you. Hell, you even let me manipulate you, the younger brother. I bought the bombs with merchandise that you fenced for me. Isn't that rich?"

"It's pathetic." Damon waited for the helicopter to land, unsure if it carried friend or foe. "The throne will never be yours. And Triad will blame you for this failure. If you stay in Jafir, I can protect you."

"I don't need your protection. The Triad will succeed, and you'll be responsible for the destruction of the Alliance." Nelson backed toward the door, the air stirred by the helicopter. "I despise you for being a coward, and I will relish watching you die."

The seconds ticked by inexorably, interminably. Nelson reached for the transceiver, harsh laughter spilling from his lips. Damon ignited the putty, threw it toward the door. Wood exploded, and fire filled the air. The force of the explosion threw Damon into the kitchenette, and his head cracked sharply against the cabinet. As he lay stunned, bleeding, losing consciousness, fire engulfed Nelson, drowning his screams.

A.J. whipped toward the sound, and Isabel took her opportunity and ran to the helicopter. Paralyzed, A.J. felt the searing heat, but could not move. The explosion echoed in her head, the sound of burning wood transformed into crushed metal. The train rushed toward her, and the car flipped again and again. Her parents wailed from the pain, and she dragged herself to the ditch beside the road. Hidden in the gully, she listened for her parents' voices, waited for them to come. Only they never did. Instead, police officers lifted her from the muck, took her to the Grayson home, the family that remained.

Tears streamed freely as she remembered leaving them, hiding as they died. She'd been a child, too young to know she couldn't have saved them. But she was older now. Stronger.

A.J. stumbled to her feet and ran pell-mell through the debris to the cabin. The front wall had been ripped away, a solid wall of flame where the door had been. The side walls crumbled, and A.J. headed to the back door.

"Damon!" She screamed his name, a plea, and wrenched the door open. Searing heat singed her hair, and black smoke filled her lungs. Fire ate across the floorboards, but had not yet consumed the entire cabin. Panic, ancient and constant, bubbled inside her as she faced the roaring flames.

"Damon," she shouted, but the now-airborne chopper drowned her words and whipped the flames higher. Frantically, she peered into the smoke. A movement by the counters drew her attention, and she stumbled blindly toward it. Hooking her hands beneath the horizontal form, she dragged the body to the door, grunting from the strain.

Beams crashed down, and fed the inferno. Steadily, insanely, she tugged and pulled, tears streaming. For minutes, hours, she towed the lifeless body farther and farther from the blaze. Collapsing beside him, she tried to perform CPR, but could barely breathe herself.

Sturdy hands lifted her away, and A.J. struggled for release. Other hands reached for Damon, and she swore revenge. Eventually, calm, comforting words penetrated the haze of panic and devastation.

"A.J., honey. It's okay. You saved him." Adam cradled her in his arms, brushing at the tears that fell heedlessly down her sooty face. "Honey, you saved him. Damon's okay."

The words pierced the howl of torment in her ears, and she focused on Adam. "Damon? I got him?"

"Yes, honey. You got him. You went into the fire, and you brought him out. I'm so proud of you." Adam hugged her tighter, waiting for the bands of panic to ease in his chest. He and Phillip had exited the tunnels just as the chopper landed. In the next seconds, an explosion rent the air and the helicopter took off. The two advanced on the cabin, in time to see A.J. running inside. By the time they'd reached her, she'd heaved his body beyond the flames. Military vehicles soon swarmed the area, and Adam had picked her up, to treat any wounds.

"Where is he?" A.J. begged, her voice ravaged by smoke. "I can't see him."

"They've taken him to the hospital. He has a concussion and other wounds. The medic said he'll be fine, once they get him to the hospital." Adam reached for a portable device. Gently, he slipped the mask over her mouth and nose. "Breathe in, A.J. You need the oxygen. Slow and deep. That's a good girl. Slow and deep. Oh yeah, you'll be fine, honey."

Days later, A.J. waited anxiously outside Damon's bedroom, in answer to a terse summons. It was her first day of freedom since she'd been placed under house arrest again, this time by fretful doctors worried about her refusal to stay in a hospital.

In the forty-eight hours, she hadn't heard from Damon, but Raleigh explained that he'd been placed on a respirator for smoke inhalation. Like herself, he'd refused to stay in the hospital, so the hospital had been moved into his quarters, the privileges of being the King.

Dr. Morley, a kindly older man, opened the door, his face tense. When he noticed A.J., he attempted a smile. "Dr. Grayson."

"Dr. Morley," she greeted, her voice still scratchy from the smoke. "I take it His Highness is not in the best of moods."

"I'm sure some people find surly an attractive state of mind," he offered diplomatically. "Please, don't stay too long. His condition has improved, but he seems to forget that he has a bruised kidney and a broken rib, not to mention his sorely damaged lungs. Five minutes. No more."

"I promise," A.J. assured the doctor. She pushed open the door with a warning knock. The sitting room was empty, and she walked to the bedroom. An IV dripped slowly from its metal hook, the clear tubes taped to pale forearms. Hazel eyes, dim and unfocused, turned toward her.

"A.J. Thank you for coming." Raspy, Damon spoke in short sentences, his lungs not quite mended.

"I've wanted to see you, but Dr. Morley forbade it. I think he barricaded my door." A.J. lovingly stroked his brow. "How are you feeling? The doctor says you're better."

Damon shifted away from her touch, and her hand fell to the bed. "I should be on my feet by Friday."

Stung, A.J. tucked her hands in her pockets. "You'll be on hand for the summit? That's wonderful. Adam told me that none of the delegates balked at continuing here. They were impressed by your security teams. Dodi Hannah has been singing your praises."

"You're rambling, A.J." Damon gestured to a chair near his bed. "Please, have a seat. We need to talk."

"I don't think I ought to." A.J. tried a grin, but it quivered. Ice settled in her stomach, and she resisted the impulse to run. "You sound ominous."

"Not ominous. Practical." Damon inhaled deeply, the sound labored. "I've asked Adam to take you with him when they leave after the summit."

"Leave?" Confusion coated the ice, and it began to seep into her veins. Was Damon sending her away?

"Yes. Your mission is completed, and I think it best for all concerned if you return to Atlanta as soon as possible. Adam and Raleigh will remain behind to finish debriefing Kronnberg. We've been unable to locate Santana, but the Alliance governments are on alert."

"And you can see no other reason for me to remain?"

Hope shone in her eyes, and Damon could not bear to look. "No. I see no reason for you to stay."

"Alright."

The easy acceptance snapped his gaze to hers, and pain coursed through him. It was for the best. "Good. I'll have Mc-Cord make the arrangements."

A.J. turned and walked stiffly for the door. Knob in hand, she looked back over her shoulder. Leaden silence hung between them. Finally, she spoke, the words bitter and fierce. "I love you, Damon, but I will be damned if I'm going to prove it again. What is it this time? You're afraid for my safety? Or is it guilt over Nelson's death?" A.J. flung an angry hand out, the fist clenched in outrage. "I can take care of myself, and I can take care of you. I walked through fire for you, and even that's not enough. As for Nelson, he killed himself. He was a sick man, and he blamed you. You did everything you could to help him. So when you resolve whichever convoluted rationale you've concocted to send me away, let me know. I might even listen."

A.J. slammed out of the room, marched down the hall and into her own quarters. With steady hands, she bolted the lock. Then she curled into a ball on the settee and began to sob. Racking sobs poured out her misery, emptied her of energy. Spent, she lay supine, unwilling to move. Exhausted, she drifted into restless sleep.

Pounding startled her awake. She stumbled for the door, her head throbbing in unison with the noise. "I'm coming. I'm coming."

Clumsily, she opened the locks. Damon strode through the door, IV gone. Before she could speak, he grabbed her hand and pulled her into the sitting room. Pressing her down onto the settee, he towered over her.

"I'm moody. Judgmental. Imperious." He rattled off the list in precise tones. "I take responsibility very seriously, and I do not tolerate failure well." Reaching out a hand, he tilted her chin up, the features familiar and beloved. Softly, he brushed the fading mark where Nelson struck her. "I let him hurt you when I promised to keep you safe. I forced you to battle your deepest fear, just to save my life. A.J., I almost lost you because of who I am."

"You think it's that simple, Damon? You apologize for hurting me, and I forgive?" A.J. looked deep into his eyes. "You didn't lose me because of who you are. You lost me because of who you've let yourself become."

Damon recoiled as though struck. "A.J., please."

A.J. leapt from the settee, eyes blazing. She wanted to hold him, but she knew if she did, she'd lose what little she had left. He had her heart and soul. She would have her pride. "I am sick unto death of this, Damon. You want to be King, fine. But you can't trample over my heart on the way there. I realize you have more than a few reasons to doubt, but not me! I have never tried to hurt you. I've been honest and open and—"

"And unbearably patient." Damon took her by the shoulders, forced her to still. Tawny eyes bored into her angry brown. Desperate, he begged, "Can't you try once more? Give me a chance to prove I'm worthy of you. A short mission?"

"Damon."

"Don't say no. Not yet." Damon reached into his pocket, removed a box. Inside the box nestled a silver band set with emeralds. "My mother gave this to me when they came to visit. It was my mother's. Not her wedding ring, but her coronation ring. She knew she might not live to see my bride, but she wanted me to offer this to the woman who ruled my heart. It's you, *ma fée*. Only you."

Undone, A.J. tugged at his hand, pulled him beside her. She caressed the stubbled cheek, and whispered, "You saved me too, Damon. From self-doubt and routine and a phobia that controlled me for too long. If we're together, we can save each other."

"The Triad will come after me again. They'll try to use you."

"So we'll find them first. We're partners. I'll make Adam open a GCI Jafir. Maybe Poppet can become a field agent for the ISA." A.J. grinned and Damon answered with a smile.

"You humble me, A.J. Make me believe in magic."

"You show me worlds I've never known, women I never knew I could be."

"I'll hurt you. I'll shut you out and"—he sighed deeply—"make you cry."

A.J. placed a hand over his heart, where the pulse beat frantically. "I'll hurt you. I'll interfere and make you worry."

Damon lifted A.J., the pledge burning to be spoken. "I'll love you. Every day. Always."

A.J. kissed him until neither could remember ever being without. "And I'll love you. Forever."